DAMAGE
LIMITATION

A DETECTIVE INSPECTOR WHITE CAPER

JACK EVERETT
&
DAVID COLES

BARKING RAIN PRESS

Damage Limitation: A Detective Inspector White Caper

Copyright © 2015 Jack Everett & David Coles (www.archimedespresse.co.uk)

Edited by: Ti Locke (www.urban-gals-go-feral.blogspot.com)

Proofread by: Rachel Roddy (www.facebook.com/rcwriter)

Barking Rain Press
PO Box 822674
Vancouver, WA 98682 USA
www.barkingrainpress.org

ISBN Trade Paperback: 1-935460-94-3
ISBN eBook: 1-935460-95-1
Library of Congress Control Number: 2015930618

First Edition: March 2015

Printed in the United States of America

9 7 8 1 9 3 5 4 6 0 9 4 7

DEDICATION & ACKNOWLEDGEMENTS

This book is dedicated to our families and friends and, in particular, to the memory of Jack Everett's wife, who died during the book's final preparations.

And our thanks go to our editors, Ti Locke and Rachel Roddy, who have done a great job of translating what we've said in UK English to what we meant to say in US English. We would also like to acknowledge the influence of our friend Rosa in the criminal character's choice of sports car!

PROLOGUE

High up in the Dales of North Yorkshire, many of the streams, even swollen as they were after the recent rains, simply came to an abrupt stop. They either soaked quietly into the broken rock just beneath the topsoil or gurgled noisily down gaping sink holes to vanish into the bowels of the earth.

Deep below those fast flowing streams and crystalline waters were long, twisting tunnels carved by thousands of years of turbulent water wearing patiently away at the cracks and fissures in the limestone rocks.

It was a playground, a serious playground with danger ever present but nevertheless, a playground for strong, fit adults. Dressed in wet suits with helmets and mountain boots and swathed in coils of rope, the Happy Roamers Potholing Club regularly descended hundreds of feet into the deep and twisted caverns beneath the Yorkshire Dales.

Mike Cargill, a senior speleologist, expected and loved the roar of water coming from all sides. Water cascaded down the sides of the shaft he was hanging in, the rope ladder with its steel rungs was slippery with moisture and demanded a firm grip and an unexcitable temperament. He reached the bottom where sloping sheets of wet rock reflected his helmet light back from a thousand facets. He checked that the foot of the semi-permanent ladder was still secure in its staples and looked up.

"Fine down here, Dave. You can send the others down, now."

The reply was tinny in his earphone. "On their way, Mike, I'll be the last down," Dave Reilly said.

Fifteen minutes later the whole party was standing at the edge of Canal Cave although, at the moment, it was more reminiscent of an enclosed mill race.

Dave nodded upslope, to where an irregular crack, about ten feet high and a crooked eighteen inches wide showed black against the lighter gray rock. "Looks fairly dry up there today, seen it pouring through there before now."

"It'll be okay. Through there, we can bypass the Steps and descend into Millar's Run without too much trouble."

"Okay folks, let's move up there," he spoke into his mike and pointed to the fissure. "I'll take the lead, Taffy'll be tail-end Charlie."

Dave looked around. "Taffy? You there?"

"Over here," came the reply, "Blue." He waved from the edge of group and smacked his hand against the light blue helmet he wore.

"Okay. Give everybody room but don't get too spread out. After me."

Mike, in the lead, climbed the rough rocky pavement to the fissure. Once inside, it became a high but narrow tunnel with his light showing up the straws and helictites covering the roof. The tunnel took them higher still until they stood on crumbling chert, covered in calcite deposits wriggling across the surface like white worms or crystalline sheets sparkling in the light. The ceiling dipped toward the end, toward the rising floor until only a two foot high passage remained.

Each of the team wriggled carefully through the restriction, those who had been before coaching the two newcomers. There was no room to stop here, they had to move on, climbing down the wall beyond using the nylon hand ropes which had been fastened to the rock, courtesy of the spelunking club. At the foot, thirty feet or so below, they reached the longest horizontal – more or less – run in the trek.

"Everybody here? Sound off."

Names came in over the small radiophone kits which fitted inside their helmets. Mike counted, "Eleven. Okay."

They tramped on through passages and small caverns as far as previous group explorations had gone. There were glittering roofs, shining curtains, pillars built from the junction of stalagmite and stalactite, formations like church organ-pipes – all photographed and recorded.

Today, they were expecting to traverse Cargill's sinkhole, a siphon that Mike had named personally because he had spent so much time under water enlarging the tight twists and turns. Beyond lay a cavern of cathedral-like proportions; Mike had glimpsed it once with battery power running low and just a few seconds of awed vision given to him. This was the first time since that day that the waters had receded.

"Ready?" asked Taffy.

"You need to ask that?" Mike grinned. "I was born ready. We'd better get a move on too. The water management team from Bradford City won't take all weekend to finish that pipeline, they've already finished the How Steen Gorge end and I'd prefer to be away from here before they open the reservoir sluices again."

Mike took the line – a light rope that he would use to signal back to the others as he reached planned points in the journey.

He stepped into the black water and, going forward on his hands and knees, began to progress upstream. Soon there was only the glow of his head lamp to mark his presence and then that disappeared along with the slight hiss of the carrier wave from his transmitter. The rope was gradually drawn into the darkness.

Dave held the line lightly in his hands, feeling it being drawn from the coil, feeling it stop occasionally, tugged at the points Mike had dipped his head below the surface to negotiate the rise and fall of the siphon.

The first fifty foot length was familiar and Mike progressed quickly. Then came a passage through what must be tumbled boulders and then a stretch which was totally under water. He went another few yards beneath the surface, the water streaming past his goggles clear enough to see grit suspended in the flow.

Here, he knew the tunnel rose a little and he would be able to breath for a minute or two before continuing. He pushed his head above the surface and reached out to grasp the rock and anchor himself while he recovered from the exertion.

But, despite his fingers being numbed with the icy cold water, he could feel an oddness about his handhold. It seemed soft – a lump of clay perhaps, turf or even a piece of clothing sucked down from the outside. He caught his breath and turned his head. He knew instantly what it was he was holding on to.

"Damn me," he whispered. "It's a body."

Mike looped a length of the line around the torso and made it fast then gave the rope three sharp tugs: the agreed signal for an emergency. Immediately the rope went tight and gradually began to pull the body – with Mike's guidance – back the way he had come.

Progress was steady and, not knowing if his victim was alive or dead, he did his best to keep its head above water.

"Chris. Mike is either dead or unconscious," grunted Dave as they hauled the limp body out of the water and turned it on its back, rubbing the slack features. "Mike, can you hear me?"

"I'm over here, Dave. I can hear you and I'm fine. Don't know how long this poor bugger's been down there but I can't imagine he's still alive. My God, I'm bushed."

"Thank God," said Dave. "I thought it was you we were pulling out. I'll start CPR," he continued. "Taffy, can you take one of the others with you and go back far enough to radio for help?"

Taffy nodded, his helmet light bobbing up and down.

"I reckon you'll have to go at least as far as the foot of the main shaft. Maybe climb to the top."

Dave was pumping the man's chest. "Look at the feller's face, Mike. Half of it is gone, he can't still be alive." Nevertheless, he carried on leaning on the victim's chest and releasing the pressure.

Mike bent close, his light shining on the damaged face. "That looks like fresh blood, Dave." He pressed the nose which had taken a battering. "Look, that's bleeding."

"Well, that's good. At least I'm working on a live one."

Experts from the emergency services for the largest county in Britain abseiled down the shaft while a bank of brilliant lights was suspended over the top. A rigid mountain-rescue stretcher followed them down on the end of a rope and within twenty minutes of their arrival, the semi-drowned man was lashed to it. Drugs were administered and he was back on the surface less than an hour later, and flown to Leeds General Infirmary by the Yorkshire Air Ambulance Trust.

The man was confirmed alive as he was taken into the hospital, but in a persistent coma. He had no identification on him, so he was given a number. When his vital signs were considered strong enough, he was taken to Widdecombe Park Hospital, where he joined six other patients in the coma unit. Despite widespread missing persons inquiries, facial image reconstruction, circulation of dental records, and DNA searches, he was not immediately identified.

Chapter 1

Leroy "King" Richards was transferred to Asket Farm open prison with six months of his sentence left to go. He had served eighteen months of his three-year sentence and had been a very good boy. Within six hours of arriving at Asket Farm, he expected to be a very good escapee. He had been assigned a bunk in a room for three. He was given clean linen, and when he had made up the bunk he was given an induction tour by an easy-going guard. Richards barely listened. He had no interest in the place; after all, he was not going to be here long enough to make it worthwhile. What he *was* interested in was looking out for any one of several of his pushers who had preceded him here.

It was not long before he spotted one, "Lofty" Pike, a white speed freak as thin as he was tall. Leroy gave him a sign from behind the guard's back and at teatime, Lofty was in the mess hall waiting for him.

"Hi, Lofty." Leroy could act magnanimous when he chose to, although as always, his eyes were rarely still enough long enough to look at anyone he spoke to. "How do I get out of here?"

Lofty, whose nose looked like a parrot's beak, bobbed his head up and down. "Out of *here*? Why man? You get a good time here, good grass, coke, anything you want. You got six months on cloud nine here, man. Why leave 'til you have to?"

Lofty tried far too hard to sound like a black brother from the 'hood. He saw King Richards's expression change from affability to annoyance and dropped the act. "Bottom of the exercise field. There's a trellis there, we strengthened it up into a ladder. We're in and out of here whenever we like."

Richards nodded. "Had to be some real easy way in an' out, amount o' shit *you* get through in here."

"Let me know when you want to move, and I'll be there and move the trellis back after you've gone over. Why the rush? Like I said, things are easy here."

Leroy Richards smiled. "Got things to do, Lofty my man. Gotta see a man who's whiter than white. Hell, he's goin' to turn out blacker than black, catch my drift?"

Lofty got the general idea and nodded.

"Soon as it's dark, man, I'm outta here. Don' be late."

Lofty grinned but his grin turned on and off when it suited him. He had known Leroy for years, ever since he and Jarvis had shared a room with him at the orphanage. He liked neither man, but at least he knew where he stood with Leroy. He grinned again because he knew something Leroy didn't, Jarvis was still alive, he knew because they had bumped into one another a year or so ago. Lofty had helped Jarvis on a fly-by-night paint job on a boat. Why, he had no idea, he had done what was asked and just covered the name up without removing the one beneath. Lofty had taken the money and left town. There was something, some weird light in Jarvis's eyes that put the fear of God into him, always had been.

Richards reached the chain-link fence but there was no sign of Lofty. The fence, or trellis as Lofty called it, had been dragged out at its foot and was taut enough to be used as a ladder. The lights from the prison buildings behind Leroy's looming shadow cast it large before him, he grasped the steel links and the shadow lurched menacingly as he climbed upward.

Leroy had a long list of contacts and had emailed several of them from the prison library. He expected a stretch limo to be waiting no more than a comfortable stroll beyond the fence. His prison grays were hardly warm enough for the late hour and time of year. He shivered and continued his climb looking—a trifle anxiously—through the fence for some sign of transport. He was confident that all of his needs would shortly be met: good clothes, warmth, well-cooked food, decent smokes and obliging ladies; not necessarily in that order.

Leroy reached the top and hesitated, it was now pitch dark, but he was more concerned with being spotted than the eight or ten foot jump he had to make. He bent his knees and jumped, anticipating a hard landing.

"Fuck!" Leroy yelled as he fell through the thorny gorse surrounding the outer wall. Inch-long thorns tore his flimsy prison jumpsuit and drew blood. His ankle cracked against something hard.

"Lofty, you bastard! You…" It took long agonizing minutes to extricate himself. Blood trickled down his neck, he cussed out the lackadaisical Lofty every way he knew and imagined every torture he could inflict on him. It did little to ease the pain.

Sore and limping from a sprained ankle, Leroy dragged himself across a newly-plowed field hoping to hide his tracks in the rough furrows. He reached the road, but no black limousine, no Lofty. Instead, there was a grimy white van and just visible in the driver's seat, a large Sikh with an imposing turban and beard.

He tapped on the glass. The driver turned and gave him a critical frown. Eventually, the widow was lowered and smoke from the interior wafted out like fog.

"You'll be Richards, then?"

"I will. And who the hell are you? Where's Winston?"

The Sikh heaved a great sigh, his impressive physique moving slowly and deliberately. "It don't matter who I am, Mr. Richards, and Winston's busy. Now, you want a lift somewhere or you want to walk?"

Leroy Richards scowled in the darkness. Winston had worked for him for years; eighteen months of absence from the scene and here he was, handing the job over to someone Leroy didn't know. There would be questions and there would be answers.

He nodded to the driver and walked around the front of the van. Inside, it was at least warm and he began to feel a little better. "Okay, take me to Perry Barr." He named the district of Birmingham where he owned a large property.

"No can do." The driver shook his head. "Not unless you want to end up in Winstone Green instead of the cushy little hole you just got out of."

Winstone Green was a high security prison similar to Barlinnie, Leroy's "home" before moving to Asket Farm.

"And why would I do that?"

"'Cause they're watching your place and have been since they locked you up. They're expecting all sorts to turn up there. Some have done already and they've been quietly wheeled away for questioning. As soon as they know you've escaped, well…"

"Hmm."

"Exactly, Mr. Richards. All your old… umm, haunts? All your old haunts will be under observation."

"You're right, my friend." Leroy knew good advice when he heard it. "So?"

"So, if you will allow me to make a suggestion, head south. Winston has a cousin in South Norwood, in London. He will put you up if you have enough money. And talking of money, I want fifty up front for petrol."

Leroy looked at the Sikh properly for the first time, really looked at him. He was very big, too big for a sarcastic reply.

"No problem." Favoring his cuts and bruises, Leroy reached into his back pocket for his wallet. A new low point in the night's events, his wallet was gone. Not only the wallet but the entire patch pocket had been torn off his jeans with his notebook of phone numbers and email contacts. "Bugger it."

"Sorry?"

"Actually, there is a problem, friend. My wallet and all sorts of stuff are back across that field in the patch of brambles I jum… tripped into." Tripped sound better than jumped. "I guess I can go back and look for it."

"You can do that if you wish, Mr. Richards. I would advise you not to, though." He pointed across the field. "Not unless you are determined to get caught." A line of lights were at the far side of the field; he could faintly hear barking dogs, it looked as though his footsteps in the soft earth had been found after all. "You are a very popular man, Mr. Richards."

The sarcasm was not lost on Leroy. "Look friend…"

The Sikh started the engine and drove off without switching the lights on. He moved to higher gears as soon as he could to minimize the noise. "I am not your friend, Mr. Richards. I am not even Winston's friend. I am a driver and a very good driver. I work for money." They had reached the bottom of a hollow in the road. The Sikh braked strongly and stopped. "No money, no driving. Will you please leave my van now, Mr. Richards?"

Leroy Richards could feel the long fingers of the law reaching out for him. On foot out there, in the dark, was not something he wished to think about. There was only one thing to do. Sweating with fear for the first time in many years, he felt for the chain around his neck and pulled out the pendant, about the only possession he'd managed to keep hidden through his prison stretch.

"This is one ounce of pure gold, my friend," he explained, emphasizing the last word. "You want it, you drive the van. Okay?"

The Sikh started up the engine, switched on dipped headlights and set off. They drove for half an hour in a silence that seemed to grow more comfortable as the miles went by.

"Kind've hungry without my plastic, but we'll see who we can shake up—or shake down—if you catch my drift, friend?"

His companion grinned, a gleam of white teeth in the light from the instrument panel. "Singh." He said. "Jasminder Singh. "South Norwood, was it?"

"Sod South Norwood. No, Leicester. I've got contacts there, but if we can stop on the way and get something to eat and a cell phone…"

"You mean if *I* can get you something to eat and a phone?"

Singh shook his head. An ounce of gold worth four hundred pounds and a little bit of chain. It wasn't much. He'd been told his passenger was a one-time drug dealer,. Well, this guy with the glossy black skin was going to learn that there were new men on the streets and Leicester was one of their stomping grounds. He was sure that he could squeeze a bit more than four hundred pounds out of his passenger.

CHAPTER 2

The observers were scattered along the only road leading into the hollow. They found easy concealment behind the unkempt trees and shrubs which grew wild along the road side. Dusk was approaching and tendrils of fog, like old lady's fingers, reached for them through the trees. Minutes later, it was a low lying blanket that hid the grass from sight.

Shelly Fearon whispered into her cell phone, and the watchers moved forward as one toward the house. The fog effectively hid the edges of the drive, and Shelly was grateful for the lamps which marked its course.

A light in the porch lit the front door and shed a diffuse orange radiance on to the brick steps in front. On the right-hand brick pillar was the name of the house: *Hey Presto.* The sign was shiny and new. Shelly made for the doorway knowing that the others were encircling the house. She stepped into the porch, raised the knocker, and brought it down with a crash, loud in the evening's silence. "Police!" That too shattered the stillness and she rattled the door handle. "Come on Faulkner, open up. The place is surrounded."

No answer. Her shout was met by an eerie silence and she signaled the officer holding the door breaker. "Unlock this door for me, will you?" Within seconds, the door had been smashed back against the inside wall. Flashlights revealed the interior: long disused, cobwebs festooning corners and light fittings, dust the only regular visitor.

"Glad I didn't shout, *we know you're in there*," she muttered and one of her companions grinned in the gloom. A single line of footprints in the dust led the officers along the hallway to a stair and up, across a narrow landing to a well-bolted door. Shelly nodded toward the bolts. "Bolts on the outside! Will you open them, Terry?"

Terry looked around to make sure his companion from the armed response team was there, an ugly looking gun in readiness.

The two bolts rasped in the guides as they were drawn aside. The noise echoed around the landing and stairwell. Terry twisted the handle and pushed, another anticlimax; it didn't move. Incongruous as it seemed, the door was locked solidly on the inside too and the heavy metal breaker had to be brought into play once more.

This time, the door panel broke away completely, falling flat on the floor inside. Flashlights swiveled from side to side, up and down to reveal nothing more dangerous than a table in the middle of an otherwise empty room. On the table was a cell phone.

One of the officers covered the room with a digital camcorder while Shelly stared into the empty space in disbelief.

"It's like the rest of the place," said someone. "Empty and unused."

"Not quite," Shelly replied. "Don't touch a thing. There's no dust in here except some spider webs up there." She pointed to the ceiling. "But the place has been cleaned. They could have left it dusty like the rest of the house. I want forensics to go over this with a microscope. Maybe they left something for us."

With a last look around, Shelly went back to the landing to call her boss. She nodded to the others as she left. "Look around, guys. Search every square inch, but don't smudge anything. I get the impression we're being taken for fools and I don't like it."

"Detective Inspector Stewart White," said the voice on the cell phone.

"It's me."

"Did you get him?"

"I think we're dealing with the invisible man here. We smashed in two doors to get in here and there's nothing but a table with a cell phone in the middle of it. We're searching now and recording everything." She paused for a moment. "Yes, I'm bringing it back. I'll put it in an evidence bag of course but I don't want to mess with it in case I lose any prints."

"Footsteps led you to the room but the room is clean, you say?"

"Yes, but the rest of the house is deep in dust and cobwebs."

"Well, they showed you the way there but not how they got out, right?"

"I figured that one out for myself, boss."

There was a silence from the other end. "Guv? You there?"

Stewart White spoke up. "Sorry, just thinking. The scenario you just described sounds familiar. Very like the crime scene that turned out to be his downfall, the one that convicted him of murdering his wife."

Shelly knew of the case, it had been front page news. The man they had been chasing, Travis Faulkner, had been found guilty of killing his wife. Her body had been discovered in a room locked from the inside; DNA evidence had convicted him.

Shelly nodded into the phone. "Very much like that, Guv. You going to call SOCO out?"

"I will, and I might come with them, get a feel for the case. There's something here that stinks." He was going to say *rotten in the state of Denmark* but thought the classical reference might go over her head.

"In the state of Denmark?" Shelly asked.

"Right," Stewart said, trying not to sound abashed.

"I'll come back and bring the phone. I bet it's as clean as if it came straight out of the box. Oh, and you'll never guess what the house is called."

Shelly switched off and I chuckled. I put the phone down and looked out of my office window. The office suite was perched above the junction of the Headrow and Westgate in Leeds center, lights illuminated the street below and flashed off the roofs of cars going by. They were heading home, I guess, but it would be some time before I joined them tonight.

I couldn't make up my mind what to tell my boss about the negative outcome of their raid on Faulkner's house. Superintendent Flowers had responded to a request from Sheffield and that had led to the attempted re-arrest of Faulkner. I tried to imagine his reactions and to prepare appropriate responses.

I recalled that Faulkner had done a runner—escaped—from a police carrier taking him to Wakefield jail. Just how, nobody knew or perhaps, weren't letting on. The mystery surrounding his wife's locked room murder and the equally spooky locked room reported by Sergeant Fearon were saying something to me. If I knew what it was, I could have decided what to say to Flowers.

I leaned back into my chair and glanced at the memo about a man found in a cave and now in Widdecombe Park Hospital. He was in a coma. It was Robert Cleghorn, had to be. I made a note to send an officer down to investigate.

It was pretty well impossible to focus on the rest of the business piling up on the desk and discouraged, I pushed it to one side in favor of switching on my laptop and reviewing the Faulkner murder case. If anyone should glance through the window from the corridor outside, I would appear to be working hard, but they wouldn't know exactly what I was working on.

There was a multitude of facts to browse through but the ones I was interested in were those concerned with finding the body and the address at which it had occurred.

Just as I remembered, the woman's body had been discovered in a locked room on the third floor of a business premises. The murderer had certainly been in the room at the time of her death. The only means of egress was through one or other of the windows. Beyond the windows was a sheer drop of forty-two feet, with nowhere to fasten a rope and no marks on the window surround. This had convinced both the investigators and the jurors that escape that way was an impossibility and Faulkner doggedly remained silent on the subject.

I checked the post-mortem report. The coroner had determined that suffocation was the cause of death. Cotton fibers in the airways matching those found in an adjacent bedroom had also been found on Faulkner's person suggesting a spur-of-the-moment attack. That last suggestion was countered by what must have been a carefully planned escape.

Still, the post-mortem findings and DNA on the corpse were enough to convict the man. I yawned. The fact that Faulkner's hobby was conjuring and illusions with women disappearing from locked chests on a regular basis, was the final nail in his coffin, so to speak.

I thought about my father's collection of "locked room murder" stories, favorites of his. My middle initial came about because Dad was partial to Arthur Conan Doyle's sleuth. I'd read all of Dad's murder mystery books, of course. Yes, the door was locked from the inside, but the door panels always slipped out easily, or there was a hidden entrance alongside the door, cleverly disguised in the pattern of the Victorian wallpaper.

I yawned again. I took the papers with me with a vague intention of reading more at home but I knew I'd promised to call Dad that night. I left a note on Shelly's desk and an email to the lab for me to be notified of any developments and went down to the basement garage.

It was past six by the time I reached the butchers but he was still there cleaning up, and I tapped on the window. He beckoned me in and came across already carrying some bones for Pip.

"How're these?" And he popped them on to a sheet of grease-proof paper.

"Just what the doctor ordered. Thanks."

As always, Pip skittered around, as excited to see me as when he was a pup. I was always staggered to see how he had adapted to a three legged life after the farmer next door had shot him. My infrequent visitors often failed to notice that one of his forelegs had been amputated.

My dad was doing his best to sound hale and hearty when I phoned. "Hello, son."

I wasn't fooled for a moment, even though I was occupied stroking Pip's ears, all it took were those two words. "Hello, Dad. What's wrong?" I could tell he was unwell but just what the problem was…

"Ah, nothing much. The odd twinge here and there. It's just old age creeping up."

I winced at the tone in his voice. I just hoped that I didn't feel that way at seventy. "Rheumatism?"

"Yes. Probably. Nothing for you to worry about. I've got an appointment at the doctor's tomorrow, he'll prescribe something, some more of those pills and I'll be good as new." He changed the subject, anxious to get away from his aches and pains. "Did you catch that Faulkner fellow?"

"No, we didn't. He wasn't where we were told he was, but we'll get him sooner or later." We chatted a bit about his locked-room mysteries. He offered to pull a couple of titles out so we could discuss them more. I knew he was trying to sidetrack me but I wasn't having it. "Now, these pills that you take, are they painkillers or what?"

Dad hesitated, though not long enough to make something up. "Yes, that's what they are and I think they stop inflammatory…"

"Inflammation."

"That's what I said. They're supposed to, any rate. Never really been right since I had that fall, you know."

"Yeah, I know, and that's what worries me."

"There's no point in worrying. It'll either get better or it won't. I'm not grumbling; I've had a pretty good inning."

I guess I was feeling guilty. I hadn't been down to see him since I'd moved to Leeds, almost a year ago. "I'll call you tomorrow to see what he said, okay? Then we can make some arrangements for you to come and visit for a while."

CHAPTER 3

Leroy looked out at the bleak row of houses in Uppingham Road in Leicester. They had driven through the night to get here and now the sun was coming up behind them. It was around eight a.m. and the streets were bustling with people. They weren't the people that Leroy remembered, though. Leroy remembered blacks and Afro-Caribbeans. Now he saw Asians, from the sub-continent, women in saris but bundled up against the cold, and men in those long shirts that fit outside of their pants. He looked across at the Sikh. "Can't be more than ten years since I was here and this neighborhood was filled with…"

"With your brothers, hey?"

"Well, maybe twelve years."

"Things change, Mr. Richards. People come, people go. The whites all moved out to Wigston Fields and Uppingham, your brothers went out to the suburbs, and now the city belongs to us." Jasminder slowed and lit a cigarette he pulled, cowboy-style, from the soft packet he kept in a top pocket. "I could have told you, but you wouldn't have wanted to listen. So now, you can pay me and we shall go our own ways. Give me the gold, Mr. Richards." It was, perhaps, the longest unbroken discourse the Sikh had uttered in the past ten hours.

"Hey, hold on one minute. I haven't even tried the door yet. Give me five minutes. I promise not to sneak out the back. You've done what I asked, I won't rob you. Okay?"

"Rob me? I think you know better than to try that. My brothers are thicker around here than yours ever were. One shout from me and you'd be a dead man, Mr. Richards." The Sikh raised his left knee and scratched the ankle. Leroy thought he had a strap around it, maybe an athletic support.

Leroy smiled—not a nice expression. His whole demeanor changed. His words lost their usual Jamaican accent; now, they were sculpted from the Oxford English Dictionary. He was showing a side of himself that few had chanced to see—and some who had, had regretted it. "Are you as tough as you talk, Jasminder Singh? Or is it just talk?"

Leroy was answered by the sudden appearance of a hand the size of a bunch of bananas gripping his right biceps. The hand squeezed, it squeezed a shriek of pain out of Leroy's mouth.

Jasminder leaned closer. "I told you I was a driver, Mr. Richards but it's not all I do. Hmm? I do debt collecting, and that can take a lot of persuasion. Most of the things I do you don't need to know about and some of them, just a few, are very, very illegal. See this?"

A gun materialized in the driver's right hand; it pointed steadily between Leroy's anxious brown eyes. "Now, good shot or not, I can hardly miss from here." He let go of Leroy's arm. Leroy rubbed his right bicep and snatched the gun expertly away from Jasminder with his free hand.

The two men looked at each other appraisingly.

Leroy said thoughtfully, "Would you consider a career change?"

It was the Sikh's turn to be a little bemused. "Doing what? I don't take orders, Mr. Richards, I don't do that at all."

"I only offer suggestions, my friend. After discussion. Though there may be times when I know more than you do and we need to act quickly."

"Go on."

"You work for me and you'll be amply rewarded. More than amply."

Singh laughed. "I do not see any sign of that."

Leroy's features froze into a mask of black marble. "Just give me a little lee-way and I'll prove it to you. I don't just deal drugs. Your driving, that's just one thing, a sideline, yes? The same for me and drugs. Cut me a bit of slack and let me call on my friend."

"Just show me the money."

"You've got one helluva one-track mind."

"I've found that money's the only thing that talks around here. Show me the money and I'll be your friend."

Leroy tossed the tiny ingot of gold at Singh. "Here, take it and if you want more, you stick with me. Reckon that's enough to buy a day of your precious time, Jasminder."

He turned the gun over in his hand and kept it for the moment.

Leroy opened the door to the van and crossed to number 412. He rang the bell and waited, certain that even an earthquake would not have moved Smiley from his abode. Not without him hearing about it, anyway.

The door opened and framed the fattest black man that the Sikh, watching from the van, had ever seen. A huge tooth-filled smile in perfect proportion to the man's girth beamed down at Leroy.

"Leroy my man. Nobody told me you was out."

"Leroy smiled back, a smile of genuine happiness to see his friend again. "Thought I'd surprise you. You got anything eatable in that fridge of yours?"

"Has a cat got claws, man? C'mon in."

"I will, I will. If you got two plates, I'd be even more pleased 'cause I got someone with me."

"I'll make it three plates. I is always happy to eat."

"Won't be a sec." Leroy went back to the van, "You hungry, Jasminder?"

"Asmin," said the other. "Call me Asmin."

"Call me Leroy—'cept when we've got brothers around, okay?"

"Could use a bathroom, too."

Leroy was already on the new cell phone they had picked up en route. He nodded toward the doorway still filled with Smiley's figure. "We've got all the modern conveniences here, indoor plumbing and all." He handed the gun back to Asmin.

"Hey, Smiley, you've done us proud."

For several minutes there was no other sound but that of mastication. Succulent chicken, mashed potatoes and gravy were not exactly a breakfast but for fast food conjured up in minutes, they served very well.

"Two-hundred-fifty a day and all found," said Leroy, wiping his mouth and picking up the conversation where it had left off.

"Ah!" Asmin caught up.

"In a little while, a tailor will be coming to measure us up for new gear. I like my right-hand man to dress as well as I do. That okay?"

"Okay, but I have questions. How did you know that Smiley would still be here and what do I call you when it's not Leroy? Boss? And what happened to your last right-hand man?"

Leroy pursed his lips. "You just ask Smiley who put all the extra-size doorways in here and who paid for the extra-strong fixtures in the bathroom and the reinforced king-size bed. Smiley and I go back a long ways. As for calling me *boss*," Leroy shook his head. "Nobody calls me boss, that's a whitey word. Leroy's good enough most of the time. If we're being formal, you know? Talking to another crew. 'Mr. Richards' will do fine. That's what my friends and my competitors call me. Most people are friends and my enemies don't call me nothin'."

Leroy finished off his coffee. "Ah, Smiley, that was good. I'm feelin' almost normal again."

"And your last right-hand man?"

"That's an ongoing matter, Asmin. We'll both find out in due course."

"Oh, and by the way," he continued. "I got a network of safe houses all over and I have money stashed here and there too. I was unlucky the night that copper, that *In-spec-tor* White caught me. Won't happen again. You in?"

Asmin looked at Leroy then at Smiley. Leroy looked at Smiley then at Asmin. There were three big grins at the table.

CHAPTER 4

I pointed to the chair on the far side of my desk and reached for Shelly's report. "Take the weight off, Shelly." I opened the folder, closed it and put it back into my in-tray. "Anything in there I don't know and need to know?"

"Not especially. We've still no idea how the perpetrator left the room but this," she handed me the cell phone, "this might prove interesting. It's as clean as a whistle and there's just one text message, received at 1535 yesterday and obviously meant for us."

I picked it up and found the text inbox. *All is not as it seems, obviously. Like my wife's murder scene.* That was it, there were no further messages. "The sender's number?" I asked, knowing the answer.

"One time use sim card. Buy them by the dozen."

"Seems that this is from Faulkner and he's telling us that his wife's murder setting was as carefully set up as this one. I think we owe it to him to solve the mystery of 'Hey Presto.'"

She nodded. "Oh, I think so. He knew we were coming. Not us specifically, but the police, and I think he's suggesting his wife's murder was a set-up in some way."

"You're right, of course. Have we got another *Fugitive* on our hands, I wonder."

"Fugitive?"

"You're too young to know about it, Shelly." Shelly giggled. "It's a bit of a cult film. Starred Harrison Ford. The guy was arrested for his wife's murder, he escaped and spent the rest of the film proving his wife was killed by a one-armed man."

"And it was an American TV series before that—before BOTH our times," Shelly said with a wry grin. "And that'll make him easier to spot, Boss. We'll interview all one-armed men in the UK. I wonder if there is some reason he wants *us* to investigate?"

"Could be, I suppose. Maybe just because we, the police, are the ones with access to the original murder scene." I sighed and chewed a knuckle. "In my experience, wherever there's a crime committed behind locked doors without a perpetrator in the room, there's either another way in and out or it's a ghost and I don't believe in ghosts."

"You get a lot of these?"

"This is my first. But if he can make us believe there's no way in and out this time, then we have to believe someone else could have done it before."

"Or he did both. We're going to have to go back to the original murder scene."

I thought about it for a while and finally nodded agreement. "But not with our workload at the moment. I'm going to have to do it in my own time."

It had been raining, but we hadn't noticed it, even with the wind slamming the raindrops against the window. The flash of lightning that lit the room followed immediately by a devastating thunder clap made us both jump, hearts fluttering.

"Jesus! Thought that was the end of all things."

I chuckled. "Announcing the arrival of Old Nick!"

There was a cough at the door. Superintendent Flowers stood there, his suit as immaculate as always. The thunder reverberated and died away, Flowers spoke as soon as he could be heard. "Faulkner?" The question was aimed at me, he ignored Sergeant Fearon completely.

"'Fraid not, I've just got the report in the last few minutes." I tapped the green folder in my tray. "We have a message left on a phone though; a phone on a table in a room double-locked from the inside and the outside."

His eyes bulged with anger. "He's playing games with us. A locked-room? It's a TV cliché."

I nodded agreement. "He sort of suggests that. He seems to be saying that the murder of his wife was just exactly that."

Flowers shrugged. He glanced at Shelly for the first time and then at her report. "Not our problem. Send the report to Sheffield and get on with some real work."

Oh dear... I looked at Shelley. "Thank you Sergeant Fearon, we can discuss your next job later, probably the Murphy thing, I think."

As Shelly left the room, one eyebrow raised as she shut the door, Superintendent Flowers did the same though it signaled quite a different sentiment. "Murphy?"

"Travelers, Joe." I paused, recollecting the case, "There are seventy-three Smiths claiming benefits from one small post office."

"Common name. Why should it concern us?"

"We've reason to believe that the seventy-three Smiths are, in fact, a single small family who spend their waking hours filling in forms for non-existent recipients of her Majesty's Government's benefits. £137,000 so far and rising."

"Fraud."

"As you say. And theft, and misrepresentation and quite a few other misdemeanors with long names." I was trying to keep the thing on a light-hearted note but it was hard work. "Either the family is a troop of quick-change artists or the Post Office staff needs glasses. Or... they were in on the job."

"Or stupid. How did they realize it was going on?"

"It was the head office personnel. They noticed the similarity in signatures and reported their suspicions to Leeds Metropolitan who passed it on to us."

"And we are going to... ?"

"I have Bell out there with a camcorder. Giro day today and they'll be collecting checks," I checked my watch, "as we speak. Once they're identified, we'll be visiting their trailer park. Sergeant Fearon will be heading out there about one this afternoon."

"What about this afternoon, won't there be more collections going on then?"

"They've made a habit of collecting the checks before eleven a.m. They like to get them paid in to the bank and cleared as soon as possible."

"I suppose they'll be entitled to some of it." Flowers seemed intent on dotting every last 'i.'

"Oh indeed, but it's the rest of the handouts we want to stop."

"Hmm, good. Venal, can't understand some people. Oh, and I almost forgot, there's a woman in reception. American. They put her on to me for some reason. Name of Cleghorn? Sister of that mixed-up serial killer, Alan?"

"Robert." I said," Alan was the brother whom he killed in Florida. The inquest has just finished. Last week, I think."

"That's it then. She wants to pick up his things. Stuff in the evidence locker. Can you see to that?"

"Sure." *Cleghorn.* A name I had hoped not to hear again. For some reason, my heart was pumping a little harder than usual.

Flowers was still hanging around. "Another thing. Do you recall a Leroy Richards?"

"I remember, yes." I remembered the face as he was taken down at Birmingham Crown Court, the white teeth, predatory smile, and the stare he had given me as he passed.

Flowers nodded, pleased with himself. "Thought there was a connection. Remembered the name from your record before you moved here. Yes, well, he escaped from Asket Farm, it's a category C prison. Didn't even give it twenty-four hours before he was over the fence. Hmm."

Flowers left and I followed more slowly, stopping as I came to the elevators.

Connie Cleghorn was a petite creature, with hair the color of ripe corn. The hair could have been genuine or out of a bottle, not that it would matter with a woman this stunning. I tried not to stare. I thought she might be in her late twenties or early thirties, which would make her younger than her brother by at least a decade—but then, I'm no expert in these matters. She certainly had an engaging smile, probably as appealing as Robert's when he was feeling affable. It would put most people at their ease—and certainly had that effect on me.

She rose from the bench as I entered and came toward me, her hand extended. "Good morning, you must be Inspector White."

Her drawl was pure American South. Savannah, Georgia, the super had said. I'd been to Atlanta several times and nearly came back with the drawl myself. I am a sucker for southern belles, with their languid way of talking and old-fashioned manners. I had to clear my throat before speaking. "That's right. I understand you've come to claim your brother's effects."

"Yes, suitcases and what-not belonging to Alan. Robert… *borrowed* them."

She put the slightest emphasis on "borrowed" and gave me a half-smile. It didn't show, I'm sure, but Robert's name had me frowning inside. He had come to England posing as his brother Alan and virtually gone berserk. He'd committed multiple murders and terrorized his sister-in-law. That was the better part of a year ago, but some of the memories were still pretty sharp.

"And how do you know about Alan's things, Miss Cleghorn?"

"Mrs. Emmanuel, Inspector." She smiled again. "I'm still using my married name until it's officially changed back."

"Ah, sorry. Guess I misunderstood. Your husband passed away recently?"

She grinned and her brown eyes flashed with devilish amusement. "Passed away? Now, that's cute. Actually, he did pass on, in a manner of speaking. He passed on to Mary Jo Chasnic—a somewhat younger, somewhat richer version of *me*." She drawled out the last word a bit and gave a short, maybe flirtatious laugh. "At least he stayed true to type."

I am a trained observer, and I saw the way her eyes appraised me. I tried to see what *she* saw: recently barbered hair, well-shined shoes, dark gray suit fresh from the dry cleaners, and I didn't have this morning's breakfast on my tie. Not that I ever had—not on duty, anyway. I pride myself on good grooming.

I've never been what you'd call a lady's man, and my flirting skills were dulled. I'd never been married, but I did go through about a dozen or so girlfriends. Still, I wasn't sure how to respond to this revelation about her personal life.

She must have sensed my discomfiture. She waved a hand in dismissal. "She's welcome to him. He was what my British grandma would have called a cad and a bounder, not that I'm sure what either one of those things is, but I can guess."

I laughed at her candid remark. I admired her refreshing *panache*, I'd guess you'd call it.

It had been quite a long time since I'd come under the influence of a pretty woman. My Sergeant, Shelly Fearon, had been the last but that romance had died on the vine. Now this woman had me fairly drooling after knowing her for less than five minutes. What ailed me?

"You were asking about the things Robert left."

Her voice jolted me back to the present. "Ah, yes."

"My right to take them, I guess you'd say." She was burrowing in a big leather bag. "It's in here somewhere." She rummaged a bit more and brought out a crumpled piece of paper. "Ah! Here we go. I got this letter from the White House—hey, the White House, no less—telling me I'd have to call in person if I wanted the stuff."

I could see the battered sheet was imprinted with the American eagle at the top with "The White House," in bold letters below. I took it from her and read it. It was as she said, with an indecipherable signature at the bottom claiming to belong to the Secretary of State.

Fine, I had no problem in handing the effects over but just for form's sake I asked her, "Do you have your passport with you?"

"I surely do." More burrowing. "Here."

I made a note of the number and asked the clerk at the Reception desk to prepare a receipt. I walked her down to the evidence room and the attendant found the belongings in no time. Fortunately they consisted of a wheeled suitcase and a bag strapped to the top, so she would be able to cart the luggage out behind her.

Being a gentleman, I trundled the baggage back to the reception area for her. She walked a couple of steps ahead of me, and I enjoyed the scent of her perfume wafting in my direction. The smell was familiar, something a girlfriend from long ago had worn perhaps.

"Well, thank you, Inspector White." She paused and gave me an oblique look from under her long, mascaraed lashes. "I love your accent. You Brits all sound so classy. James Bond. You know?" She paused and pursed her lips. "Um… are you married?"

Well, that was bold. I laughed a little self-consciously. "I love your accent, too. And no, I'm not married." I shifted on my feet, feeling rather like a poster boy for *Bumpkins R Us* under the gaze of this much-too-attractive lady. "I suppose I've never met anyone who'd put up with my weird working hours, or just me."

We reached the door. "If you came home at all, Inspector, it would be an improvement over my dear nearly-departed husband. My ex was what we call a 'good ol' boy', spent all his time hunting, fishing, hanging out at a place called Doc's with his buddies, or gallivantin' around with some other woman."

She looked me up and down. "You know, I don't know a soul in this town. Would you have dinner with me this evening?" She wrinkled her pert little nose. "I don't know a thing about British food, you could help me. My treat of course."

There was no logical way I could sidestep her invitation to dinner without appearing rude; not that I wanted to refuse her. We arranged for me to pick her up at her flat. I felt flattered except I wondered—what could be her motive? I was sure I hadn't swept her off her feet with my *savoir-faire*. And I was hardly James Bond.

But the lady would bear watching.

CHAPTER 5

The morning after Leroy's arrival in Leicester, he sat at Smiley's breakfast table, his fingers sticky with toast and honey. Sky TV was on the box and he was making notes on a slightly greasy scratch pad. There was no mention of his escape on the news. He switched to the BBC, nothing there either.

"No use looking at the national stuff, Leroy. You might have made it onto one of the Yorkshire channels but we're not goin' to see it here. You think everyone's forgotten about you? You worried someone knows our connection?"

"Not here and not now. I thought that might be so the night I got caught on the canal. Somebody squealed for certain and I reckon I know who. Didn't think about it at the time, I was too worried by the bloody copper who brought me in."

Smiley watched Leroy get himself worked up.

"I was in the water, was swimmin' away from the boat. He could have let me go but, oh no, he had his reputation to make, din't he? Dived in and pulled me back to the bank. Then made out I'd been drowning. Now that is just plain meanness." Leroy's voice had fallen back into character. He wiped his fingers on a handkerchief.

Smiley listened to the story and eventually said, "He's a copper, his job is to catch folks like you, Leroy. Why would he let you swim away?"

"Pretty soon I'm going to show that *De-tec-tive In-spec-tor* what being mean is all about."

Leroy shook himself and changed the subject. He nodded to the back door. "Where does that go?"

"The backyard. Brick walls, totally private. You know that. You need to escape, you go up in this house. There's a pole with a hook on next to your bedroom door, remember?"

"Been a while, Smiley. Yeah, I saw the pole."

"There's a hatch in the ceiling straight above. Push that up and pull the ladder down. Go up there and pull the ladder up behind you an' bolt the hatch closed."

"And that's it? Rats in a sinking ship?"

"Nah. You n' anyone you're taking with you go across the boarded walkway, there's a flashlight there, get up there and take a look."

"I will, Smiley. Bet on it. Where does the walkway go?"

"You go on 'til it stops and there's another hatch. That puts you in the end house in this row which is just like this one 'cept the backyard has a door in the wall, straight across from you. Just go downstairs like you own the place and walk out."

"That's rich, my man. Rich. And that's it?"

"Oh no." Smiley rolled his eyes. "That door in the backyard goes into a garage? Inside there's a four-by-four?"

Leroy nodded.

"You can damn near drive that ve-hi-cle straight up a wall, it'll get you anywhere you want to go. There's two buttons on the dash, red and yellow, yellow opens the outside doors, red closes 'em."

"You got some nifty preparations, Smiley."

Smiley grinned. "An' if you ain't drivin', suppose you just want to hide? Lift the front bench seat, climb in and don't make a peep. It's padded, there's bottled water, there's energy tabs. You're safe."

Leroy smiled almost as big a smile as Smiley's. He shook his head. "You're my guardian angel, Smiley. Anyone else know about it?"

Smiley shook his head. "Not now. Remember Daemone?"

Leroy nodded, suddenly sad.

"He used it once, no, twice an' got away both times, but he gone now."

"God rest his soul," said Leroy sincerely.

"What about you, Smiley? You ever used it?"

"Me?" Smiley roared with laughter. "You wait 'til you see how you get there. I couldn't get up the stairs, let alone fit through those dinky little holes in the ceiling. No, if the *po-lice* ever come for you, you get away and I'll swear blind I don't know you." He parodied a Jamaican accent: "I don' know him officer, never saw 'im before he come through ma door."

There was a loud rush of boots on the staircase and a moment later Asmin came through the door from the hallway. "You want some breakfast, Asmin?"

"Yes, Leroy. I do."

"Then get it down you, we'll be going for a ride shortly. I got questions to ask and answers to get. Don't make any plans for the next twenty-four hours, got quite a few people to see."

They visited in quick succession a bank, a hardware store, and an angling supplies store. After the last stop Leroy said, with a satisfied expression on his face. "Now we head for Doncaster in Yorkshire, know where that is?"

Asmin gave his new boss a look which Leroy interpreted, quite correctly, as 'Does a bear crap in the woods?' They stopped for lunch on the way and arrived in Doncaster a little over two hours later. They drove up to a commercial premises, concrete, with black metal doors that folded to one side. Leroy asked Asmin to stay in the van and was gone for an hour. Asmin slept until he came out and climbed back inside.

"We can go back to Leicester now."

"Oh."

"We can go back in the van or we can leave it here and go back in a Jaguar. Don't worry if you're attached to the van, you won't hurt my feelings. How do *you* feel about it? If you do stick with me, I don't think you'll need your van."

It didn't take much thinking. Asmin nodded. "Reckon the Jag'll be faster."

Asmin got out and took a number of bags and bundles out of the rear doors of the van. "Personal things," he explained to Leroy.

The personal things only just fitted into the Jaguar XK. "Should have gotten a four-door." Leroy said, watching the process with a grin on his face.

"I'll move them out when we get back," Asmin said, a little embarrassed.

Leroy nodded. "Five litre direct-injection V8 engine, Asmin. Gives out seventy-nine horsepower. Won't slow us down. Oh, take us north first. You've got a snazzy little SatNav there, set it for Garforth, it's a small town just a little off the A1."

They settled down into the aptly named *Celestial Black* Jaguar. Asmin set the SatNav and started the tastefully quiet engine, he seemed almost asleep, in a dream world. He pressed the accelerator and the two men sank back into the *scraffito*-finished leather of the front seats.

Once they had gone a mile or two and Asmin was comfortable with the feel of the vehicle, Leroy passed him a polythene bag, inside were bundles of bank notes. "Ten thousand," he said quietly and watched the slight twitch of Asmin's eyebrows. "In fifties."

Asmin's lips stretched in a smile. He stuffed the bag into a side pocket in the door.

"That's what I like to see, my man. A flash of those pearly whites. Now, on to Garforth, I need to see an old friend."

"Not going to Winston's house, are you?"

"That was the idea."

"Doubt the police will have given up on you yet, Leroy."

"Hmm. What does Winston mean to you, Asmin? Is he a friend?"

"He's my paycheck, Leroy. Or he was. He's paid me to fetch and carry from time to time, that's it."

Leroy nodded, satisfied with the other's answer. "That's good." He passed something else to Asmin, something heavy, and continued talking. "I thought he was my friend. I treated him like one, like a brother. But I found out it was all just for show. He ain't much of a friend to anyone."

Asmin took his eyes off the road for a second. Leroy had given him a gun. He knew what it was, a Browning semi-automatic. He didn't remind Leroy that he already had one. Without a word, he slipped it into an inside pocket.

Leroy saw Asmin secrete the gun and the way he did it reminded him of William Jarvis, years ago. Back in the home, Jarvis had had a coat with a secret inside pocket. All manner of things found their way in there including food, drinks, in fact just about anything not nailed down. Sometimes Jarvis shared them with him and Lofty but not often. Leroy had suspected him of stealing cake from the food parcels he used to receive but he had to admit he was too scared to confront the youngster. Jarvis had a vicious streak, revealed to all by the many ways he had invented of killing cats and taking joy from the acts.

Leroy could hardly believe it when he heard he had drowned.

He didn't stop grinning for a week.

CHAPTER 6

Dad's report from his visit to the hospital was not good. Not as bad as I feared it would be but not good. It appeared that his sciatic nerve kept touching the spinal cord where the discs had worn thin. That touch was causing a red-hot dagger of pain, anti-inflammatory pills were the only answer. He and the doctor had a long conversation, he was to get off his feet as much as possible to let the swelling go down.

I arranged with an old colleague to parcel up Poppa and deliver him to me the following weekend. That gave me time to get the house ready and warn him to get a suitcase packed.

I made the phone call from the Gents restroom for privacy and when I got back to the office, Sergeant Bell was waiting for me, standing conspicuously out-side my door. When I first came to Leeds, Sergeant Bell and I had not imme-diately hit it off. He was a somewhat brusque individual as well as a doubting Thomas. Relations had improved since then; I had found his strengths and played to them, it improved his self-esteem.

"Okay Sergeant Bell, come in, sit down."

He followed me to my desk and dropped a report on the blotter. Reports were another, er, strength of his.

"Got them bang to rights." Popular phrases were another.

"I take it we're talking about the Murphys?"

"Murphys, Smiths, travelers, whatever you want to call them."

"What do you call them?" I knew it was a mistake as soon as I said it.

"Waste of…"

"Yes." I nodded to cut him off and nodded. "As public servants, you and I are not supposed to express these sorts of opinions. There's good and bad in everybody."

He looked at me a little oddly. "Sir? We followed them back to their park and raided three vans. We could have paid all our salaries for a year with the money we found stuffed into every nook and cranny of those vans. Cushions, mattresses, they all rustled when we picked them up."

I heaved a great sigh of relief. "Aha, and what else?"

"Statements by the dozen, three confessions, so far."

I could see Sergeant Bell wanted a pat on the back and I guess he deserved it though I had already complimented him on other matters this week. I didn't want to over-inflate his ego. I gave him a handshake, a mental congratulation and turned to other matters.

I managed to get one report finished for Flowers before the next interruption. Despite our cooled personal relationship, Sergeant Fearon was still more welcome than Bell. I looked up with a smile.

"Are we still on for the house in the woods this afternoon?"

"The 'Hey Presto' case? Did we agree on this afternoon?"

"We did."

"Then it's fine, unless something more important turns up."

"Great. I also wondered if you wanted to see the original murder location in Sheffield."

"Now that is something I *do* want to do."

"We could go straight over there afterwards. It's only thirty miles and motorway all the way. I've arranged a provisional visit with a contact down there."

I nodded. "Can we make 'Hey Presto' three-thirty then? I'll shave a half-hour off my lunch break."

She frowned. "A lunch break? What's that? A perk for you senior officers?"

I opened a drawer and took out a red file. I slid it across to her. "You'll be able to check out the perks we get, yourself, very shortly."

"Huh?" she said as she picked up the file.

"You requested a place on the Inspector's Course a little while ago. It's been approved." I took a great deal of pleasure from the smile that lit up her features. It was like the Shelly I'd first met. She'd been pregnant at that time by her ex-husband and she'd had a miscarriage a month or two later; it had knocked the stuffing out of her and out of what might have been a great relationship between us. The least I could do was recommend her for the Inspector's course.

Shelly's eyes became a little damp and she turned away, probably hoping I hadn't noticed. She knew I'd given her a glowing recommendation.

The house outside Leeds was just as I'd pictured it from the recordings and discussion. When we arrived, two SOCO officers were chipping plaster off the walls in what had been the locked room. No, not SOCO now; they were called CSI—Crime Scene Investigators. It had been nearly a year since they had changed the name to CSI; same people, different name; I must try to get into using their new one. They were on the final wall with the others already down to the brickwork on one side and to the studding in the other two. It was pretty obvious that there weren't—and never had been—any openings.

"I think you can give the rest of that a miss," I said. "It's an outer wall and we'd have seen evidence outside." I studied the floor as they stood back. "That's close boarded; no sign of disturbance. Ceiling?" I looked upwards. "Got to be there."

The older of the two officers spoke up. "Suspended ceiling tiles. We thought of that first and examined it. Above that one there's the older one, it's polystyrene tiles. No sign of disturbance there either."

"I want it stripped, though, Jerry. If you give me a tool of some sort, I'll give you a hand." He gave me the barest eyebrow movement—*if he wants to be stupid…*

We pulled all the suspended tiles down and started on the polystyrene stuff that had been stuck to the ceiling plaster. Jerry found what we were looking for, a plus for good relations. The tiles were about eighteen inches square and one had been dropped in from above and stuck in place with a bead of adhesive around the edges. It certainly wasn't apparent from a visual inspection, only when we saw the slight difference in materials did we realize it.

The tile was directly over the table and it concealed a piece of plaster board above that had been let into the rest of ceiling.

"That's it then guys. Not magic after all."

Much sooner than we expected, Shelly and I were on our way south. I was driving because I wanted Shelly to navigate, she would need to do a fair amount of that on her Inspectors course. "I'll give Ned a call," Shelly said, tapping a number into her phone as we waited at a traffic light.

"I think I'd have tried the ceiling first," I mused after she had told Ned we expected to be early.

"I think I would too," she agreed, "but why not work from the walls up? They were being cautious; they'd have got the blame if anything had been missed."

"Yes, that's true. I don't think Superintendent Flowers believes that to err is human."

"It's next right, according to the SatNav." And a minute later, "Now left into Cardinal Street."

Shelly pointed. "There's Ned—I mean D.C. Stokes, the one in the dark brown sports jacket, the one talking to that bald-headed guy."

She braked to a stop just as the man with the shiny pate walked away. We got out and Shelly gave Ned a mock salute. The street was mainly offices at street level with flats on the upper floors.

After the introductions, Stokes took us across the road to a five-story Victorian building with access blocked off with yellow and black tape. He took us up a side passage to a door at the back and pulled out a bunch of keys.

"No point in ripping the tape off and announcing our presence, sir. How long will you need?"

"Oh, not long. Er, Ned?"

Ned gave me a broad grin showing that he liked familiarity." Right you are, guv." He opened the door and relocked it from inside. "Shelly and I were rookies together, you know?"

I nodded. "Yes, she told me, so let's see what we can make of this crime scene. If there's time later, I'll get us a beer, Okay?"

We were climbing the twisting concrete staircase when my foot slammed into something which went off like an explosion. "Damn!" I switched on my flashlight, discovered the remains of a bottle that had been left there, and brushed my pants down to remove any bits of glass.

We carried on up the passageway, our footsteps on the hard red-tiled floor echoing around the space. The room in which the murder had taken place was like the Leeds site, bolts on both sides of the door. There was only one reason I could think of for them being there and that was because the murderer wanted it that way. It was clean, white-painted walls and ceiling except for a light rose with exaggerated segments picked out in gold and a ceiling molding—broader than normal—highlighted in lime green. The high ceiling was old, apart from a crack running all the way across, it was plain. There were no furnishings and I was about to ask when Shelly got in first.

"There was a settee, an office chair, two guest chairs and a desk here. They've been taken away, they're back in storage."

"Right." I nodded and began a slow walk around the space, stopping to take samples of dust which was only noticeable because it adorned a cobweb. I dropped it with some of the spider's furnishings into an evidence bag.

I completed the circuit. I looked at the floor: typical heavy duty brown linoleum and waxed, probably weekly, by the office cleaners. There was nothing, no clues of any description. I shook my head and as a last resort, I went around the walls again, tapping every six inches and listening. Only around the bank of four light switches was the sound different, as you'd expect.

I shook my head, my frustration must have been obvious. "Disappointing after our success this afternoon," I said. I certainly wasn't in the mood for drinks and didn't mention my earlier offer.

CHAPTER 7

Winston Umbok sank the black, smiled and punched the air in delight. "That's three games to one, Freddie. Ha ha, not your night, is it?"

Freddie, whom Winston employed as a bodyguard but whose duties encompassed chauffeur, companion, and grunt, grinned back. He was accustomed to losing; it made life much easier. "We leavin' Boss? Gone eleven."

Winston nodded. "I guess so." The club steward would be around shortly, switching off the lights. Winston loved the once-a-week outings and treasured every minute at the tables. He had a snooker table at home but it wasn't the same as a night at the club, where everyone could see how he could put the balls away.

He dropped the cue ball into a corner pocket and straightened up, taking his cue apart and laying it in the velvet lined wooden box. "That's a *Jack Everett*." He would say on most occasions. "Handmade. You don't see many of those, these days." He snapped the clasps closed and left the box on the bar, knowing it would be locked away until his next visit—a privilege of being a member of the small, exclusive club.

"The 'Solace of India' is next, I reckon. We'll see if the curry's getting any better. Get the car started; I'll just pay a visit." When Winston came out of the restroom, he high-fived the steward who was waiting to lock up. The car, a gleaming white Porsche Cayenne, was grumbling quietly to itself just outside. He opened the passenger door and slid into the rear seat still thinking of the way he had kissed that final black into the pocket.

The car was speeding away from the club when a sixth sense warned him that something was wrong. There was a chuckle from the front; a voice that was definitely not Freddie's. "Creature of habit, Winston, ain't ya?

The question registered in his brain long before he identified the man driving the Porsche. As oncoming headlights outlined the driver's features, he knew. "Leroy?"

"Correct, my man. See, you haven't really forgotten me, have you?" It was more of a statement than a question.

Leroy's voice froze Winston's bone to the marrow. He leaned forward and did his best not to sound fazed. "How could I forget, Boss? Huh? Been countin' the days. Good to see you—bit of a surprise though, you gettin' out like that." Winston took a deep breath. "Where's Freddie got to, then?"

Leroy's chuckle was no more comforting than before. "Freddie decided not to join us. He's… let's just say he's taken a side trip." Leroy thought about the dumpster where Asmin had dropped the unconscious chauffeur after relieving him of the car keys with a smile. "So don't you worry about getting a curry tonight; we have business matters to discuss."

"Shall we go to my place?"

"Oh, Winston, man." There was no false jocularity now. "Guess you'd really appreciate that, eh? There's more police 'round your place than a rat has fleas. No, we called earlier, see? We picked up everything we needed for a business meeting."

"You called at my house?"

"That's right, across your backyard. Nobody watchin' there. It's in your name, of course, but we all know where the money came from. Don't we, Winston?"

"What's that mean?"

Leroy stamped on the brakes and sent the car skidding to the side of the road. He switched on the interior light and turned to look at his former lieutenant. He pulled a wad of paper out of his pocket and flapped it in front of Winston's frightened eyes.

"Bank statements, Winston. Tell quite a story, hey? Tell how you transferred all of *my* money into *your* name—how you been livin' high off the hog? *Too* high, Winston. New posh home, flashy expensive car, jewel-covered women." Leroy saw the other's eyes widen in the low light. "Oh yes, we met Shaylene. Obliging girl, handed over all that gold and the two diamond rings and the other stuff when I explained how it was my money that bought 'em. Real meek, she was."

"Leroy…" Winston licked his lips. "Leroy, I'm sorry you think so badly of me. I've been earning my own money since you went away. Okay, it *was* your money bought me the house—had to move away to keep the cops from seizing everything as proceeds of crime. They'd already taken your old house before I decided it was best to move your funds out of your old accounts."

"Ah, I see, that makes it all right then. Sellin' drugs to my clients which makes the profits mine anyhow since you used my money in the first place. There's no problem though." Leroy started the car and doused the interior light. "You can transfer all that money into my new account, my old money and my new money. You do that and I'll think about how to reward you."

Winston was shivering, his hands clenched into impotent fists. He was trying to think of something convincing to say. "Sure, Boss. We'll go to the bank tomorrow."

"No need, we can do it online. Got all the routing numbers."

"But my laptop's back at the house."

"Oh no, man. I knew you'd see things my way so we brought it with us. And there's that backup machine you keep under the floor in the trunk." Leroy slowed the car, turned off the main road and down a bumpy track. "I think this is the right place." He came to a stop under a high-arched railway viaduct; Asmin was parked a little further along in the Jaguar. Presently, he joined Winston on the back seat of the Porsche.

Winston looked out at the darkness and knew that this was not going to end well. What could he do? Leroy would have a gun for sure, he was helpless. His shaking fingers typed the necessary details for the wire transfer, then he passed the laptop over to Leroy—who passed it back over the seat to Asmin.

Leroy nodded. "Send it off, my son, then show our friend the way home."

The look on Winston's face was one of mixed relief and gratitude. He thought he was getting away with it. He had dreaded the coming of this day.

His relief was interrupted as Asmin reached across and clamped a huge hand on Winston's shoulder. Winston tried to duck and run but the arm behind the hand was like the branch of an oak tree, immoveable.

"What do you want me to do with him, Leroy?"

Winston glanced at Asmin. It hadn't been that long since he'd arranged for the man to pick Leroy up from the Asket Farm prison and dump him out on the moors somewhere.

"Asmin? Come on, man! Let me be—you work for *me.*"

Leroy's teeth glinted white in the moonlight. "Wrong, Winston. Not any-more, not since he saw how *you* been working for *me.* Throw him down the bank, Asmin."

The big man's hand pulled Winston out of the back of the car like a sack of groceries and hurled him away. Winston rolled head over heels down a steep earthen bank leaving clothes and skin on tree stumps and stones in equal mea-sure. He came to a stop at the bottom and, totally demoralized, struggled to a sitting position.

Leroy called down to him, "Remember what you said when I got caught by that copper in the canal? *Should have swum faster.* That's what you said, Winston. Bet you didn't think I heard that, did you? I wondered why you cried off that job, Winston."

"I didn't mean nothin', Boss."

"Well, just in front of you is a stretch of water. You show me how fast *you* can swim across. We'll help you, give you some incentive; my man here—used to be *your* man—is going to shoot at you. Asmin's going to give you a ten seconds start so I'd start now, if I were you."

Asmin counted to ten and then fired three or four shots around the dis-turbed water where Winston floundered. The splashing died away, the water was black and unreflective. Beyond and where the mist began, there was no sign of Winston.

CHAPTER 8

I met Connie a few days later. "I wondered if I'd see you again," I started. "I don't get the chance to socialize much—because of my job. But I'd welcome the opportunity to show you around." I had to admit, the chance to look around appealed to me, too. "Actually, it would give me a chance to get to know the area as well. I've been here almost a year and still haven't seen much more than the city."

"And you live here?" she drawled.

I was far more interested in finding out more about the woman sitting opposite me than talking about scenic beauty spots. What did she want from me? Was her whole coming on to me thing genuine, or did she have other motives?

"I live about ten miles from here, in the country."

"Ten miles is nothin.' I go ten miles to get to a Red Lobster."

I grinned. "Yeah, I hear what you're saying but five of those ten miles are across the city where the traffic is as bad as I hear it is in New York, and there's no public transport over the other five."

I could see her turning this over in her mind. "Public transport? Like a bus? This place is seriously weird."

I chuckled. "No trains, no buses and you need a bank loan for a taxi. So, maybe you're right."

She nodded. "Guess I'm lucky then. I don't need taxis. Robert's involvement with the secret services gave me a couple of perks. I've got the use of a dinky little car and an apartment to match while I'm over here."

"And how long is that going to be?"

"I'm flavor of the month for some reason. The Director kind of cottoned to me; I can stay up to three months if I've a mind to."

I took note of that: it seemed a little too easy. The Director of what? The CIA? I wondered if Connie worked for the US government too, or even if she was who she said she was. I knew Robert Cleghorn was alive, albeit in a possibly permanent coma. Did she? I shook off my thoughts and took a sip of my drink. Connie was looking at me curiously.

"And are you likely to be here for all three months?" I asked.

"Could depend on how this evening turns out. Pour me a little more of that good Jack Daniels, my ice is getting dry." She had managed to look coy as she peered at me over the rim of her glass.

I reached for the bottle and poured her some more but none for me. As I put the bottle down, she gave me a look somewhere between hurt and incredulous. "I thought you Brits were big drinkers?"

"Sorry, Connie, not this Brit. Besides, I'm on a murder case and I daren't be hung over tomorrow." I thought maybe she pouted a little. "Day after that's Saturday though. Let me take you out tomorrow evening and it'll be a different matter."

She picked up her glass and stood up, a little wobbly and supporting herself on the table, came around to my side. I looked up just as she was bending down and our lips sort of collided. It was off center and tasted of whiskey but I have to admit despite my reservations, it was very pleasurable.

It was dark on the canal towpath and the man with the roll of carpet over his shoulder moved carefully, watching his footing. There was a small cabin cruiser moored just here, it was the only craft in sight. The man made his way across the gangplank without stopping. He did not pause on deck as he pushed into the cabin. There was a gasp for breath as he dropped the heavy roll of carpet. He bent and rolled the carpet along the floor, revealing the man's body concealed inside.

The final couple of feet of carpet had rolled back through the door, he bent and lifted the edge high enough to make the body roll further into the cabin, rolling up the carpet as it came free. Finally, he re-rolled the carpet without the body inside and left it out on the deck.

Inside once more, he pulled the door closed, locked and bolted it on the inside and then went forward to the bulkhead, beyond which were the bedroom and galley and tiny bathroom. He then kneeled, pulled at the foot of the bulkhead and disappeared.

Moments later he reappeared out on deck and walked back along the narrow decking at the side of the cabin to lock the door from the outside. The roll of carpet went over the side and sank with barely a ripple in the dark water. Any evidence that adhered to it would be food for fish and insect larvae before long.

Back to the towpath and a brisk, seven minute walk brought him to the Leeds Hilton. He was whistling "You'll Never Walk Alone" slightly off-key but without a care in the world. He was sure no one had seen him.

Flowers was agitated and it wasn't down to me because I was fifteen minutes early into the office. Even so, he was perched on the end of my desk, waiting for me. "Problems, Superintendent Flowers?" I was formal because some of my staff were even earlier than me and around and about.

"Is there ever a day without problems?" he asked. "May have been once but I'm damned if I can remember the time."

I nodded and said nothing, knowing that anything I said would sound smart-aleck and upset him.

"There's been another damn murder, could be a Faulkner thing. Body's down in the morgue, it was found inside a locked houseboat. Sound familiar? I tried your cell phone around ten last night but there was only the answer service and by the look of it, you haven't checked in with that."

Oh, oh. I remained silent because he was right.

"The pathologist wanted the body back here so I told the Crime Scene Investigators to take shots of the body *in situ* and camcord the whole thing. He's laughing at us, Stuart. He left the body on a boat not more than half a mile from these offices."

I chewed my bottom lip, it sounded as though Flowers was right again. "Same MO?"

"I haven't seen the pathologist's report yet but—locked inside and out? This time though, the victim was male."

"Are you giving me the case?"

"Yes, of course. Millet already has three murders on his hands." Flowers was talking about the other CID inspector. "You've only got fraud, armed robbery and drug pushing."

"Also organized prostitution, serial arson and the fifty or so mixed crimes that make their way across my desk every day."

"That's why you've got a squad of sixteen. Delegate Stewart, delegate. You want a course on delegation?"

"No, sir. We'd be further back than ever."

"Put something on the back burner then. This one has to take precedence. The Chief Constable's already making noises and not just murmurings, either."

Aha, that explained it. "Did you tell him you're putting it on my tab?"

"I did and I might say that he didn't raise an eyebrow, didn't make any derogatory remarks."

I heaved a big sigh. "I guess that settles it." I looked out of my still-open door, there was no one around. "Okay, Joe. I need to start making placements. Would have to be the day that Sergeant Fearon starts her Inspector's Course."

"I know about that Stewart. I've arrange a replacement. A Sergeant Patterson, she'll be reporting to you within the hour I hope."

"Well, thank you, sir. That is a big help." I meant it and I hope he realized it. "Got a file?"

Flowers pointed to my in-tray. "It's the green one, don't lose it, there's a lot of other stuff in there."

He might have been being a bit sarcastic but I didn't think so. I pulled all the orange case files out and left the green one on the top. "I'll rally the troops." I doubted the files would boost my popularity but I had to dish them out.

After that job was done and the grumbles had died down a little I nodded at Sergeant Bell. He came over. "Alec, there's a naughty boy on the loose from Asket Farm. Chap called Leroy Richards. When he went down on my evidence, he promised me all sorts of retribution."

Alec Bell was a dour Scotsman, and he gave me a thin-lipped smile. "It's something they all do, sir. Normally comes to nothing."

"Oh, it's happened to me before but in this case, I wouldn't be surprised if he's the exception to the rule."

"You'll be wanting me to watch your back, then?"

I returned his smile in much the same style. "Not exactly. What I'd like you to do is to just keep me informed if his name crops up, whereabouts, activities and so on."

"Okay, Inspector White. I can do that. I'm already after some other nasty little buggers who're importing East European prostitutes into the north of England. But I can do both."

Not the happiest of sergeants but then… I put on a rueful expression. "Knew I could rely on you Sergeant Bell, it's why I asked *you*. Keep things going and you might find a bottle of single malt will miraculously find its way into that locked drawer in your desk." I winked and turned away to leave him wondering how I knew about his little cache and how I could put stuff in there.

I found a tall ginger-haired girl in the corridor outside my office when I got back. She was walking up and down in very high-heeled shoes with very loud and disapproving footsteps.

"Sergeant," I said, opening my office door, "You *are* Sergeant Patterson?"

"Yes. Yes, I am."

"Well come on in. Give me a few moments." I crossed to my desk to get her personnel file. I read it, and once the main points were firmly in my mind, I looked over to where Sergeant Barbara Patterson had stopped her noisy pacing and was looking me straight in the eye with a mixture of anger and embarrassment on her face. Take a seat." I tapped the file. "Now that I *know* you're Sergeant Patterson."

She crossed to the chair with one stride but remained standing as I sat down at my desk. "I needed to read your service record, check your photo ID before we got down to pleasantries. If it comes to that, if your file hadn't assured me of certain skills, I wouldn't have asked you to stay."

"Oh?" she said, guardedly."

"You're replacing a very able sergeant and I need someone familiar with the sort of crimes we're investigating at the moment."

Barbara Patterson had not taken up my invitation to sit. She stood in front of my desk looking down at me and I realized she was actually trying for a little intimidation. "I wasn't aware this was a selection interview, Inspector. White." She was still bristling with annoyance, if not with anger.

I smiled, I chuckled, in fact and it seemed to diffuse the situation somewhat. "No, I don't suppose you were. Let me explain and for God's sake sit down, Barbara." She did sit and a little more tension seeped out of the office. "Let me explain. Umm, if you were applying for a nursing job, would you expect to get a position in the operating theatre if you'd never worked on a ward?"

"No, I don't suppose so."

"I was given a brand-new murder case less than thirty minutes ago, before I'd seen your file. Without the experience you've had, I'd have you doing different work here. As it is, you're going to fit right into this nasty little business."

"Okay. Thanks." She made to stand up.

"There's no need to stand yet, I know how tall you are already." I chuckled again to make certain she didn't take the remark amiss. "Now, I noted you had an involvement with the Stablinski murders, your DCI spoke very highly of you. He suggested, here…" Again, I tapped her file. "… that your contribution brought the matter to a good conclusion."

She nodded. "I found out that one of the perp's alibis was a total fabrication. He certainly got a very severe interrogation as a result."

"You also found some blood spatter that SOCO—I mean CSI—missed. How was that?"

"I just got lucky. They were on a coat which had been thrown in a dumpster truck three streets away."

"But you looked for those sorts of things and you looked over a much wider area than you were expected to. That's what produces results, that and a good nose for detail." She actually grinned at me. "Your desk is in the big office to the right, I'll be there to introduce you in a minute." She got up and I followed her to the door. "Don't get too used to your chair, we'll be going down to the local canal shortly."

"Fishing?" She raised her eyebrows and finally laughed.

"Exactly right but we're after a disappearing act. Umm…" I frowned, trying to hold on to one of those thoughts that come and go like smoke. "Ah, yes. Got a camera?"

"Not with me but there'll be one in my car."

"Great. I'll introduce you around the office and then fetch your camera. I'd like you to meet me at the exit gate onto Albion Street. Okay?" I made hurried introductions to everyone still in the office and Barbara left, which was lucky, I guess, because I was just about to follow her down when Shelly Fearon passed me.

At least she was about to but stopped right in front of me. "Stewart, I never did tell you why I stopped calling 'round, and I think, maybe, I should."

"Your choice, Shelly. I just assumed…"

"Let me explain, I shall be away for some time and I'd like to."

"Okay, go ahead."

"It had nothing to do with you, Stewart. When I lost the baby I thought everything would go back to normal but I was wrong. I suppose it was like post-natal shock."

"Not surprising, Shelly."

"I thought I'd get over it pretty quickly but somehow, maybe with *him* going off too, I just couldn't get on with men friends, seemed wrong somehow. Didn't seem a lot of point in trying to force the issue."

"I can see that, I'm sorry. Is there anyone who could help you?"

"I've consulted my doctor who's referred me. She says there's no reason I shouldn't shake this thing off but there's no telling how long it will take."

"It's a shame, Shelly but if you get over it, well, that's what matters isn't it?"

She smiled a little uncertainly. "Seems unreasonable after all the help and kindness you've shown me but…"

"Hey, you're still the same person you were before the accident. It'll just take time to get things sorted."

"I'll let you know if they do get sorted."

"When…"

"You still want me to do this Inspector's Course? It might have come at just the right time."

I nodded. "Of course. Show them what you're made of."

Her eyes flickered with light, just for a moment.

"Good luck," we both said at the same time.

CHAPTER 9

Leroy and Asmin dropped the Porsche off at the same factory building where they had exchanged Asmin's white van for the Jaguar. Leroy drove the Jaguar and Asmin tailed him back to Leicester in the van. Once they were back in Smiley's living room, Leroy punched Asmin lightly on the shoulder.

"Earned yourself another little bonus for tonight, my friend. What you might call service above and beyond."

"Won't catch me arguing, Leroy, so long as it's not too little. The only thing I regret is that Winston still owed me a ton."

Leroy sniggered. "Let's get the computer set up and we'll get my money transferred out of that offshore account to somewhere a little closer to home—like Barclay's at the end of the street. Some of that money is mine, stands to reason that some of it's yours."

Leroy put the laptop on the table while Asmin laid out the notebooks and schedules they'd picked up at Winston's home. They opened the account they had set up for the funds from Winston's account to be transferred into.

"Here it is, Coral…" The pause was followed by a list of expletives, Leroy was just short of apoplexy.

"And here it is empty," said Asmin glumly. "Anything we can do?"

"Fuck you Winston." Leroy looked at his watch: 4:13 a.m. "Nobody I can call at this time."

"Hmm, unless…" Asmin rubbed his beard.

"What?"

"It'll cost us at this time of night but I might know someone, Boss. A specialist. It'll cost."

"How much?"

"Could be a grand to get him out of bed."

"Just get him here."

Asmin took a cell phone out of his pocket; it looked like a toy in his huge hands. "Dara?" Asmin's language was in no tongue that Leroy recognized. The Sikh wrote something down then dialed another number. "Vishram?" And again, there followed another conversation in Asmin's language, finishing off with Smiley's address in English.

"He is coming, Leroy. From Hinchley, say forty minutes. Fancy a sandwich?"

"So long as its bacon and eggs. That a problem?"

"Not a problem. The Sikh does not have to be vegetarian, it is a personal matter. We do not eat meat that has been ritually slaughtered, other than that…"

They had just finished their early breakfast when there was a subdued knock at the front door. Asmin went to let the newcomer in.

"Vishram, this is your client, Mr. Richards." Vishram and Asmin had been speaking rapidly in Punjabi as they came into the kitchen and changed to English once they were inside, a matter of courtesy. "The computer is through here." Asmin went into the living room, Vishram followed. "And the notes, the passwords, and coding are here."

Vishram grunted and sat down. He studied the notes and typed the same codes that Leroy and Asmin had tried. Eventually, he sat back with a further grunt. "Whoever set this up knew what he was doing. There's professional, proprietary software on the machine, he must have known you would try and transfer funds. The software has automatically diverted the funds to a different account."

Leroy rolled his eyes at Asmin, who muttered something in Punjabi.

"At 11:40 pm, a command was issued to transfer a sum of six million, three hundred and sixty one thousand pounds to Coral Independent Bank in the Channel Islands."

"Ah," said Leroy, "that one's mine." He made a sound of satisfaction.

"Thirty milliseconds later, before the transfer had taken effect, a second command altered the destination. The money was routed elsewhere."

"And where was that?" Leroy's breath was coming in short gasps.

"I don't know. It would be possible to find out but I'd recommend you save the money. It will probably take the rest of the night and will do you no good. The money could be anywhere in the world and will certainly require different passwords and different security protocols to find it."

"Such as?"

"Such as iris recognition maybe. Ah—fingerprint scanning, there is a fingerprint pad on this machine. But it might also involve voice analysis. Whoever did this knew what he was doing, I have performed similar services myself for people who feared for their lives. Does this sound like a reasonable conclusion to you?"

Leroy nodded slowly. "Son of a bitch." He scowled and paced around the room for almost a minute, thinking, looking for other avenues to explore. "Thanks, pal. How much do I owe you?"

Vishram told him and Leroy reached for his wallet without protest and counted out eleven hundred pounds in red fifties. "Thanks for coming."

Asmin saw him to the door and locked it after the expert had gone.

"He knew I'd be coming for my money at some time and worked all this out. I hadn't reckoned on losing all that."

"Winston hadn't reckoned on having to disappear. I doubt we'll see him again—new identity."

"That's true, Asmin. I'm going to have to make some other arrangements."

Asmin grinned, white teeth shining through his beard. "I've no doubt you will, Leroy."

———

At around six feet, I'd never considered myself a short man. Standing next to Barbara Patterson, however, I began to have second thoughts, until I realized that the two inches she topped me by were due to the high heels she affected. She was an impressive woman and probably outweighed me by ten pounds, all of it distributed in just the right places.

Calvin Schmidt, on the other hand, had no such effect on me. He was stoop-shouldered, graying, with pale washed-out blue eyes. The pathologist had completed his post-mortem and the murder victim was neatly sewn up when we arrived. I had some questions but they could wait, I preferred to see the body first.

Schmidt nodded at my request and drew the sheet down to the navel. I looked and felt as though I had been knocked sideways.

Barbara was quick on the uptake and knew exactly what my expression meant. "You know him, sir?"

I nodded. "I do. Ned Stokes, Detective Constable Stokes from Sheffield. I was talking to him less than twenty-four hours ago."

"Sheffield? That's thirty miles away, what's he doing here?"

"Exactly what I'm wondering." I didn't add that he could be here because he'd been showing me around the scene of another murder. That would mean that it *was* Faulkner or, someone else continuing to set Faulkner up. Either way, it was another nail in Faulkner's coffin.

"How did he die, Cal?"

"Well it would be a guess, I think someone crept up behind him pulled something over his head; rammed their knee into his back and held on. I'll know more once the lab has tested the nasal samples I took." I winced both inwardly and outwardly but tried to hide my feelings. It was then I had my first doubts that it could be Faulkner.

"Poor bugger, what a hellish way to go. What time do you think?"

"He was found around eight o'clock last night, but he wasn't killed where they found him."

"No?"

"No. His clothes were covered with thick fibers from a heavy duty rug. Sort you get in lobbies. Nothing on the boat to match them."

"So he was killed elsewhere and…"

"Carried to the boat in the carpet." Barbara finished.

"Absolutely."

"You two make a good double act. You put two and two together and come up with five before I've got around to the extras."

"What extras?" I asked.

"His shoes. The heels had been dragged across a red waxed floor. The kind that…"

"That you paint quarry tiles with."

Schmidt laughed. "He likes these little mind games, Sergeant Patterson. You'll have to come 'round to my place for a game of Trivial Pursuit."

"Any time, Cal. Once these people stop killing each other."

"Bit of a leap to think of quarry tiles."

"The hallway in Sheffield was floored with them. Maybe he went back for another look by himself?"

I led the way back to my car and drove us down to the canal. The scene of crime was a brightly painted cabin cruiser. A few days ago, it would have been inconspicuous among the craft that had taken part in the gala. Today, it was very noticeable, especially with the yellow and black police tape and the lone uniformed officer waiting for us.

He saluted as we walked across the towpath. "Morning sir, been expecting you."

"Good morning. Has there been a guard around the clock?"

"Ever since the body was discovered, sir."

We walked up the slightly wobbly gangplank and gained the deck.

He nodded at the sliding doorway. "Had to smash their way in, I'm told. The door was locked on the outside and…"

"And bolted on the inside." I nodded grimly. "I'm getting a bit tired of this guy's theatrics."

"Ah. Seen it all before, sir?"

"You could say that, yes." Although I hadn't, of course but I was getting a feeling of familiarity after the Sheffield scene and Faulkner's woodland retreat.

Up close, we could see the door was partly glazed, enough to let some daylight in but not big enough to move a body through. Broken glass and splintered wood lay everywhere. Nobody had cleared up the debris after the official break-in.

Inside, a brightly-patterned carpet covered most of the cabin floor. There were rich blues mixing with pale yellow and orange and the area near the entrance was covered with fragments of glass and wood. No sign of blood, which tallied with the murder being carried out elsewhere. And when I thought about it, we also had no evidence of a fight, no bruising on the body and so forth.

Sergeant Patterson had remained outside and she called me onto the deck. She was kneeling on the gunwale and peering into the green water. "The pathologist mentioned a carpet, sir. I'm sure that's what I can see down there."

My movement had caused some ripples in the water but once they had subsided, I could see something lighter colored than the muddy bottom.

"Could be, we'll get a team out right now to recover it while there still might be some evidence on it. If that's what it is, I want this boat taken apart piece by piece. The guy's a bloody escape artist, either that or he's a copycat taking the piss, but either way he cannot disappear into thin air. Look for a hidden entrance or exit. He's playing with us and I want to know how his stupid little tricks work. Do you follow me?"

"Oh yes, sir. Loud and clear."

———

Mal Hemingsby was waiting for the last of his dealers with the weekly takings. This particular guy, Reuben Ogavy, had some big cocaine hitters on his patch. Mal always looked forward to counting the money. Some weeks, the takings could run to a hundred grand.

Three short rings, one long and two more short, Reuben's own code on the door bell, announced his arrival. Mal refilled his near-empty whiskey tumbler and sauntered down the long passage.

He looked through the spy-hole in the door panel and recognized Reuben's features before he turned the heavy security lock and pulled the door fully open. Outside was a steel gate. It looked ornamental but there was nothing decorative about the welded joints with heavy hinges on the outer gate. Mal unlocked it.

"Took your freakin' time, Reub. Where yo' bin?" His heavy midland accent showed itself undeniably in the eight short words.

Reuben pretended to cough, not that he needed to pretend much.

Hemingsby, in the act of pulling the iron gate open, sensed something was wrong before he noticed the cord wrapped around the other's throat, concealed by his hoodie. It was drawn tight by one of the two men who stood behind and to the side of the doorway. He tried to slam the heavy grill back into place but was too late. A black hand appeared from beyond his field of vision and smashed it into his body, slamming him back inside where he tripped and fell over onto the floor.

The black round opening of a sawn-off shotgun followed him down and stopped six inches in front of his eyes.

A dozen thoughts flashed across his mind, the final one being: *Was this the reason his minder had not turned up tonight?*

Reuben performed a curious little skip and jump to avoid treading on his boss as the two men pushed him inside. They wore full-face ski masks and seemed to know exactly what they were doing. Mal was lifted unceremoniously to his feet and he and Reuben were prodded viciously back up the passageway into the living room. Behind was the sound of the steel gate being closed and the door itself thudding shut.

The man holding the shotgun was black although only his hands gave this away. The other, when he entered, might have been a lightly toned black or even an olive skinned Mediterranean. He was tall and spoke with a deep baritone voice and an almost cultured accent.

"The money, Mal. Give it to us and you will save yourself a lot of pain." He turned to the man with the shotgun. "Isn't that right, my friend?"

The other nodded and grunted.

Mal mouthed a wordless snarl.

"Oh dear." The barrel of a suddenly visible Uzi smashed into Mal's face and he fell back onto the settee behind him as broken teeth and bloody tissue filled his mouth.

"Yo'm a walkin' dead man, Reuben."

The poor, unfortunate underling was too scared to do or say anything.

"You are not making this easy on yourself, Mal." And again, the barrel took him across the nose, smashing it to pulp as the metal tore into the right cheek. Blood dribbled down into Mal's collar.

"The money, Mal. Speak now or I shall get really angry. I'll start with some target practice, arms and legs and feet. I've always found there's no substitute for real pain, Mal and, oh yes, I'll pay real attention to the kneecaps."

To emphasize his intention, the man fired a burst from the automatic into the cushion next to Mal's knee. Foam exploded and feathers flew in a cloud of scraps that hid the look of terror on Mal's face.

Incongruously, Mal sneezed and that seemed to take away any further thought of resistance. "Okay, okay. The second bedroom, under the vinyl flooring, under the bed." His words came bubbling through the bloody hole in his upper lip.

"Say that again. Speak slowly so we can understand you."

Mal repeated himself and pulled a handkerchief out of his pocket to wipe the mess from his face. He looked, appalled, at the bloody cloth in his hand.

When the money had been located and bagged up, the two robbers duct-taped Mal and Reuben together, with Reuben gagged and tape stuck across his mouth. The thieves could not bring themselves to deal similarly with Mal, his face was too badly injured, and the danger of suffocation would have been too great. Instead, they forced the victims into a bathroom and into the bathtub.

As they left the house, Mal was cursing both the visitors and Reuben as best he could. He promised painful retribution on them all although, in fact, none could understand what he was saying.

Once they were in the car and speeding away, they peeled off the ski masks and let out a whoop of joy.

"By the 'eck, Asmin, you had me believing you was a bigger bastard than me."

Asmin grinned into the darkness. "I never talked so much in all of my life."

"So polite, such a gentleman. I'll never believe anything you say, ever again."

"You don't think Hemingsby can cause problems, Leroy?"

"How can he? He never heard me say a word, he's never met you, you was totally new, man. Listen Asmin, I used to be just like him, pushing stuff, counting the take every week but I stopped all that and concentrated on one big job at a time. Di'n't work, did it? That bastard White got me put away and that other one, Winston took all my money."

"And what are your plans now?"

"I stay in business, I stay undercover. Nobody knows what I'm doing. We gotta grow our funds, Asmin, we gotta be able to afford to play in a bigger league."

The "we" was not lost on Asmin.

CHAPTER 10

picked Connie up just after seven that evening and stopped at the Aagrah Indian restaurant for a takeout. By 7:45 p.m., we were back home and I was introducing her to Pip. It was quite hilarious watching her trying to stroke him as he danced around on three legs playing bashful.

The meal was warming up again under the grill as we shared a bottle of Merlot on the couch. Connie had made herself at home by kicking off her shoes and resting her heels on the coffee table.

"I'd better get the plates out," I said as my glass ran dry. Connie stood up and asked where the bedroom was, I pointed her in the right direction and she grabbed my hand and pulled.

"I always feel hungrier after sex, don't you?"

I agreed, though I would have preferred a little more finesse. But still, it came to the same thing in the end and I allowed myself to be towed along.

We stood close together with my arms around her. She unbuttoned my shirt and with it out of the way, started on my belt. I made that easier by undoing it myself then reached around for the zip on her dress.

I picked up my discarded trousers and folded them, dropping them over the back of a chair. Not the act of a passionate man but I was still a little bit uncomfortable at being stage-managed. Mind you, I was even more embarrassed on turning back to find a totally nude and nubile woman about to clasp her arms about me.

We fell in an untidy but very delightful heap on the bed; muscular legs twining around mine, ample breasts awaking interesting responses. All of my earlier reservations were forgotten for the moment as my desires overcame mental warnings.

"Well, well, Stewart! So you *are* human, after all. Gotta say, I was beginning to wonder."

"Umm," I replied provocatively... I hoped. "I've nothing against abstinence so long as it's for Catholic priests and such, but—"

Things were just about on autopilot by now, and I was happy to sit back and let it take me where it would when suddenly there was a chilling development.

"Is the dog the only one in this house to welcome me, or what?" A loud voice called from downstairs.

"Oh my God." I groaned, and crashed. "I don't bloody believe it."

"For God's sake, who's that?"

"Dad."

"Tell him to go away, Stewart. I'm all a-quiver."

"He must have come all the way from Birmingham and he's turned seventy. He's come a day early."

"And I'm just about to... you are not going are you? Damn you, come back. You can't leave me like this!"

I looked down at my rapidly shrinking assets. "My friend has other ideas, and believe me it's just as bad for me. I freed myself from her arms and feverishly pulled my pants on.

There were a few frantic moments as I heard him pacing around the hallway. But I managed to get my pants fastened and stood at the top as he looked up. "I was just about to take a shower, Dad." But I clattered down the stairs as he limped through to the study, leaning heavily on his walking stick.

"Wonderful sight, son." He lifted the stick and pointed it at the window. "There's a full moon rising over those apple trees and that river flowing alongside them. You've said it was a pretty place but this is absolutely beautiful."

I was at a loss. I had some rather beautiful scenery upstairs but no way to enjoy it. "Cup of tea?" I asked. He nodded and followed me through to the kitchen and there was a surprise reunion: Pip suddenly remembered who the voice belonged to and rushed out of his basket to greet the old man. The scientists who insist a dog has a memory measured in weeks should really get out and look at reality. Dog and man were on my padded rocker, wrestling with each other as if it they had been apart no more than a day or two. Dad never mentioned the new three-legged and one-eyed arrangement.

After the tea and back in the living room, I offered him a nice malt and I noticed him wince as he bent his knee and sat down carefully. He saw me watching him. "Growing old, son. It's a price we all have to pay, I'm afraid. There's no alternative."

I didn't know what to say.

He smiled sadly. "Doesn't bear thinking about, does it?"

There was a small cough from the doorway which drew our attention. Dad's eyes were the size of saucers.

Connie stood there, demurely dressed in her rain coat and carrying her handbag. "Well, thank you for the use of your telephone, Inspector. I've called a taxi and we can finish my statement later, at a more convenient time. Bye."

The collar of her raincoat was part up-part down and her hair was standing straight up in back but I couldn't very well tell her. I brazened it out and introduced her to Dad. She refused my offer to walk her to her car. She opened the door and smiled impishly. "See y'all later."

I was pondering how many people "y'all" signified in the American South as she stepped out.

I turned to find Dad viewing me with an amused expression. He said, "Well at least that fancy Indian food you bought needn't go to waste."

I shook my head—crafty like a fox.

The next morning, I was at my desk twenty minutes early. Sergeant Patterson had called me at home at 6:30, before I'd even thought of breakfast. She told me there were several reports awaiting my attention; was she trying to show how efficient she was or getting at me for making her wait?

She wasn't present when I'd arrived so I got on with the reports and was, maybe, half way through them when Sergeant Bell tapped on the door and came in.

"Want to hear something that doesn't quite smell right?"

I nodded, despite the mixed metaphor.

"Remember Winston Umbok?"

"Umbok? Wasn't he a hanger-on with the Leroy Richards gang? I remember he was supposed to be with Richards the night we busted him."

"The very same. In the course of my inquiries on your behalf, I discovered why that was."

I kept my expression polite and interested and waited.

Sergeant Bell tapped my desk for emphasis, "He was Sergeant James Callaghan's snout. Callaghan had obviously tipped him off about your impending bust."

I remembered a little about Callaghan though we'd never worked together. I could see him in my mind's eye, a Northern Irishman, big, bluff, friendly sort standing with his short legs spread apart. Liked to slap people on the back. Not one of my type at all.

"So what about Umbok? There has to be more."

Alec laughed. Canny lad aren't you? I wondered how long it would take before the penny dropped. Yes, they fished his body out of the River Aire, near Allerton Bywater."

"Sounds an appropriate name, where is it?"

"East of here, was a mining village. The Wakefield Police pathologist suggests it was accidental, there's nothing to suggest foul play. They fully expect the coroner to bring in a verdict of drowning by misadventure."

I'd got as far as "Hmm," when he continued.

"Funny, less than a week after Richards' escape and I'm told by a *usually reliable* source," he popped up two fingers up on each hand, signifying quotation marks, "that Umbok was the money holder while Richards was inside."

I got another "Hmm" out and smiled at Bell. "That's good work, Alec. Keep it up."

After he had left, I returned to the reports. The first concerned the dust sample I had lifted back at the Sheffield murder scene. It was simple resin dust that might have come from a piece of furniture or several types of statue imported from China or other eastern countries.

The words brought back the melancholy memory of Ned Stokes's murder and that led straight into the next report, the boat where his body had been found. That rankled me—if I had a periscope, I could've seen where the little cruiser was moored from this office. The team who had pretty well taken it to pieces above the water line, had found that the entire front bulkhead slid upwards by about two feet. So much for murderers disappearing into thin air. The MO had also confirmed cotton residue in Stokes's airways, looked like suffocation from a pillow or bed linen.

The murderer examined his features in the mirror and tutted at the rebellious strand of grey hair which persisted in flying off the top of the toupee and ending up hanging down the back. He had tried combing it with water but it dried out too quickly and continued to have its own way. Hair spray? He would have to get some.

He heard the daily newspaper come through the letter box and thump on to the floor. He put the disappointment at his new wig's behavior out of his mind and strode through the hall to pick up the paper. The headline read:

HOUDINI KILLER LEAVES BODY IN LOCKED BOAT
Was it Travis Faulkner, wanted for viciously killing his wife?

He read the article twice, but nowhere was there a mention of who had been appointed to lead the investigation. Were the reporters not doing their job or were the police being unusually reticent? Perhaps the police were keeping the matter low profile so that the Great British Public could sleep safely in their beds at night. There was no mention of the way the man had been killed and no suggestion, either, that they had found and arrested Faulkner either.

Infuriated, perplexed, annoyed, he tossed the paper away from him in disgust. Why should they still have doubts? Could it be anymore obvious? The man was dangerous, he was out on the streets, he had the necessary skills of an illusionist, a little basic, rough around the edges to be sure, but it should be obvious that Faulkner had to be the guilty party.

The only thing that prevented the case being closed was the missing man. Here, he had to admit, Faulkner had been very clever or very lucky; the man he had arranged all this for could not be found.

Clever or not, he would have to be even cleverer than Faulkner with his next victim. Someone Faulkner would have wanted dead, someone the man hated.

He sat down and lifted the toupee off his head, put it on the table and leaned, head in hands over its polished surface. His reflection blurred as his mind's eye turned back to the first murder in Sheffield.

He had returned to the building and unlocking the office doors, had expected to find the camcorder hidden in the desk. It had been his intention to record the investigations but not only was the recorder gone, so was the desk and every other scrap of furniture. He had been standing there, shocked by the thwarting of his plans, when the sound of a car door closing with a slam had drawn his attention. He had run to the front window and watched Stokes get out of a dark Vauxhall. Stokes needed only to walk around to the back and he was trapped.

Prepared, he waited in the suite to see where Stokes was going. A few minutes later, there was the sound of a key in the lock. The policeman entered and turned to close the door just as the other dragged his favorite device over Stokes's head and pulled it tight. There was a minute's struggle which grew weaker and weaker. Stokes died without uttering a sound.

The method he had employed was not intended for Ned Stokes, but it didn't matter. It had worked smoothly. He had gone through Stokes's pockets before anything else and the contents suggested his next course of action. It was something that appealed to his sense of humor, something fun. The policeman had a diary in his inside pocket, the current day's page was blank but turning back, yesterday had the notation: *Shelly with Inspector White from O.C.S. Leeds*; that would be the two cops he'd seen yesterday.

He wrapped Stokes's body in the door mat from the front entrance and rolled it into the car's trunk at the multi-story for disposal later.

The boat was a godsend. It was one of Faulkner's cast-offs, converted for use in magic shows at river and canal galas. The trick was to enter the cabin, roll across the floor, and strike a hidden latch. This allowed the front wall of the cabin to roll up just enough to get out onto the deck. An assistant would slide the door open and bring in a member of the audience to pronounce him *vanished*.

Now, the trick was to get the body in its roll of carpet into the boat alongside Granary Wharf without anyone seeing him. Not a trick of any great achievement, the Dark Arches, a series of cavernous tunnels beneath the railway station where the river Wharfe poured through the man-made water course, were gloomy and home to a few homeless people who would look the other way even if a pitched battle had been going on. He had walked through as though he owned the place and stepped aboard the cruiser at the water's edge.

With the diary note about Inspector White from O.C.S. Leeds and knowing exactly where the organized crime guys had their office, he had motored along the canal and moored the boat as close as he could get to the back of the tall buildings beyond the mainline railway station. Somewhere up there, Inspector White would be getting ready to go home.

He was just fastening the trunk when a man came up to him. At first, the killer thought he had been spotted but the man said. "You can't leave your car there, you know."

"And you are?"

"I am Inspector Patel of the NCPA. This is private property, for which a permit is required."

"I'm sorry, Inspector...?"

"Patel. Now be quick and move it before I issue you a ticket that will require you to report to the police."

"Yes, Inspector. I will. Sorry about the mistake."

"You *will* be next time. I don't ever give second chances."

No, thought the killer, *neither do I. I need a different method though; he could never be one of the chosen.*

Monday morning. The incident room was full of officers waiting for me to put in an appearance. I had already pinned all the available information to the glass wall so, hopefully, everyone had soaked it all up before I got there.

Coppers were a peculiar sort of people—me included, I suspect. Like horses, you could lead them to water but not make them drink. Had I not given them this break, a period in which to review what we knew and discuss it among themselves, they would not have paid me as much attention.

I had worked with most of them for twelve months now but they were really only just getting to know me. They probably thought they were pretty familiar with my likes and dislikes but none of them had more than scratched the surface.

I smiled to myself, it almost reached my face. Another of Dad's sayings had come to mind as I waited for them to stop talking. 'Never tell anyone all you know; only what you want them to know.' True, it was the only way to make them go in the direction you wanted.

"Morning, men." I opened. "We've got the Faulkner murder details up here on the wall and I've included the Stokes murder. If anyone doesn't know why Ned

Stokes has been lumped with the others, you probably shouldn't be here. Yes I know the MO's are different but I only consider coincidence when all else fails. "

I grinned, making sure nobody thought I was making sarcastic comments.

"Maybe you've got it all worked out? Joined all the dots up? Who committed the murders and why? Anyone?"I looked around the room, faces – both perplexed and amused – looked back at me, one or two remained poker faced. It was Harper who broke the silence, a D.C. who had been on my team since day one.

"Seems to me, Guv, that it's either Faulkner who's been tagged as the Disappearing Man or someone is working very hard to make it look like him."

I nodded. "That sums it up very nicely: it's Faulkner we still have to find or someone we don't have a clue about. A someone who wants us to think it's two people. Anyone else with ideas?"

Peggy Allerdyce put a finger in the air. "We're a bit light on motives, Boss."

"Okay." Peggy was a recent arrival among the plain clothes ranks. "Like to elaborate, Peggy?"

"I can try. If any of you can remember the report on the murder of Faulkner's wife, you'll know they'd been together for twenty years. They had a thriving business together and friends and relations described them as a perfect couple. Even their housekeeper swore she'd never heard them arguing and you know what housekeepers are…"

"Oh, whoa, Peggy. Everything you say is true and maybe they did dote on each other but the husband's DNA argues for murder. The fact that he was some sort of semi-pro magician swayed the jury… well, I don't want to open that case again but – okay – there are unanswered questions."

I shook my head. "We've got to get to the bottom of those as well as these follow-on murders. I'm going to introduce a squad system. I know you've all got case-loads – we've all got case-loads but this will spread the work fairly."

"So, Sergeant Beach will take A squad, Sergeant Levy – B and Sergeant Meredew – C. I'll put lists of the DCs up shortly.

Alex Bell put his hand up and I signaled him to speak.

"What about me, sir?"

"Hey, I'd forgotten all about you." Bell's eyebrows rose as everyone chuckled. "No, I lie, Sergeant. You're my link man. Every piece of hard evidence will be passed to you by the other sergeants. I want every one collated, I want any connections you make reported to me, okay?"

I looked around the room. "A Squad will take the Sheffield end, B squad – the house in the woods and C – the cabin cruiser and forensic collating. If we can't go forward, we go back."

This produced a whole lot blank stares.

"Look at Sheffield. The murder site has been cleared and, I presume, their officers carried out a house to house questioning. I put Sergeant Beach in charge of Sheffield because he joined us from there. He'll have contacts, he knows the ground, he should be able to get the info organized quicker than anyone else. What wasn't asked, who wasn't questioned, who and where are the other tenants in that building? Key holders, did Faulkner have other rooms there, know other people…"

I continued for several more minutes, talking about the work I expected the other squads to cover. I'd just about run-down when I heard the door open and close; I turned to see who had come in.

"Ah, for those of you who haven't met our new colleague, this is Sergeant Barbara Patterson." I looked at my watch and then remembered she had phoned me earlier that morning. "Sergeant Patterson has replaced Sergeant Fearon who's now tackling the lofty heights of inspector training at the Police College."

I turned back to Patterson. "Good morning, Sergeant."

She looked weary and rather less fiery than the last time I'd seen her. "Morning, sir. I've been home to see my parents, seemed logical to get involved with the Sheffield end of things on my way here." She held up a heavy bag. "Collected the case notes."

"That's great Sergeant. Thanks. Give them to Sergeant Beach when we're finished here. He's the one with the smart hair and the blue and white tie."

I'd lost track with Patterson's interruption so made the best of a bad job. "Any questions? Everyone get the general idea?"

D.C. Franks – another of the men who had been with me since I'd moved here – stood up, frowning. "Boss, I've looked at the stuff on the wall, can't fault it. Both murder scenes – Sheffield and Hey Presto, the house in the woods – have Faulkner's DNA all over the place. So why," he looked across at Peggy Allerdyce, "why do we think there could be another perp? Is it just because the M.O's were different?"

It sounded as though there might have been a bit of a debate going on. I answered quickly.

"Come on, Bob. Don't you think you or I could place DNA evidence from a suspect at a scene they'd never been to? I remember a case where DNA was turning up everywhere, places where the suspects simply could not have been. We went back, like my point about Sheffield a few minutes ago, and we found that clothing had been left at a dry cleaners. One of the employees had taken samples of dandruff, hair, sweat from a shirt and even urine from underwear and carefully placed them at various crime scenes. That was a doozy, as they say. I'll tell you how we caught the guy another day."

"O'Hara." I nodded to another officer, waving a hand.

"How concerned is the Chief about these cases, sir?"

I grinned. "Don't you worry about that, O'Hara. It's the Chief's job to be concerned and it's the Superintendant's job to tell me about his concerns. And it's my job to get you lot to handle them while I handle the worry. Right?"

There were a couple of shrugs in addition to O'Hara's raised eyebrow – his right one, I think.

"Okay. Let's get some work done."

On my way out, I stopped to see if Flowers was in his office. He was there and he nodded me in. I mentioned the business of forming squads and pointed out how much more efficient it would be and the five people in each one would do the work of six with no extra cost.

Whether he bought it or not, I'm not sure, but at least he knew I was making the effort.

———

I talked to Dad later that evening – asking him about settling in, was the bed comfortable, was he getting enough to eat?

"Son. Food's been the last thing on my mind since your mother died. God knows I used to love her cooking but a sandwich is as good as a feast, these days.

"Right…"

"As for the bed, I don't give a damn so long as I wake up the next day – and I did this morning so I'm happy. But…"

"But what?"

"But I'd love a cup of tea.

———

I had two strange phone calls that evening.

The first one was a call with no one replying when I gave the number. *Was that Connie*, I wondered. I checked the number but it wasn't one I was familiar with so I wrote it down to check the next day. If it had been Connie, I don't know what I would have said after our abandoned night of passion on Friday, so I didn't call back.

The second call came after Dad had gone to bed so I was sitting in my favorite armchair, now otherwise vacant, with a tumbler of whiskey. This time there was a voice: low, hesitant—but definitely male.

"Inspector White?"

"That's right. Who's this?"

"I'm the man you're looking for, Inspector."

"Sorry?"

"My name's Faulkner and I'm not the man you should be looking for. I didn't kill my wife and I didn't murder that policeman. No matter what evidence you have, it's wrong."

"I'm willing to believe that if you can offer some proof."

"Really? An open-minded police officer? Listen, I'm on a ship in the middle of the ocean. I've been on it for eight days and that can be proved. Can *you* prove I didn't kill my wife?"

"That's a tough one at the moment, sir. I don't think I can."

"I'll call you occasionally as I circumnavigate the globe, just to see how you're progressing. Oh, and before you ask, your office gave me your home number a little while ago. I told them I was your father. I understand from what they said that he's getting on in years and is a little fragile, so they didn't mind breaking the rules this once. Information is king, Inspector, and it's so easy to come by. Goodnight."

I put the phone down then dialed 1471 again, wondering if the previous call had been from the same number. It wasn't... and the number reported was a cell phone.

I got up and threw the whiskey away. It seemed to have gone sour.

CHAPTER 11

Gale-force winds lashed heavy rain across the façades of the shops along Castlegate in Newark. Dennis McGuire was the fifty-three-year-old manager of the Rock Bank and Friendly Society. The bank was situated in the old town and it served the scores of farmers and horticultural companies which were the lifeblood of this immensely fertile area.

McGuire sat behind the wheel of his car in the parking lot at the back of the offices waiting for the downpour to abate. The clock in the dashboard still showed twenty-three minutes before any of the staff would turn up—early starts were a habit formed over the years since his first clerical job when he was a spotty youth just out of school. The fact that his dad ran his own farm and breakfast was always promptly up at half past five a.m. also had something to do with it.

Two minutes had passed and there was a lot less noise on the car roof, he opened the window an inch or two to get a better view. He could see across the empty parking lot now and there was a definite tang of ozone in the air from the earlier lightning but as his ears had told him, the force of the rainstorm was spent.

Somewhere nearby, the sound of a jackhammer replaced the thunder, some-one else was braving the weather. Dennis took his chance, getting out and making a run, windswept umbrella in one hand, a battered old briefcase in the other. He stopped briefly in the narrow passage leading through to the main street and clicked the car locking fob. The indicators flashed briefly and he walked through to the other end.

Across from the offices—perhaps a couple of hundred yards—the old castle was just visible through the falling rain. Dennis turned right and the wind caught his umbrella and turned it inside out, another flurry of rain all but blinded him and he located the main door by touch. Somehow, he got the first key into its lock and turned and then the second. Peering through rain-spotted glasses, he punched the code into the electronic security system. With two digits to go, he felt a presence looming as he finished the sequence and opened the door to stumble with relief into the dry interior.

Dennis's sixth sense was right. Two shapes materialized behind him and slammed the door wide open and pushed him across the lobby. The door closed behind him with a bang and he was pushed roughly toward the inner door, which had its own security system.

"Just do everything we say, granddad, and you and your family will stay safe and sound."

"My family?" Dennis quavered, "what about my family?"

"Nothing to be alarmed about. Your daughter's just left number eleven Willow Avenue, she's got your granddaughter, Natalie, with her. Everything's fine, and it'll stay that way as long as you behave. Now, open this door and take us through to your office."

"There's very little money in the branch," he quavered again as he did as he was told.

"Ah, but it's Friday, Mr. McGuire. There are all those payrolls to service, all those workmen coming in to cash their checks. There's the big delivery coming in this morning."

Dennis felt the fight go out of him. They knew about his family, they knew about the cash delivery and his routine early arrival. General instructions were to comply with any demands like this, but almost two million pounds were expected at nine-thirty this morning. It was difficult to accept that it would be stolen just because of him.

McGuire went around the offices, opening the doors and every now and then, turning to get a look at the men who were following him. They both wore identical dark blue or black zip-up boiler suits with attached hoods, their faces remained hidden within the cowls, there was nothing he might recognize later.

"Now," said one when the last lock had been unlocked and the last blind lifted, "and don't think of lying, we know enough to tell when you're lying and if that happens, Imogene may find the knife that's just touching her throat at this moment will get even closer—and we don't want that, do we? Just tell us what happens when they bring the money in."

McGuire's mouth became a thin, bitter line across his face. Imogene. They hadn't mentioned his wife before, but now, this new threat changed him. He resolved to do exactly as he was told, the hell with the company he had worked for all these years; nothing mattered except his family now.

He sat down in his office chair, and looked at his captors. He had been proud of his rise to authority, of facing customers across the counter and later, across this very desk, deciding who would and who would not receive loans for a mortgage or a car, which farmer would expand his dairy business, which farm would buy the extra field. Now, the boot was on the other foot.

Bang! The fist crashing down on his desk top brought Dennis back to the present. "The routine, McGuire."

Dennis took a deep breath. "They should be here at nine-thirty, though it can vary by a few minutes."

"Go on. What happens when they get here?"

"Nothing. Oh, I see. Well, I open the door to the vault and they bring the boxes in. We make certain the seals are unbroken then I sign for them and we stack the bills in trays inside the vault."

"We'll talk about that in a minute." The man changed the subject abruptly. "Panic buttons. Where are they located and any other alarms?"

Dennis thought for a moment. The knowledge was ingrained in his memory but it wasn't easy to recall everything in the present circumstances. "Umm..."

"Come on, your wife must be getting quite uncomfortable by now." He took a cell phone from his pocket and read from the screen, "01636596577. I've only to call that number, I don't even need to say anything and she will be even more uncomfortable. Quite unpleasantly uncomfortable."

"Panic buttons, you said. There are three in the teller's area, I... I'll show you. There's one here, right under my desk and another in the vault." The thief turned the phone over and over in one hand and then he held it up, close enough for Dennis to see his own home phone number across the screen. "Oh, and there's another under Mrs. Campbell's desk, that's the office with the yellow door."

The one in charge put the phone away. "That omission might have been a nervous slip, but if there's anything else you've forgotten, now is the time to tell me."

Dennis frowned and shook his head. "That's it."

"Very well. This is what will happen this morning. You will open the rear door and greet your Mrs. Campbell as usual. Moira," he used the woman's given name casually, as if he had known her for years, "will be expecting you to open the door in..." he checked his watch, a huge gold thing, "exactly six minutes."

Depressed and dismayed, Dennis nodded. They seemed to know everything about the business.

On the opposite side of the road, a black three-liter BMW Series 7 waited, almost inaudibly, the motor idling. A wisp of smoke escaped through the driver's barely open window from Asmin's cigar. The car had a top speed in excess of 150 mph although Leroy and Asmin did not expect to use that power. Having spent the best part of the last four days with the head clerk of the little bank,—a member of Asmin's circle of acquaintances—they had a very good idea of the amount of money in the expected delivery and had no reason to doubt that all would go very smoothly.

It went without saying that there was also a Plan B.

They watched as the security van arrived and two men exited the vehicle and waited as four steel boxes were discharged through the chute from the van's interior. Each man carried two boxes and marched into the bank's front entrance.

Barely two minutes later, they emerged, returned to the security van and were on their way.

"Boxes seemed heavy." Asmin let the window down another inch and dropped his cigar stub onto the road.

"Two million quid gotta be heavy," said Leroy, pleased with the results of their homework for the job. "And look, here come the boys." He checked the road in front and behind. "My side's clear, pull it over there."

The two men who had entered the bank with the manager, opened the rear doors of the BMW, threw in four bulging rucksacks, and then jumped in themselves. At exactly that moment, they heard the sound of police sirens.

"Plan B?" asked Asmin.

"Plan B," agreed Leroy.

Twenty-five yards along Castlegate was an old stone-built archway. It had at one time been the way through for horse and carts delivering coal, beer, flour and various other commodities to the businesses which had once lined the road.

As Castlegate modernized, alleyways like this one had become superfluous and turned into paved walkways or built over entirely. Mellor's Gap was still in pedestrian use but had had a concrete bollard sunk into the ground at the inner end to prevent wheeled vehicles, such as a three liter BMW, for example, using it as a short cut.

Ignoring the prominent "No Entry" sign, Asmin swung the BMW over the pavement and into the alley with mere inches on each side. He lost the passenger-side rear-view mirror but otherwise, the car fitted the opening. It purred over the cobbles, straddled the hole where the bollard had been earlier that morning and swerved between the parked cars which lined the old street.

Behind them, a giant truck pulled across the outer end of the passageway blocking both ingress and egress. The driver jumped down and leaving the door wide open, tossed the keys down a nearby drain. A white van with black lettering identifying it as a "Public Works Department" vehicle picked him up and just as the van moved off, the rear doors opened and the concrete bollard from the far end of the alleyway rolled out and came to rest in the middle of the street.

Leroy bared his teeth in a wolfish grin, and watched through the darkened glass windows. The handful of puzzled coppers who did not spare a second glance for the BMW had no idea where the bank robbers had vanished.

"Everything go as we planned, Arjan?" asked Asmin, half turning his head.

"Like a dream. Though I don't know how the police knew so quickly. I thought the little man was shitting himself with fright, I even believed him as he showed me the alarm buttons and said that was all."

"Did you search him and the women?" Leroy asked.

"He wasn't carrying no guns, Boss. Or knives."

"What about a cell phone? Maybe he had a cell phone with a speed dial set up."

Arjan, now his hood was pulled back, was a handsome, dark-eyed man rather younger than his countryman. His unlined face suddenly blossomed with furrows. "Balls, Leroy. I never thought of that. I'm sorry, boss."

Leroy had not thought of it either, until just now. That fact was not something he was about to admit to. "You live and learn, Arjan. You live and learn. I may fine you a tenner for that." He grinned. "No, no ten grand."

Jarvis saw the TV news item about the search for Richards. He'd forgotten Richards until the camera zoomed in on another prisoner standing casually by the fence. *Lofty Pike*, he thought, *older but still the same skinny features*. It was then he considered Richards being Leroy: the third of the young orphans. Well he was black and the name was the same. So he had gone into dealing drugs; that did not surprise him, the fellow was soft and a low life. The two of them must have been five or more years older than him but he could have sorted them with one hand.

Chapter 12

I called around to see Connie on my way in to work, but no one answered the door and I didn't have her cell phone number. I gave up and went on to the office although the delay made me ten minutes later than normal.

The first person I saw was Barbara Patterson. She was waiting outside my office. "Sir." She nodded.

"Sergeant?"

"Can I come in, sir?"

"Certainly, but can I just check my email first?"

"Well, yes, of course but I honestly think you'll want to know what I've learned… sir."

"Okay, make it quick then."

A triumphant grin spread across my assistant's features and I'd swear that, despite her striking height, she performed a quick jig as I unlocked the door and ushered her in before me. I took off my top coat and hung it on a hanger before turning around. She was clutching a slim file which she opened as I sat down and put in front of me.

"What am I looking at?"

"The DC Stokes murderer used the same MO, sir. I did some research in our records. This is what I found."

At first, I assumed she had found witnesses to a man with a description similar to ours until, belatedly, I realized *we* didn't have a description. I picked the file up. "You shouldn't do this, Barbara, not 'til I've had at least one cup of coffee." I started reading, not quite certain what I was looking for until I noticed that Patterson had underlined the pertinent facts—bless her.

Five murders in the last three years, in Lancashire and Merseyside. Each victim suffocated with a pillow case or similar and no DNA evidence at all; the only difference to ours was the lack of a locked room, and no pillow cover left behind.

"Hmm." I went over it again—one person questioned had seen a car, might have been a classic model and there was a partial registration: PIG. And apart from that, nothing.

"Well, Sergeant, the same perp or maybe…"

"A copycat killer. It's quite possible that these murders were well documented. A reporter from the Granada ITV region did a series on them. Did quite a detailed job, by all accounts. The last murder was six months ago."

"Ah! When Faulkner's wife…"

"Turned up dead."

We grinned at each other. I sat back and clapped. "That's bloody good work Barbara—oh, hope you don't mind me using your given name. Bit of a slip up."

"Not a problem, sir. So now, all we have to do is prove it—the same or a copycat."

"I'll have to have a word with the Super before you put this on the glass wall. There's a possibility that he may not want it known to the public that we're hunting a serial killer. One thing I am sure of, he'll tell me he wished the perp had stayed in the Granada region."

"Fine."

At which point, Sergeant Bell knocked and entered, nodding to Patterson.

"I'll let you know what he says." I spoke to Sergeant Patterson then turned to Bell. He was clutching a DVD and was about to pop it in my computer.

"What is it, Alec?"

"Footage from a filling station in Hinchley, that's near Leicester."

I frowned, trying to figure out what this had to do with the investigation.

"Two men in a white van stopped there for fuel. The attendant mentioned it because they were an odd couple."

I was still confused. I really needed that coffee. "Go on."

"Well, I managed to get this record for you…"

"Who are they?"

"Wouldn't you like to see for yourself?"

"Any other time Alec but the stuff in here," I shook Patterson's file, "is dynamite."

Bell tapped the mouse pad and prodded buttons and the disc spun. "I think it's Leroy Richards, boss, you'll know for sure. The other one, the interesting one, is Jasminder Singh." He looked at me expectantly.

At least I'd got as far as what he was showing me, nothing to do with the murders, all to do with Richard's threats. I shook my head. "No. Sorry, Alec. The name doesn't mean a thing to me."

Alec grinned, he was going to educate me. "According to our records, Jasminder—or Asmin as he's known to his friends, had a big thing going in West Yorkshire a few years ago. People smuggling on a grand scale, ship's captains and boat owners in the scam with him, connections in Pakistan and the Punjab. Illegals by the thousands, must have increased our population by whole percentage points at a time." Bell rubbed his hand across his mouth as I watched the black man and the huge Sikh talking.

"Each of these illegal immigrants had been promised jobs and somewhere to live and each of them paid five grand for the privilege."

I remembered the bus loads of similar unfortunates I'd chased in my early days in Leeds. "Hmm. I remember something similar when I first arrived here. The switching buses case?"

"Oh yes. I'd forgotten that because I wasn't involved. Stuck here in the office even more at that time."

I resolved to make certain Bell got out more—God knew *I* was getting to feel incarcerated here. "So this Asmin was never brought to book?"

"No." Bell shook his head. "Lots of his fellow citizens got short sentences but we couldn't amass enough evidence to get the Crown Prosecution Service to bring a case against him. Last I heard, he was possibly involved in a grooming ring, could still be under surveillance."

I made a face. The idea of young, vulnerable girls being forced into prostitution was abhorrent; it made me feel physically sick.

"What have you done about these two, then?"

"Nothing sir. Oh, we've checked the registration number—belongs to a Peugeot car in the Leicester area—but I wanted to speak to you first, sir."

"Well, keep your eyes and ears open, Alec. I really must see the Super right now and, er…do you have any contacts in Leicester?"

"I have as a result of these inquiries, yes."

"Okay, see what you can dig up about Richards and Singh."

"Official or on the QT?"

"Keep it quiet until we've located them. I don't want them bolting like rabbits in the headlights." I picked up the file again. "Quite honestly, there's enough in here to give us all nightmares without these other two and I've got to keep a lid on this for the time being."

"It's big?"

I nodded. "Big and there are far-reaching implications."

Joe Flowers waved me in while he was speaking on the phone. I could hear phrases: *deep cuts* and…*expect police to cover an area this size*. It went on for some time—*why do we have to do all the saving?*

He looked at me, raised his eyebrows as he listened. "Do they really want anarchy on the streets?" Another lengthy pause. "What was that, George…"

So it was George Munroe on the other end, the assistant chief constable who handled the budget.

"I know. Everybody's in debt and actually, it's not my personal fault…"

It was obvious that Munroe had had the last word and had put the phone down to stop Joe in mid-sentence.

"My God, Stewart, I hope you've brought me some good news. Have you caught Faulkner yet?"

I told him about the phone call that purported to be Faulkner and told him too, that I thought it was genuine."

"Why do you say that?"

I plopped the file down in front of him. "Skim through this, sir. The main points are highlighted; then see if you agree with me."

Flowers's expression changed from frustration to anger to concern in under sixty seconds. Not something I was used to seeing. He looked up and grimaced. "Bloody hell, Stewart, if this *is* the same man, all hell is going to break loose. There's already a TV program been put out and it's just a question of waiting for TV and newspapers in this region to catch on. Politicians, counselors, they'll all be looking to make capital out of it."

He thought some more and his expression got darker. "Any way we can keep it from the chief until we can put a positive light on it?"

"I don't know about that sir, I have to say that that's your end of things. Mine is catching a man who's left no useable evidence at all up to now. He's found a method of murdering for fun and he doesn't need to change a thing. The only DNA that's been found was almost certainly planted."

"So the bastard's free to kill any time he likes?"

"Or *her*, sir." I thought I'd just throw that in for good measure. "Though, there's a degree of strength required to this sort of thing—and height too." I was being more formal today by not calling him Joe in an attempt to show how serious I was.

"Like your new sergeant, Stewart. She's pretty Amazonian, bet she could manage it."

"She's certainly the type, physically. Anyway, I need your guidance, sir." That put some formality back into the conversation. "So far, only one officer, Sergeant Patterson, as it happens, knows about these extra victims. I've at least twelve others on the case that should know. Have I permission to spread the word?"

"Good God, no, Stewart. That decision is above what *I'm* paid for too. The Chief can carry the can for this, it's his job to decide this sort of thing and it'll be his ass on the line. Give me half an hour, I'll get back to you."

Rather less than the half hour later, we were all called to the general staff room where the Chief Constable, no less, would condescend to speak to the troops. He kept us waiting rather more than the half hour before his feet could be heard descending from the ivory tower—I may have been feeling a little irritated.

War was declared in no uncertain terms and we might be fighting with extra militia from Lancashire and Merseyside. Detective Chief Inspector Clive Bellamy would be in overall charge, the Chief Constable's favorite. The Chief was taking it seriously.

On my way home, I called again at Connie's with the same result, no one home. I don't know what I would have done if I'd seen someone glancing down at me through the curtains. Probably written the woman off. This was most unlike me, so unprofessional. Why was I so concerned about this woman? I shook myself out of it; concentrated on the drive.

Later still, over supper, Dad told me about taking Pip for longer and longer walks. He described local places I'd never seen or noticed. Time had always been at a premium and the area I had chosen to live in was still a mystery to me after the best part of a year. I knew less about my immediate environs than I knew about Leeds, the city I worked in. I poured him a Guinness and a Carlsberg for myself. We relaxed, him in my favorite armchair and me in my second favorite.

"Hey, do you remember that time I disappeared for an afternoon?" I asked. "You almost called the police?"

"When you got your first bike?"

I nodded.

"Thought they'd find you down a drain, that day."

"It was the wind. Blowing half a gale but it was behind me and I never realized."

"You must have gone ten miles or more."

"No problem going. Peddling back was the tough part."

Dad shook his head and we passed on to other memories; when I was a kid and him still a young man.

"Your mum used to say some funny things, you know. *I'd sooner feed him for a week than a fortnight.* You had an appetite on you in those days."

Mum had some nice little turns of phrase I recalled. *Told you to wash your ears out, I could plant potatoes in there.* I could still hear her now, she had a voice like cream poured over bread pudding.

He chuckled. *You fall off that branch and break your leg, son, don't say I didn't warn you.*

"I used to climb some big trees. Makes me feel weak at the knees to remember them."

"She knew a lot of sayings like that—God knows where she got them from."

"From her mum and dad, I'd say."

Dad pried himself out of the chair. "I'm off to bed, son. Pip's walked me off my feet today." He went out to the hallway.

"And shut the door," I called after him. "Any one'd think you were born in a field with the gate wide open."

Another of mum's catch phrases. There was a long cackling laugh as he shut the door.

CHAPTER 13

Leroy turned on the BBC news channel and heard the name of his nemesis, D.I. White, mentioned in connection with a high-profile murder case. His eyes popped and he muttered, "I was wond'rin' where my man had got to."

There were no interviews and no pictures, however, so he pulled open the newspaper. Leroy really wanted to see a picture now; there was no memory of the man's face left. There in 62 point capitals, followed by a somewhat more restrained font, the front page story read:

MASS MURDER HUNT IN NORTHERN ENGLAND

Five deaths admitted by the police and still counting.

D.I. White is appointed senior investigating officer.

He skimmed the rest of the article. The reporter was relaying what had come to him from a "usually reliable" source, though no one from the regional Police Headquarters would confirm a word. The murderer, a man *The Mirror* was calling "the Spook" because of his well-organized disappearances, was killing left, right and center throughout Yorkshire.

"Hmm. So that's where he's hiding," he mused. "Bloody Yorkshire. Leeds, what a hell-hole to go to ground in. Mills and coal mines and foggy moorlands…"

Leroy grinned and drained his coffee. He realized that Stewart White would have his hands full and with such a high-profile case, he was not going to be able to stay out of the limelight. Every newspaper and every TV channel would be reporting his whereabouts and any progress made. He considered his feelings on the matter and recognized that they had cooled somewhat. Less than a year ago, he would have driven a thousand miles to kill the bastard D.I. White, but for now the policeman could wait. He knew roughly where he was, and he could find him anytime.

Another little nugget of information appeared on the final line. White's middle name was Sherlock; his father had named him for his favorite fictional detective.

"Get out of town, man!" He threw the paper across the room. "I don't believe it."

The murderer saw the same newspaper article and smiled. He had expected to read about the body he had placed on the boat but now they had discovered more of the others. "Well, if he's Sherlock," he thought," that must make me Moriarty. Welcome to *my* world, Sherlock."

Not that he cared too much about names. His mind examined the past. He had been christened William Jarvis although everyone called him Billy. On most Fridays, his father beat up his mother and would then go looking for his son. It didn't take Billy long to wake up to the fact that this would be his life for years to come. When Billy was ten years old, he climbed out of the bedroom window, and half slid down the roof of the outhouse. When his father climbed the stairs, Billy was closing the backyard gate.

He never returned.

A truck driver took him west and left him on the edge of Newtown. He enjoyed two days of freedom before he was picked up for thieving food from the market. He refused to give an address and ended up in a Welsh orphanage, where he stayed for two years.

The orphanage was just a place to put boys, runaways, intractable children, children with low intelligence, the abused. Billy learned to keep a low profile, even to aping other children to evade notice. No one in authority bothered him, half the staff did not notice whether he was there or not. There was nothing about him that made him stand out, he made sure he was average in every way, anonymous. He met Leroy Richards and Lofty Pike but paid them little mind. His father's fists had hardened him and taught him that aggression was king.

Once a month, the orphanage took the boys to church to improve their souls; once a year they organized an outing to improve their minds. Billy enjoyed the outings. The second outing was to an urban park with a boating lake. He and his roommate of three months, Gabe Henderson, shared the oars in a rowboat.

Gabe spent more time looking over the side at the shoals of tiny fish than rowing. Billy wasn't so happy with being left to work the oars and helped his partner to see the fish at close quarters by kicking him in the ribs until he fell over the side of the boat. Gabe went down and up three times while Billy sat stolidly and watched until he failed to surface a fourth time.

He raised the alarm, shouting that Billy Jarvis had fallen overboard and from that day onwards, he answered only to Gabe or Gabriel or—to the staff at the orphanage—as 497, the number Gabriel was known as on the register.

When he attended *his own* funeral, everyone thought he was crying for his friend but they were wrong, quite wrong.

At twelve years old, Billy, now Gabe, ran away from the home. The extra two years or so had added to both his street skills and his height, he lived in Cardiff at first then later, on the streets of London. Big cities, he found, were where the big pickings were and at fourteen, he was pimping for six teenage prostitutes, finding punters at pubs and taking them to the five up, four down house he rented close to St. Pancras.

As money accumulated, he tried to buy into a Soho club and was taught an early salutary lesson: brute strength always beats brains. Gabe was bright, a good little fighter and a fast learner, but the three-hundred-pound bouncer at "Pink Melons" waited for his boss to give him the nod. When it came, he showed Gabe out into a back alley. The beating he took that day, far and beyond anything his father had dealt out, put him in hospital for a month. His injuries, both internal and external, were severe enough for the nursing staff to wonder if he would survive. The old maxim had proved right: *a good big'un always beats a good little un.*

But he did recover and while doing so, Gabe saw that the bouncer had done only what he had been paid to do. He laid plans accordingly. Gabe bought an old car from a drunk and taught himself to drive, late at night, on a deserted former airfield. It didn't take long for him to drive smoothly and confidently.

When he deemed himself a decent driver, he bought leather gloves and waited outside Pink Melons in the early hours, waiting for the club's boss to merge. On the first night he saw that the boss did not drive; he had a driver who pulled up in front of the club, effectively blocking any man with a gun and a score to settle. The boss didn't come out until the driver was in place.

However, on the seventeenth night, the owner stepped out and was clearly annoyed that his chauffeur was late. He lit a cigarette and walked back and forth in front of his club. Gabe plotted his trajectory, accelerated, rolled right over the curb and propelled the man into the plate glass window of Eddy's Bistro. The body ended up propped against a sign on the wall which said *Never suffer from indigestion again.*

Satisfied with his vengeance and certain he had left no trace of himself in the car, Gabe left it on the pavement and walked away as a few late pedestrians began to gather.

He went back to his place, packed his bundles of bank notes into a large scuffed suitcase and his clothes into a much smaller one. He took the first train leaving King's Cross-Saint Pancras and left the capital.

He took lodgings in Stamford, Rutland County, at a small bed and breakfast hotel. His morning local paper was less than interesting but he needed to get a feel for his new surroundings. He needed some cover. He knew he looked young—he could pass as a college student. In fact, there was nothing stopping him from actually being a college student—or a student, anyway. Gabe leafed through the paper, until a picture of a headstone at a local graveyard caught his eye; the photograph showed three angels looking down at a freshly covered grave. Now there was an idea: Gabe went out, bought himself a brand new notebook and pen before visiting several graveyards.

He came back with a list of names which appealed to him and checked out of his hotel. Three lodgings later and the first two of his names used and scribbled over in his notebook, his name had become Arthur Lemic.

The original Arthur Lemic was born in 1953 and had died in 1959; the new one preferred to be called Art. Now it was time for another career change. Art enrolled at New College, Stamford in a twelve-week course in computer studies. It was designed to teach the basics, but he leaped ahead of the curriculum, studying through the day and asking questions at night school. The subject he really wanted to learn about was not taught, he worked his contacts and hired a man to teach him and ended up knowing far more about hacking than his teacher, a graduate of HM Prison Ashwell in Rutland.

The money he had made in London would last him for a long time though, of course, not forever. At the moment Gabe lived frugally but later on he expected to sample the high life exemplified by big houses, fast cars, and foreign travel. He'd need money for that, more than would fit into his suitcase. His studies had suggested the easiest and quickest route: identity theft; new identities were there for the taking and with them came bank accounts, credit cards.

But where to find new identities? That was easy, they were in the trash. He discovered he was not alone in his quest and the garbage trucks from wealthy neighborhoods were already being fought over by organized gangs. He watched the others bent on the same quest, he learned quickly which garbage trucks came from the wealthier areas of the town. He avoided the gangs doing similar things by working in the early hours of the morning, directly patrolling the streets of rich neighborhoods. He used a discreet pencil flashlight to sort through the trash, looking for bank statements and invoices for high value goods.

Gabe took a very ordinary job driving a delivery vehicle with a driver's license he had obtained by reporting the original as missing, He asked for signatures on an official-looking form he'd created, even though no signature was needed for the company he worked for. He built up a library of hand-written signatures which he scanned into his computer. It was comparatively simple to obtain replacement credit cards and make cash withdrawals before the owner became aware of the problem. He made a policy of using his "replacement" cards only once.

In the first month of his operation, he netted close to £150,000 and in the second, over half a million. After that second month, he had to move. There were mysterious knocks at his door which he suspected were police. He packed up and moved to King's Lynn, which was full of itinerant fruit pickers at this time of year. He disappeared into the crowd and laid low.

He met an Afghan, called Ali Al Alayah, in a pub. He was one of the fruit pickers; they played darts and as their acquaintance lengthened, Ali taught him to speak Arabic—his hometown language—just for fun. A few words to start with, then a few more, and then a flood. Art soaked it up like a three-year-old on amphetamines; he didn't know he had such a gift. Ali said he had a Kabul accent.

It took Art a month to assimilate the Kabul version of Arabic and Ali thought they were friends for life. Ali showed his new friend his passport, bragging how he had arrived in England without papers and was now a British citizen.

Art was really interested and as they passed a water-filled levee, he had a coughing fit and pretended to vomit. Concerned, Ali put an arm around the other's shoulders. They overbalanced and tumbled down the bank; Art scrambled back to the pathway, but Ali didn't. Art had the passport.

Art didn't shave for a couple of days. With dark stubble, he resembled the photograph in the passport. He tried it out on a return trip to France. The passport worked perfectly on the outward trip, but watching the treatment given to would-be immigrants on the French side of the channel, he was less certain that his passport would get through the Border Agency checks.

Ali Al Alayah's body might well have been found by now, he had left it in the water to seem like an accident. However, the authorities might be looking for the passport or its user.

Art, or Ali, as he had now become, had a good meal at the Port of Calais and then made his way circumspectly to the Sangatte camp in the Pas de Calais. He mixed with the hundreds of refugees and speaking nothing but Arabic, he got to know a few of the thousands who had arrived at this last stop before reaching their illusory land of milk and honey.

By day, they wandered around telling stories of their travels, begging food and standing in line for handouts from the Red Cross and other charitable organizations.

By night, they caught buses to the Channel Tunnel entrance, climbed the fences and risked their lives attempting to board freight cars or hiding in trucks that would be driving on to the vehicle rail transports.

Ali decided against waiting his turn to try this route to the United Kingdom. He destroyed the passport, took a local bus to the docks and taking out a bundle of English currency, approached a lorry driver. The deal was quick and easy; the notes disappeared into the driver's cab, Ali disappeared into the two thousand cases of French wine.

He expected to be discovered and with no wish to implicate his driver, he got out of the trailer before the inspection team and dogs reached him.

Ali was now an illegal immigrant who had to be processed through official channels. Another change of name—assumed from two different people at Sangatte—he became Fakhri Hussain, a Shiite Muslim from Kabul. Shiites were a minority and often the victims of religious harassment; hopefully, it gave him some explanation for his entry to the U.K. He would live with this name for some time.

CHAPTER 14

Barbara Patterson was late again but still managed to get to my office before anyone else came along. "Sorry about the time, boss. I just arrested this scrote and wheeled him into Leeds cop shop."

"That's okay, what did he do? Steal your bike?"

She shook her head and made a face. "Playing cop-a-feel in the Headrow. Must admit, he was fast. Managed a big squeeze." She massaged her left breast, *a rather nice one,* I thought. "Cuffed him while he was distracted."

Did I believe her? "And that's why you're smiling?" The expression seemed a little strained.

"No, nothing to do with that. I had this thought last night and I reckon this guy we're looking for is a copycat."

"What is it makes you think that?"

"Well, all those murders in Lancashire and Merseyside, really. Apart from the locked-room business, those murders were carried out just the same as ours."

I nodded. "Yes, you said so before. I can see your reasoning, but it's not as easy as that." She had not thought this through and, actually, I thought she was trying to sidetrack me. "Suppose our perp just added the locked-room trick recently, hmm? The one constant we have is the pillowcase inside the plastic bag, if we assume the Stokes murder to be someone else, that is. How could our perp have known about that?"

Barbara pursed her lips. "I read the reports from over there and the killing method was never reported. Okay? Let's get along to the incident room and gather up the troops."

I looked around the somewhat crowded room and projected good humor. "I'd like to thank our colleagues from over the hill," I used the local vernacular for the Pennines which separated the ancient kingdoms of Lancastrians from Yorkists, "...for joining us today. They're here as observers but more than that, they're police officers." I gestured toward the four men and women I had met earlier.

"I've acquainted our guests with our progress on the investigation and let them in on our cunning squad method of dividing the job up."

I beamed at everyone impartially.

"I'm open to any ideas, suggestions or incredible conclusions from anybody. I can tell you that forensics have turned up nothing new on the boat despite taking it to pieces and with the negative results from 'Hey Presto'—for you guys, that's the name of the house in the woods—and from the Sheffield offices, nobody here's a happy bunny."

The relentless cheerfulness had exhausted me, I sat on the corner of a table.

A man I had been introduced to as Sergeant Briar from Merseyside spoke up. Nothing fresh then, sir." He shook his head. "We went over the sites three times and he might as well have been invisible. Absolutely nothing."

"Same as ours, sir," added another. "Murder scene as clean as an operating theatre, not even a boot mark on the mat, let alone a sign of a scuffle. He either kills without any trouble—must be a strong guy—or he cleans up meticulously—and in that case, he's never in a hurry."

"That's been said by our boys too. It implies he's damn well organized." I turned to my squads. "Anything more from the scene of the boat murder? Neighbors, passers-by. What about the TV and press requests for information?"

"We've had maybe half a dozen calls, sir." That was Melodie Connolly from Sergeant Levy's squad. "Fruitless."

"That car registration… PIG?"

"Not been used since 1964," put in Alec Bell, "when the prefix letter was B." He was referring to a time when all car registrations had been given a letter to add to the plates, starting in London in '63 with the letter A.

I scratched my head and let the thoughts run around my brain, unsure whether to reveal them to the boys and girls. There are always times like this, there was no direction, nothing to work with, and so I had to tell them about Faulkner. It was all I had.

"Well…" And who should walk in on us but Flowers? I nodded to the Superintendent and re-started, seeing no reason to stop, "The one fly in the ointment has always been the Faulkner murder. The fact that Faulkner was found guilty suggests that he must be responsible for all the others but I'll give you this… I received a call from Faulkner and he said he was calling from a ship in the middle of the ocean and had been there for a week."

A murmur rose and fell.

"In which case, he couldn't have been guilty of the boat murder," said Barbara, stealing my thunder. "Did you believe him, sir?"

"I did, actually, Sergeant Patterson. Why would he lie? If he's really calling from thousands of miles away—which can be proven—why bother tracing my home phone number and lying?"

"Mind games," muttered Flowers.

"Sir?" That was Fletcher, one of the lab technicians, standing with just his head around the edge of the door.

"Fletcher?"

"Your carpet, Inspector White. The one they fished out of the canal?"

"I remember. What about it?"

"Nothing special. Bog standard wool and nylon mix but it's what was on it that's interesting." He came all the way into the room and went silent. He might have been looking at Barbara Patterson.

"And what is it that was interesting?"

"Three different types of blood, sir. Fortunately it had not been under water long enough to compromise the samples. One animal and two different human samples."

"Identification on the human samples?"

He shook his head. "Type O, type AB but neither DNA is in our database."

"And the animal?" I thought I'd be quite good at extracting teeth.

"Chicken or some bird."

"Chicken?" Fletcher nodded as he took one last lingering glance at our Amazon.

"So, Inspector White," Superintendent Flowers was at his driest. "Do you have any suggestions?"

I nodded and thought furiously. "I do, sir. I think that all the murders have been the work of one man, even the last two, although they've had this carnival trick added and the new MO, of course. In order to prove this, we need to ask why he should go to such lengths as to fit someone else up. It gives us a new avenue to explore. The killer must know Faulkner... he must have a reason for laying the blame for the murders on this guy. Find the reason and we'll be getting somewhere."

I looked around the room at the puzzled faces. "Concentrate on all the Faulkner connections, and his wife's: business partners, neighbors, friends, family, lovers. Let's get to work and let's turn something up."

Flowers bent a bit closer. "Still say it could be a woman."

"Takes a lot of strength to kill like this."

He too, took a long look at Barbara Patterson. "Quite."

CHAPTER 15

The front room of the house on Uppingham Road had been the pride and joy of its owners since it had been built in 1870. The room was used infrequently by family after family for Christmases, birthday parties, weddings, birth celebrations, and funerals.

Even now, with totally different occupants, Leroy had rarely seen it occupied. Today, though, was different and the atmosphere was thick enough to cut with a meat cleaver.

Leroy had been going on walks for days now, supposedly taking the air but in fact arranging a meeting out of Asmin's hearing or the friends of his who dropped by. These friends were those same ones who had pulled the building society job in Newark, Leroy considered them trustworthy on that performance but they were not his soul brothers.

He sensed the difference before he opened the door into the room. His body tensed as he composed his face into a visage of calm authority. He pushed the door open. There were five people inside, Asmin and four Sikhs. They watched Leroy cross to the small table where he took the top from a bottle of white rum, poured and added coke and some ice out of the ice box. "Anyone join me?" he asked, smiling. "No?" he chuckled, giving no sign he could see this was a hanging party.

He looked slowly around the room and smiled again. "Must be my money you're after."

Asmin was sitting deep in the oldest and biggest armchair in the corner, the only piece of furniture he could fit into. He remained quiet, listening to the others as they broke into furious chatter in Punjabi. Suddenly exasperated with them, he interrupted. "Do not be rude to our host, speak in English. You say you have concerns to discuss with Mr. Richards, the main man. Do so in a civilized way."

Leroy raised his eyebrows and, since he didn't know any of these Sikhs by name, he nodded to Asmin. "Like Asmin says boys, you gotta problem, let's hear it so we can clear it. But none o' that jibber-jabber, how'd you feel if I spoke to you in my mother tongue, eh?"

Leroy's mother-tongue was English but it didn't stop him from reciting a few Creole phrases that he remembered from his very early boyhood. "Kisa ou ap fe

Ia? Kisa ou vie? Tout bagay anfom?" *(What are you doing there? What do you want? Is everything OK?)*

The men looked mystified and Leroy smiled more broadly, "That's from Haiti but I won't be talking at you like that 'cause I respect you, see?"

Leroy swallowed the rest of his drink and gestured with his empty glass. "I s'pose it's about money, hmm? Prob'ly, you think you deserve more?"

A Sikh spoke, "That's right. That's why we've come."

A second said, "We think twenty thousand between us is disrespectful and you can say that in any language you want to."

The third said, "And that's what we'd have got if we'd been caught. Twenty. Twenty years each."

Leroy looked at the Sikhs. They were indistinguishable cannon fodder to him. He nodded and shrugged. These disputes were familiar, he could handle them easily. *"If* you'd got caught, you'da got maybe eight years max each. But you didn't. Now, let's get things straight, you finished workin' for me now? You don' want anythin' bigger? Like what we hijacked that money for? Hmm?"

There was a palpable silence that stretched on until Leroy judged it time to speak.

"Now I don' remember—an' I was there, doin' the controllin'—I don't remember there ever being a likelihood of you being caught." He slowed down a little, let the heat cool a degree or two. "It was a walk in the park for you guys; the hardest job was lifting that bollard out of the ground and who was it arranged the strap hoist to pull it out with?"

There was a murmur that sounded like grudging approval to Leroy.

"That's right."

"There was two mill in that van and we split a hundred grand between the lot of us. Now we did the math, Leroy…"

"Mr. Richards," said Asmin quietly but very, very firmly.

The speaker corrected himself. "Mr. Richards. And that don't seem too fair."

Sammy chose that moment to enter his front room. He took stock of his visitors and grinned at Leroy. "Anyone want a beer?"

"Me, Sammy, please," Leroy responded. Then to Asmin, "you feel the same as your brothers, Asmin?"

Asmin leaned forward and carefully straightened the seams in his trousers. "I thought you should learn how my cousins feel, Mr. Richards. Me? I reckon you had your reasons for splitting the take how you did and I reckoned you'd tell us all in good time."

Leroy was never anybody's fool and he knew who held the power in this room. It was clear that Asmin was a force among his fellow Sikhs, not the mere van driver he had purported to be when they had first met. He was quick on the uptake, strong and good with weapons. A linguist. What's more, he spoke

English with a precision to which Leroy could only aspire, and these disgruntled four respected him.

"I never told you because I've been working out the details. I got this put together while they had me moldering away in prison but I needed to work on the bricks and mortar. I need some troops, I need special transportation. And I need a few men who can be trusted and who've got the brains to understand what'll be going off—that's you, boys. Least, I thought it was."

He looked around the room, judging the mood. "I think we could all do with a beer, now, Sammy. If you don't mind." Then back to Asmin's men. "Anyone want to be a millionaire?"

Sammy brought in a tray of ice cold beers from the kitchen and handed them around. "Anyone staying for lunch? It'll be southern fried chicken from down the road, butter-fried corn, and salad."

"Nice touch, Sammy. Salad—healthy." Leroy knocked the top off a bottle and chugged it back, letting the amber liquid ease the tension out of his throat. He had a .38 tucked into his waistband at the small of his back and a .32 in his right sock. They were there if he needed them but he was quietly confident that the crisis was over. He and Sammy swapped glances.

"Now?" mouthed Sammy.

"Soon as we got the flicks over." Leroy replied in little more than a whisper. Then, to two of Asmin's men who were standing with their backs to the only wall with some clear space in front, he said. "Can you guys move a bit, we're going to have a film show, so you can all see what I've been on about."

Sammy closed the curtains while Leroy busied himself with the projector. The projector was an old one but it threw an excellent picture on the wall. They were looking at a tall square building with a flat roof. Four floors below, open streets surrounded it. The camera zoomed in and panned along the windows. Most of the windows were bricked up, those that weren't were fitted with thick steel bars which would let very little light through.

The building was gray. Not only stained by a layer of soot but every door, every window frame was painted in dull, battleship gray. It had a look of solidity from the concrete roof down to the chain-hoisted steel doors along one side. However, the front ground floor had gaily painted windows with colored glass and doors with half-life-sized cartoon characters to either side.

"That is one evil place," said the youngest of the Sikhs. "Look at those bars, enough room to get a gun barrel through but not much more."

"You're right," said Leroy, "it's a bloody fortress. Okay, fellers, what I'm about to say needs no interruptions so save any questions 'til the end."

He took a deep breath and spoke without any theater.

"This building is maintained by the largest drug cartel in the U.K. What I learned in prison is this... the top floor is a meth lab, see those vents there," he put a finger into the projector beam and pointed them out. "It's said that it feeds the whole of the Midlands and the South."

Leroy coughed and took another beer, pried the top off and took a drink.

"The third floor is offices, packing and such like, and on the back wall, which is the other side, there's chutes like builders use to drop stuff into lorries. Just to keep up appearances, they use dumpster trucks and top off each truck with broken-up plasterboard, packing cases, cardboard and so on."

"What goes in the dumpsters, apart from rubbish?"

"Di'n't I say? Heroin and cocaine. Now, these two top floors can only be reached by industrial elevators, no stairs despite what health and safety might say. Those elevators are big enough to lift a Ford Transit to the higher floors."

"Bribery must be a big item."

"Damn right. A lot of palms have to be greased, I'll tell you that for nothing."

"Security?" Asmin asked.

"Yep. Let me tell you about the rest of the place first. The second floor is for entertainment. Lounges and bedrooms, the cellar is one big bar and there's pole dancers who double up as good time girls. They earn five times the money of street prostitutes and they're five times safer."

Leroy saw contempt on Asmin's face and various curious expressions on the others. He put his hands up in a defensive position.

"Okay, not your cup of tea. But it's still there. Now, the ground floor and we're finished with the tour.

"We're not interested in the ground floor but just for completeness, it's a charity. It's a charity for autistic kids and it's staffed by volunteers who have such children themselves. There's no entry to the floors above, it's completely sealed off. It's a nice touch don't you think? It has all the local residents thinking that everything that goes on there is for charity."

Asmin asked, "Does the charity know about the activities on the upper floors?"

Leroy thought, then said, "You asking if the charity is just a cover? I'm reasonably sure that they don't know or don't want to know what goes on upstairs. They use their space rent-free; a "gift" from a generous supporter. And our operation won't take place when they're in the building."

Leroy raised an eyebrow. "Everybody okay with that?"

Nobody looked at Leroy, all eyes were on Asmin.

Leroy continued, "So that's why I needed the rest of the money from Newark. For guns, ammunition and for… What? Emergencies, did someone say? Like exits? There's those chutes, big enough to take a man, even a man like Asmin who is to be in charge of this job and will be from now on, my full and only partner."

Leroy beamed around the room. Asmin, still in his corner, was wearing a dour expression and struggling not to break into a grin. Asmin covered his almost-grin with a question. "You seem to be saying that we can raid this place—how do we get in?"

"Ah, yes. Someone interrupted me. That nest egg from Newark is for two helicopters and two pilots. Big Sikorsky troop movers."

"F—" said Asmin. "Damn me!"

"Whatever you say, my friend. Helicopters, pilots, and pucker Warwickshire Police uniforms, since it's near Birmingham, which will get us into the place and so long as we stay away from the back, where they have spotters operating when they have product to be moved…"

"So they'll naturally try to escape down the rubbish chute, where they think they're not covered. And helicopters will take us off to where?" Asmin had summed up the operation. Almost. "And… why the guns and ammunition?"

"Precautions, Asmin. There'll maybe be a few rats who don't want to leave a sinking ship."

CHAPTER 16

I was summoned to DCI Bellamy's office; he pointed to a chair. "Make yourself comfy, Stewart. Sorry it's come to this. I had enough problems as it was without the Chief Constable dumping this on me on top of everything else. Besides, I'm sure you're more at home with things than I'm ever likely to be."

At least the chair I was offered had an upholstered seat; I pulled it closer to the desk and settled in. If this turned out to be a long job, my bottom wouldn't turn numb. "I only wish I could agree, sir."

"Clive, please Stewart, in here anyway. So what can't you agree with?"

"Whoever our perp is, he's damned clever. Leaves nothing to chance. We can do with another viewpoint, Clive, another input. He makes me wonder if he's been police trained, or maybe a pathologist's assistant. Even the cleverest of crooks leave some trace of themselves."

"You're adamant that it can't be Faulkner. I ask this because the old man is just as certain that it is and he's hoodwinking you somehow."

I bent forward, did the *man to man* look. "I haven't told all of this to anyone else because I don't want it broadcast to all and sundry but if we're to work together, then you're not all and sundry."

He smiled at my turn of phrase. "Trust, Stewart. Goes both ways."

"Sure. Okay, I can't prove whether or not Faulkner killed his wife. Witnesses say they were unusually close and that they had a rather open relationship, by all accounts. However, *if* we agree that whoever killed Mrs. Faulkner also killed Stokes and the others: then Faulkner is not our serial killer. On the day Mrs. Faulkner was murdered Mr. Faulkner was in an all-day meeting of the Rotherham Planning Committee with the Mayor and several other dignitaries. They report Faulkner did not leave the meeting, not even for lunch. I will remind you that the killing occurred fifteen or twenty miles away."

Bellamy nodded slowly. "And your reason for keeping this under wraps? Tell me again."

"Because our friends in the press will pay a fortune to any policeman informing them of the facts. I don't want our guys exposed to that sort of temptation. And I don't want it public knowledge because *I want the real murderer to continue thinking we believe Faulkner is guilty.*"

I could see the idea dawning on Clive's face, "And if the real killer thinks he's in the clear, he's more likely to make a mistake."

"Absolutely. Over-confidence," I replied, although I hadn't actually got that far myself, it had just been a gut feeling that it was the right thing to do. Bellamy had just crystallized my thoughts.

———————

The incident room was quiet when I looked in. Most of my team was out, though Barbara was at her desk, her fingers flickering over the computer keys as she feverishly skipped from one page to another. I thought she hadn't noticed me and I was about to go on to my own office when she looked up.

"Bird details."

"Sorry?" I said.

"Details of birds, boss. Do you know how many birds fall into the poultry category? There's domestic hens, guinea fowl, ducks, geese, turkeys, peacocks, simply hundreds—"

"Got a reason for this compendium of all things poultry?"

"Well, I thought I'd try and narrow down our search for blood types but it's a can of worms."

"And we have a pathology service to do that sort of thing. It might be quite interesting though, if we could figure out why there was poultry blood on the carpet in the first place. The variety probably doesn't matter."

"If you say so, boss." She looked a bit hurt.

I explained, "Might be enough just to know its animal blood. But you're going after this with lateral thinking, certainly outside the box, it could be useful later on." I leaned over and whispered, "We are dealing with a magician, right? Does that help you narrow your search?"

She shrugged and kept typing. I couldn't figure her out; she looked thoughtful, grateful, tired. She even looked a bit nervous and something else I couldn't put my finger on.

———————

Sergeant Bell came into my office a short time later. He smiled—he smiled a lot more these days than when I had first met him, not such a dour Scot these days.

He said, "You may wish to send Shobna Guish of the Leicester Constabulary a bouquet." He paused for me to ask what the hell he was talking about; which I did.

"Who is this person?"

"A woman, not sure whether she's young or old, sir, but she mans—if that's the right word—the town center CCTV screens..."

"Sergeant, if you don't get to the point soon, I'll have retired before you've finished."

"She positively ID'd Jasminder Singh who..."

"Aha, Leroy Richards's driver. Yes, I remember."

"Yes, well, he doesn't just drive a white van anymore. Lately he's been seen behind the wheel of big black Jaguar and each time he's been spotted, it's the same camera on Uppingham Road."

"I think you're right. If you can find out this lady's home address, I'll send her a big bunch of flowers and you might just brief her to keep a lookout for Leroy Richards, as well."

"Already did that boss, she's got his pic stuck to the wall."

"So as soon as we spot him, we can take him whenever we want."

"We could just let Leicester know and let them pick him up—he's an escaped prisoner, after all."

"We could and he'd get, what, eighteen months and he'd be out again?"

"I suppose..."

"And we'd have to do this again. If we just keep an eye on him, we can see what he's up to and catch him for something worth more than a year and a half."

Sergeant Bell nodded. "Yes, I guess I like your thinking, boss."

The phone rang. I looked at the caller display and I saw it was Dad. I picked it up and raised my eyebrows at Bell. "Yes?"

"You going to be home at a reasonable hour tonight, son?"

"Can't see why not. Fancy something different to eat, perhaps take you to an Indian?"

"Oh no need for that. We have an invitation to dine with Margaret. You, me, and Pip are going out."

"Margaret?" That must be the lady my Dad had been waxing lyrical about.

"New girlfriend?" asked Alec Bell as I put the phone down.

"Not mine, my dad's."

I drove Dad and Pip to the tiny village of Main Wearing which proved to be a lot further than a mere stroll along the river bank, the odometer said fifteen miles and I didn't like the idea of my dad stumbling that far along the river in the dark. Just the thought of him tripping and falling down into that swift water was enough. Could be the river bank was a shorter route than by road, but I still worried.

Like mine, Margaret's home was a country cottage but with roses growing not just over the front porch but everywhere else too. The roses would be a big plus point with my dad. He loved the things and had won more prizes for his hybrid teas than I'd had hot dinners. One year, his Crimson Velvet scored best in show; no doubt that would come up, or had already come up, in conversation with Margaret.

Margaret Grimmond was a delight. I could see how she'd taken Dad's fancy. I'd envisioned a rather chubby elderly lady in a flowered apron, but Margaret was slim with thick shining silver hair down to her shoulders. Her face was serene and almost ageless; a sort of fifty going on eighty look that certainly kept me guessing. She walked quickly, meeting us halfway down the path and giving Dad a swift peck on the cheek. "Welcome to Orchard Cottage," she said, looking at me. "Everything's just about ready so I hope you're hungry."

What was almost ready was home-made steak pie with black gravy that had more than a hint of red wine in it and new potatoes. There were other vegetables which Margaret made Dad carry into the dining room in big tureens to set on a lime-washed oak table. The meal went very well, the hour or two afterwards, likewise, with a nice desert wine to loosen our tongues. As the driver, I had to limit myself but I didn't notice either of my companions showing much restraint.

I told Margaret a little about me, Dad told her more with embarrassing anecdotes and the only thing I really learned about our hostess was that she was a damn good cook. The apple pie with nutmeg that she served after the main course was enough to make me hope that she invited us over for dinner frequently.

It got to going home time and Dad was obviously pretty reluctant but then, he didn't have to get up early the next morning to get to work. All the way home, he mooned like a schoolboy over his first date.

"You know, son, she reminds me so much of your mother."

"Like that night she locked you out because you were singing rude songs all the way down the street?"

"Oh, son. That's cruel."

And I didn't know whether he was really hurt or joking. "Sorry, pop, Just the wine." And it was the wine and a very full stomach that put me to sleep until the alarm went off.

Fakhri Hussain, nee William Jarvis, moved back to Hammersmith. He used his new persona, courtesy of the U.K. Immigration Service, and continued to acquire language skills and religious knowledge in order to conduct business in the Muslim quarters. As he learned he managed to disappear in full sight of the people looking for him.

He was a regular visitor at Finsbury Mosque and he became to all intents, a fervent Muslim. He spent months learning the new ways of thinking and soaking up the culture which seemed less and less alien to him as time passed. He abstained from drinking alcohol, ate Halal meat from food bowls with his right hand only, conducted ablutions with his left, found the east and prayed in the direction of Mecca five times a day. As is the case with many adult converts to a new faith, he became more devout than the devout. He started to feel that this was what he was meant to be, a follower of Islam.

It was a serene and comforting lifestyle and time passed at a leisurely pace until... and here, Fakhri did not quite know what caused him to change his colors like a chameleon.

He was returning to his home from the last prayers of the day on the underground railway when two white boys—teenagers—began taunting him. He ignored them for a while but the maneuver served only to make them angry. Finally, one of them drew a switchblade and made to cut him on the face. Real or feigned, it switched Fakhri from a placid Muslim to his former vicious, street-wise self. None of his old skills were forgotten. He remembered giving the knife wielder a dead-arm and simply taking the knife from the other's nerveless fingers. The other boy rushed him then and the knife was in his hand...

Fakhri had no memory from that point on and it wasn't until he saw the papers on the following morning that he learned that both youths were dead. There was CCTV in the underground; he realized at that precise moment that Fakhri had to die.

The truck driver who picked him up at a trucker's service area on the A4 asked him where he was going.

"Anywhere," he said, "just can't stand London anymore."

"You foreign?" asked the other, glancing across the cab. "Got a sort of odd accent, bit like Iraq maybe, somewhere out that way."

"I've been out there, Afghanistan actually, didn't realize I'd picked up an accent. Got injured, got my discharge, pension isn't enough to live on. So now, I'm looking for work."

The implication that he was ex-services sweetened the driver some, he told him about the fruit picking in the West Country and eventually dropped him off at Bath. He made his way to the Somerset orchards and secured a job for the rest of the season. He now called himself Harpal Kumar, a name he had culled from a newspaper though he had no idea if the name was Afghan or not. Not that his present companions cared. He dossed down—slept—with two Nigerians in an ancient barrow that the English Heritage people had not gotten around to fencing off.

The barrow—an ancient dirt mound last used for burials three or four thousand years ago—was larger on the inside than it appeared. The doorway was cramped, only a yard high leading to a tunnel seven yards in length. The interior was lined with field stone and a camping light and a gas stove kept the night chills at bay.

Harpal embarked on another long hazy existence with nothing harder than picking apples and taking full wicker baskets to the trailers day after day. The farmers paid without fail, just enough to cover the cost of food, clothes, and a journey to the pub every two or three nights. A habit he fell back into easily.

The money he had previously amassed was safely in various bank accounts but difficult to get hold of while he was living out here in the sticks. It was something that he could take care of when the fruit season came to an end. He retained his passport, kept it on his person at all times, so he could verify his identity if necessary.

When he received his final pay packet, Harpal left without saying goodbye, and took a bus to Bristol where he wandered around the docks. He asked a few questions and found an Irish fishing boat that had lain over; the captain had an EU warrant to catch pollock and was returning that night. Harpal paid the man a small fortune to take him along and he spent thirty hours doing little more than making endless mugs of tea for the crew.

Ireland would assuredly be a safe place to settle for as long as wanted. He could get hold of his money, he could—and did—hitchhike to Cork where, just before reaching the city, he asked the driver to stop and let him out. He climbed down from the cab, said "thank you" and began walking, turning into the nearest country lane he found and exploring the various tumbledown buildings that littered the countryside.

Back in the nineteen-eighties when EU money was flooding in to the country, financial grants for land or building improvements or new builds could be had almost for the asking, old houses were just left to rot while new ones were built to replace them.

Harpal found a cluster of three where the walls were still solid but the roofs had long-since collapsed. He took timbers from two of them to lay across the empty roof space of a third and covered them with the old gray slates that lay ankle deep inside the old buildings.

By wintertime, he was snug. There was wild fruit still hanging in the hedgerows and fish to be caught in the streams and an occasional foray into Cork for a sleeping bag, tinned goods, a pair of boots, and a warm by the fire in a public house with a glass of Murphy's to hand. Winter set in and passed him by.

But such times always came to an end. Always, there came an incident which brought things to an end and moved him, quite unwillingly, onward.

Harpal was in Cork, an early spring day when all should have been enjoying the sunshine and—perhaps—more than one or even two, glasses of Murphy's. A fight started, two men in an argument stood face to reddening face, sizing each other up. A fist was thrown and another, other men became involved and within seconds, the argument had grown into a decent-sized brawl with tables being thrown and glasses shattering all around.

A heavy bar stool flew across the room, catching Harpal on the temple, no great injury but enough to blind him with fury. The bar was lined with full or part-filled bottles of all sorts and sizes; an arsenal of missiles that Harpal saw no reason to ignore. Very soon, there was a hail of deadly glass bottles. Skulls were cracked, men laid out and mirrors and windows smashed.

The bartender and a friend tried to grab him. Harpal smashed the barman over the head and when the bottle shattered, he thrust the jagged end into the other one's throat. The angry red mists cleared. *Time to go*, he realized as thoughtless reaction suddenly gave way to crystal-clear judgment. Vanish before the Garda arrives.

Harpal had never wavered from his Afghani persona except in the matter of an occasional drink, he imagined that he had stayed well below the radar until he saw his assumed name on the front of the *Irish Times*.

He went into Cork and bought a railway ticket to Dublin. Despite his linguistic skills, Harpal had, so far, failed to master the Irish brogue, not so much the accent but the choice of words. His passport was unusable since it had no stamp from when he had entered the republic. He changed his plans, and exchanged his ticket for one to Dundalk, close to the border with Northern Ireland, crossed over by foot, and thumbed a lift to Belfast.

For a while, he'd considered staying there but England beckoned, life would be familiar and a lot easier. Crossing back into England was no problem. He had simply boarded the ferry and debarked in Liverpool like the rest of the day-trippers.

CHAPTER 17

Dad was still dreaming the dreams of the just when I woke up and was still in dreamland while I showered, dressed, and made toast. I was reaching for the marmalade when I noticed the light flashing on the answer-phone. It was Connie.

"Hi, Stewart. Just thought I'd let you know that I'm out of town for a few days in case you were considering giving me a call."

Although she'd never been at home when I called, her tone didn't seem sarcastic so I took her words at face value. Disappointing but probably for the best; I had decided to forget about her. Between Dad and the job, my life was pretty full at the moment. And the thought of Dad giving me that knowing I-can-see-what-you've- been-up-to look was not a happy one. Then I realized that *that* was probably the very look I was giving him over the Margaret business—except that he just ignored it. I chuckled. *Damn, we are alike in many ways*—not that I minded that one bit.

I sometimes got the impression that the corridor outside my office was a race track. Alec Bell beat Barbara Patterson to my office that morning, a serious expression on his face. "Not much to say about the Faulkner murders, sir. No one's coming up with anything, I'm afraid. They're all pretty worried and maybe an encouraging word from the Boss would help."

I knew what he meant. There is nothing worse than beating yourself up day after day and nothing to show for it. "Okay, Alec. I'll come by shortly and try and inject a bit of fire."

But that wasn't all Alec had to say. There was more, two more things, to be exact.

"One of my contacts, Sahid Gupta, is familiar with our new friend Jasminder Singh. Word is out on the streets, in a very hush-hush sort of way, that Singh and a few of his persuasion are planning a big job. No one knows exactly what it is, obviously, but it's something in the Midlands."

"Hmm, that's a mighty big area, Alec. Can't really pass the word without more specifics."

"I know that, boss. Just keeping you up to date. But there's another matter you should know about, even if the teams are focusing on the Faulkner case."

"Okay, spit it out."

"I've a snout," he screwed up his features as though he'd used a dirty word, "who says there's an armed robbery going off in Huddersfield."

"Oh?"

"Tonight."

"And why should it be of interest to us and not the boys in blue?"

"Aha, this is the good part. Because it's going to happen on premises flagged by the NICIES…"

I smiled slightly. I didn't like working with the National Criminal Intelligence Service and neither did Sergeant Bell.

"…who in my estimation and that of my colleagues don't have enough intelligence to fill a condom." he said.

"You're right, Sergeant Bell, If they had the place flagged, I'm definitely interested." I rubbed my hands together. "It's on our patch and I've certainly had no word from that quarter so…"

"Thought you'd go for that sir. In fact I'd have bet on it."

"You didn't, did you?"

"Certainly not, sir."

"Right, what's good for the goose…"

"I'm waiting on information as to time, boss. My guy is certain it's tonight but I told him, we can't go off half-cocked…"

"That's good enough. Let me know as soon as you do."

It was ten o'clock, and Barbara Patterson hadn't come in. I was worried, okay—she was a bit of a loose cannon but definitely not the type to just not show up for work. I called her cell phone and got her voicemail connection, tried her home number with the same result. I checked her address, made some excuse and left.

She lived ten miles from the station in the opposite direction to me, in a row of small semi-detached houses. She was home, or at least her car was and I pulled in behind it. A van was parked in the drive next door cutting off any view of their front garden and everything else in that direction.

I rang the doorbell and waited. When there was no reply, I went through a gate to a side entrance. The door there was wide open; in fact, it was almost hanging off its hinges, it rattled as I moved it.

"Barbara," I shouted and stepped inside. I walked through the kitchen where there was washing up waiting to be done. There was no one in the living room beyond, untidy with blankets piled on the sofa. It looked as though she had slept the night there. A small fish tank had been broken, there was a big damp patch on the carpet with dead fish scattered about.

I crossed the room and stood at the foot of the stairs. "Barbara," I called again. "Are you here? Are you okay?"

"There was a sound from the room I'd just come through: something falling and maybe a voice. I turned and looked back to where the blankets were being pushed back. A red head with eyes of much the same color tried to focus on me.

"Christ, Barbara, you've hung one on, haven't you?"

"Boss? What're you doing here?"

There was a smell of whiskey in the air now and the thump I'd heard was the whiskey bottle hitting the floor and emptying its dregs on to the carpet.

"I'll make coffee, shall I?" And without waiting for an answer, I went into the kitchen and filled the electric kettle. The water boiled while I looked for coffee. I found a jar of instant coffee and spooned some into a mug, also sugar, quite a lot of sugar, and some tap water to cool it to a drinkable temperature.

Barbara had got as far as sitting up with her head in her hands when I returned. She took the mug and drank about half of it in one go. A minute or two later she pulled in a huge breath and patted my hand as though I was the vulnerable one. It probably signaled *thanks*.

"What've you been up to, Barbara? This will look pretty bad if I have to report it."

"Bloody hell, boss, give me a break, eh?"

"Just tell me, girl."

She finished the remainder of her coffee and tried to start two or three times. "My parents..." she said eventually. "They got themselves into problems with... debt problems with this loan shark."

This was not what I was expecting. I thought maybe a love affair gone bad. I organized my thoughts and asked, "One of those TV advert organizations?"

"God no. Those're like angels of mercy besides these people. They were going 'round and breaking the door locks to get in and see what they could take."

I patted her shoulder. "Well let's get the police involved, that's what we're here for." I chuckled a little, trying to lighten the situation until I saw her expression.

She shook her head. "It's me now, boss. I bought the debt so they wouldn't be bullied anymore. Dad's in his seventies, mums not far off. They were ready to commit... well I don't know what they were ready to do but they were desperate, I couldn't think of anything else that would've been as quick. But now they're..."

"They're what? Who?"

"You look at my back door, they came in here last night, they pushed me around, pushed me into the aquarium."

"Ah, right. I see."

"It's more difficult now. They're really polite but it just goes up—what's owed—just goes up every day and they'll write to the newspapers and I'll…"

"You'll have to resign?"

She nodded.

"When do they come?"

"About six when I'm at work, other times when I'm not."

"Okay. Go and have a shower, get dressed and we'll make some plans. Got anything with the name of this organization on it?" "

She got up and rummaged through some papers that had been behind the fish tank. She handed a cheaply printed letterhead. *Pay Day Lends* it said, *advisor: James A. Naylor.* Below was the one word: *balance* and the sum £16,000.

I left the house and sat in the car while Barbara put herself to rights. No wonder she'd been tired and out of sorts at work, coming in late with odd excuses. Her parents lived in the country, I believed, between Leeds and Sheffield.

A shadow fell across the window. "That was quick," I thought Barbara was ready but it wasn't Barbara. A man in a three piece suit looked down at me and I wound the window down. "Can I help you?" His three-piece was stuffed with muscles.

"Maybe you can if your wallet's full." His voice sounded like a heap of rusty cans falling off a shelf.

"I don't know what you mean?"

"I mean, if you happen to be," he nodded at the house, "her boyfriend or something, you might help her out."

I was getting the idea and I got out of the car, opening the door sharply enough to catch him across the belly. "Sorry."

"You'd better be, sonny."

"I stood up, topping him by about three inches. "Less of the *sonny*." I closed the door firmly. "I have a feeling you're asking for money."

"Look, your girlfriend's up to her eyeballs in debt. Doesn't matter how she got there but she owes me about seventeen and a half grand. You can help her."

He tapped me sharply in the chest. "She's a policewoman, right? She shouldn't be getting herself into this sort of pickle."

"You touch me again, asshole, and I'll get her to arrest you for assault."

"One word to her CO or whatever and she'll be out of the force faster than she can say *knife*."

"Her CO doesn't give a shit. I know what you've been doing to her parents and I know the threats you've been making to Ms. Patterson."

"Nothing illegal."

"Breaking and entering's illegal. Assault is illegal. Probably breaking property and killing tropical fish is illegal."

He was still truculence personified.

I pulled out my warrant card. "It so happens I'm her CO. And if I ever see you again, I'll have you charged so fast your feet won't touch the ground."

Mr. Three-Piece looked at me for a moment, then across at the house, then back at me. He looked at my warrant card and opened his mouth to speak.

"Don't," I said, "say another word. Go and really believe that this is the luckiest day of your life… Mr. Naylor."

Mr. Naylor left. He got into his BMW and gave me the finger as he drove off. I chuckled, usually, that gesture at such a point in a conversation means it's all over.

I went back into the house. "How're you doing Barbara?"

She came into the room, approximately A1. "That was him who was talking to you. That…"

"Yes. We reached an understanding. I don't think you'll hear from him again and if you do, we'll have him in court so fast… well, we'll have him in court."

"But my record! What if he goes to the local rag…" She reached out then and put her arms around me. "Thanks."

"It's okay…"

She made to kiss me and I moved back a little. "It's okay, Sergeant Fearon. Really."

"Fearon?"

"Oh, bloody hell."

Back at the office, just to make a change, I phoned Dad. There was no reply and eventually, the voicemail cut in.

"Any news on the time, Alec?" For once, I was ahead of Sergeant Bell.

He laid a finger alongside his nose and lowered his voice. "W.R.T. Paper Mills, just before the evening shift goes off at 10 p.m."

"Oh? Why this place? Do they pay the late shift off in cash or something?"

"It's the product that's interesting."

I shook my head. "You've lost me, sure your source is reliable?"

Alec gave me a long look which seemed to say *Oh ye of little faith* and said, "Copper-bottomed, sir."

"Right. We don't want to alarm anyone and we don't want to set tongues wagging. Put a ten man team together and we can meet at Lennox's café on the bypass and make certain no one says a word to their wives or brothers or …"

"Absolutely, sir. Er, weapons?"

"Inspector Masters in C19 owes me a favor."

C19 was the armed response unit, I looked at my watch, it was six o'clock. There was always a presence at C19 but I was banking on Masters still being there.

"Product, Alec?"

"Paper."

The team of ten officers from our crime squad and six C19 officers assembled at Lenox's. The proprietor would have been very pleased with so many customers but, of course, the café had been closed for almost four hours and we were just using the parking lot for a few minutes.

This was my first raid with my troops since leaving Birmingham a year or so ago so I wanted to do it right. I made certain to pat my guys on the shoulder and shake hands with Maurice Masters and his team.

"Your boys lead, mine follow, okay, Maurice?"

"Only way I know, Stewart. Death or glory for us, paperwork for you." His big face split in a grin. "Tell me about the target."

"I'm told it's a paper manufacturer though they don't advertise the fact. Just a single line in the phone directory, no web page or online presence."

Masters looked across the expanse of patchy grass between us and the factory building. "Looks quite a big place from here but I looked on Google Earth—looked long and thin."

"You're right. There's a backyard enclosed by a high wall—that's what you can see from here. It's about a hundred feet long, thirty deep. At the front there's a pair of loading dock doors and an office door to their left."

"I've got ladders in the van, we'll put someone at the top of the wall, just in case anyone tries to get out by that route. Umm, we're going to let them get in the building first, right?"

I nodded. "Easier to round them up that way."

"Easier to let them open the place up for us too."

I heaved a bit of a sigh. "The only thing we're not sure of is the numbers. I don't know how many we're going to be up against."

There was only one man with a sawn-off and four more armed with pickaxe handles. We made quite a noise coming in, the guy with the shotgun broke a window at the back and crawled into the yard.

"DROP THE GUN AND RAISE YOUR HANDS," Maurice's man also had a megaphone. The man raised his hands, the shotgun still grasped in one.

"OH CHRIST," prayed the C19 man in an exasperated voice. "DROP THE F... DROP THE GUN." The gun was dropped.

The other four stood around dejectedly, waiting to be cuffed. "We'd better get hold of the management." I said, more to myself than anyone else.

"I'll get that, boss." Sergeant Patterson beamed at me and strode off toward the offices.

By the time the thieves were in the van and the C19 guns were put away, the MD and the foreman from the last, late, shift had arrived.

"What I can't quite understand," I said, "is why paper." I pointed to the three pallets that had been towed to the doorways ready to load into the small truck outside. "It's hardly a king's ransom."

"Could be." He said, seriously. "It's currency paper with watermark and security structures already incorporated. "King's ransom, just depends what's printed on it."

———

The five would-be thieves were charged and locked up for the night by half past eleven. I drove home; Dad had gone to bed and left me a note propped against the kettle. *Chicken pie in the fridge—don't forget to warm it up first—very nice.*

No, I didn't feel hungry.

CHAPTER 18

Asmin drove the Jag as usual and Leroy settled back into the sumptuous cowhide seat. The car still smelled of new carpets and leather, the doors still shut with a hardly audible click, the walnut and enamel still had that subdued gleam of understated luxury.

"What made you make me your partner?" Asmin asked as he took the car west on the A47 to its junction with the M6.

"Truthfully? Because you're the only one who never asked me for nothin'."

"Apart from payment to get you away from prison."

"Except that. You've done more than I expected of you, Asmin. You been more loyal than all my past friends."

"Except Sammy."

"Except Sammy." Leroy looked at the sky laced with dark clouds. He scratched the side of his broad nose with a manicured fingernail. "And why did you agree to become my partner? And while we're askin' questions, why din't you say nothin' when your boys asked for more money?"

Asmin smiled. "Could have been that I thought your natural charm would win the boys over."

Leroy snorted and laughed.

Asmin smiled and said, "But, just as truthfully, I knew you had a .38 tucked in your pants and a backup in your left sock. And absolutely truthfully, based on the time I've been with you, I reckoned you had a reason for being… frugal."

"You could say *absolutely, bloody stingy* and you'd be right. But for this job we're on now, I needed every last penny. It's costing a lot more than we got from that bank job. In fact, I think money is the only reason no one's tried it before."

Leroy turned in his seat to face Asmin. "Of course, it could be my West Indian soul brothers is shit-scared of Mad Charlie Morgan." He seemed to be looking for a reaction.

Asmin just raised his eyebrows a fraction. "Why? Is he an alien with super-powers? Is he bullet proof?"

"None of those things, my friend. He's a sly, slimy old bastard, is what he is. Hard as boot leather, handy with his fists and as evil as any I've ever seen."

Asmin shrugged and the car snaked just a fraction. "Just a man, then and as long as he isn't bullet proof, I don't care." He took his hand off the wheel and gestured. "We've been over the plan enough times and the men know their positions, as long as they do as they're told, it's pretty well foolproof."

"And they will do as they're told?"

"Oh yes. Fear and honor have always intermingled in our culture. Personally, I don't care if they fear me or respect me as long as they obey me. They are family and I am the head of that family."

"Really? They're all your relatives?"

Asmin glanced quickly at Leroy and grinned. "Not literally. But here, in this district, I am regarded as a person of authority."

A pair of matte black Sikorsky helicopters rested like two huge crows in the woodland clearing, part of the Cannock Chase National Forest. As the two gang leaders climbed aboard, they were given black balaclavas to match the police uniforms they wore. The pilot showed them where the weapons were stored and briefed them.

"Journey time's about twelve minutes, take-off to landing. Two of your ground force have two-way radios for when we get closer."

"I thought we had cell phones for that?" Asmin tapped his top pocket.

"These are more reliable. Keep your phones as back up but you shouldn't need them. We're leaving nothing to chance and of course we need confirmation that everyone has left the place before we put the choppers down. And there's champagne on ice in the onboard fridge."

Leroy gave him a harsh look. "Plenty of time for drinking after it's all over. Anyone celebrating before then loses fingers—or worse."

Asmin nodded grimly. "No argument, Boss. How long before we go?"

The pilot consulted the large-faced watch on his wrist. "We'll get the covers off and then I can tell you."

Canvas covers were pulled from the aircraft to show the insignia of the West Midlands Police Force with which they had been decorated. A line of realistic numbers had been stenciled on below the graphic.

"They look real enough," Leroy said, peering across at the other helicopter.

"A good copy from some choppers already in service. They'll pass muster and we've got the current call-signs in case we have to answer communications."

"Who's going to call us?" asked Asmin.

"Ha! Air Traffic Control for Birmingham for one. Could be other police aircraft too."

Asmin sat down and looked for his straps. "Got a plan B, Mr. Pilot?"

"Oh, I know this area like the back of my hand. There's not a bridge, not a wood, not a tunnel I don't know, a thousand hiding places."

Five minutes later, they were aloft and on their way to the target while Leroy and Asmin were testing the radios and their cells. Leroy gave the order to those on the ground to start their action.

———————

Police sirens and flashing lights emptied the roads to the front of the fortress-like building. A pair of Land Rovers pulled to a screeching halt, ten armed men leaped out and ran to the various entry points and began beating on the doors. Like the real thing, one of them carried a door breaker and began battering at the main door. Upstairs, once they had the elevator working was another door which had obviously been reinforced; it took a lot of effort to open it.

At length, it swung back and what appeared to be office workers were in the midst of gathering paperwork and dropping boxes of the stuff down the chutes at the rear of the building. A shout went up even as Asmin's troops ran in and fanned out across the floor space. Men followed the papers down the chutes to tumble into the dumpsters below. An ordered confusion followed which left the floor empty of evidence and people.

Flying separately in the two choppers, Leroy and Asmin saw the exodus from a hundred and fifty feet above, a surreal bird's eye view which contracted dramatically as the aircraft descended to the roof. It started raining as they jumped to the surface and everyone was soaked by the time they reached the access ways. Entries to the top floor were not as heavily reinforced as at the administration level and they were soon inside to find the place already deserted. As had been expected, this floor was an extensive meth lab with tables covered with bottles and glassware and the air heavy with the smell of chemicals.

Although everyone was armed, there was a sort of collective sigh of relief to find there was no defense here. Shoulders relaxed, steps were firmer as they descended the stairways to the packing floor.

Here too, there was no one to bar their way.

"I wonder how much of the goods they tried to stuff into the chutes before they left," Leroy muttered. "Give everywhere a good look," he ordered, "there could be one or two in hiding around here." There was still no sound except for the noise of their boots echoing across the empty space.

"Ah. Now this is what we came for." Asmin pointed with his gun at the stacks of cardboard boxes entirely lining one wall. Each was sealed with masking tape, each had a label with details of contents and delivery. "Just waiting to be shipped out."

"We've struck the mother lode here, Asmin. We can build villas in the Bahamas and live like kings for the rest of our lives. Let the ground force know we're all done up here."

Asmin used his cell and when he'd finished, replied to Leroy's vision of the future. "There is a hill I know in Kashmir that overlooks the most beautiful lake. I have dreamed of having a home there." He smiled distantly. "The Caribbean holds no fascination for me." Asmin almost believed his dream.

"Well, that's all right, partner. Whatever floats your boat..."

A burst of automatic fire interrupted their plans, it was followed by a second.

"They've found someone hiding out." Asmin said, looking around. "One of those offices down there, I think."

All six armed men converged on the room and Leroy and Asmin leaned casually on a long counter between two of the chutes. Another, longer burst of fire was followed by two shorter ones, it was not possible to see who was firing at who; the noise echoed all around them, confusing the hearing and now, it seemed to be coming from several offices.

"What the hell's goin' on?" Leroy asked. "Can't be that many rats still on the sinkin' ship."

There was a lull and into the silence, drifted an eerily familiar voice. *"Oh Leroy, Leroy. You should not've called on your Uncle Charlie like this."*

A man stepped into view, an automatic weapon dangled idly in one huge hand and then, several more armed men came into view and the huge room shrank in size as more and more and more men made their appearance from all sides.

"Mad Charlie," Leroy whispered as if his mouth was filled with bile.

Asmin's eyes went from Mad Charlie to Leroy. "Ah, this is your Mad Charlie, then?"

Charlie produced a mock smile and said in a liquid Caribbean accent. "We was cell mates, me an' Leroy. No secrets between us, was there my dear?"

Mad Charlie was a six-foot, three-inch West Indian flexing arms like legs of pork and his smile was one of pure enjoyment. Leroy breathed heavily and tore off his balaclava. "You knew, you conniving old bastard. Someone told you, who was it?"

"I knew, my dear. I knew, I know everything. I don't run the biggest set up in the UK without knowing everything. I got more people in the Metropolitan Police on my payroll than the prime minister. Ha ha!"

Leroy raised his gun.

"Oh don't even think of it, my dear. You'd be dead before you got your finger on the trigger. No, no, you was braggin' about your puny little setup in Leicester an' pumpin' me about mine. You must come an' see what I got here before we take you down to the entertainment center."

That invitation chilled Leroy to the bone. He looked at Asmin; his eyes were dancing and darting from one side of the room to the other. At length, the Sikh threw his weapon on the floor with a clatter and said, "They tell me Mad Charlie's pretty handy with his fists. I reckon I can take you, do you want to try?"

Charlie laughed. At least Asmin and Leroy assumed that was what it was. The drug chief must have given some signal to his men, he moved forward and they relaxed a little.

"I'm goin' to enjoy this, my friend. I told my boys not to shoot you, glad I did now."

It seemed to Leroy that he was being ignored but there were several muzzles still pointing his way so he quietly put his own gun down on the counter top.

The two huge men went at each other like cave men—no finesse, nothing that resembled the noble art—they just stood in the middle of the floor and punched each other as hard as they could.

The sound of meat being pummeled echoed off the bare walls around them as body punches rained in from both sides and from all angles. Charlie grunted with every blow he made, Asmin remained completely silent except for heavy breathing.

Charlie suddenly shifted his aim from Asmin's body and landed a hay-maker to the Sikh's jaw. Asmin staggered and went down. Charlie scrambled in for the kill and swung another punch to Asmin's head. Asmin shook his head, attempted to rise, and failed.

Leroy waited no longer. The writing was on the wall in great big letters: *Asmin's finished.* Mad Charlie's fist connected resoundingly against the side of Asmin's head and as all eyes were drawn toward the action, Leroy flung himself down a chute. Guns sounded from above as he plummeted downwards, but he ignored them even as holes appeared in the fiberglass to either side of him.

He emerged from the chute dazed and with an ankle that was going to be useless in minutes, bleeding and bruised but alive. Briefly, he considered trying to raise one of the choppers but his radio had gone and his cell was a broken and flattened slice of high technology.

Maybe, he wondered, *it was one of the pilots that had been in Charlie's pay.* Leroy limped across the backyard, keeping close to the wall and crossed the street outside. He headed toward the Birmingham heartland.

CHAPTER 19

The mind works in funny ways. I was driving into work and wondering how Shelley Fearon was doing on her Inspector's course. From there—I think it was that slip of the tongue with Barbara Patterson that led me on—I wondered about Dad and his feelings for Margaret. I remembered the saying—*there's no fool like an old fool* and that brought things full circle, to Connie. I tried to decide what my feelings were for her.

There was no doubt that she was an attractive woman but was there more than that? Or had she just come along at a time when I was feeling lonely?

That was as far as I got because my Bluetooth chose that moment to go off. It was Alec Bell. "How far are you from the office, boss? Joe Flowers knows there's some intel from all three squads, he's on the prowl."

"Five minutes, as long as I can take the elevator." I put my foot down and the BMW roared its approval.

Alec was in my office with the door closed, sitting in my chair. Was he pretending to be me? I didn't ask. I was seething quietly, the first time in months I hadn't been in twenty or thirty minutes early and something unsavory had hit the fan.

"Hi." Short and sweet. "What've you got for me, Alec?"

Alec got up and left an open the file on my blotter.

"No, no. Give me the shorthand version."

He pressed his lips together, gathering his thoughts. "'A' squad first. They've located the ship that Faulkner's on. He's got a job as purser and using his middle name, William."

"Purser?"

"Well, think you'll find he's got accountancy qualifications… Manchester, I…"

I cut him short. "Does it prove him innocent?"

"Damn right. He was in the middle of the Indian Ocean when DC Stokes was murdered." He pronounced it like Taggart used to on the TV series, rolling the "r's"; *morrdered.* "Now, 'C' squad may gild the lily here. They've got lists of his declared business dealings, contacts, fellow council members from the Council minutes and files. He was in an all-day meeting the day his wife died. Some heavy names there from Rotherham and there were others from Sheffield…"

"Yes, we knew that."

"So he's clear. Someone's trying to frame him. We've got to find out why and from there, who."

"You said all three squads?"

"Yes. 'B' squad have come up with something that's a glaring mistake on somebody's part or it's just downright weird. Remember the blood samples from the carpet?"

"Don't I just. Bird?"

"The other one. Belongs to a dead person, not a recently dead person either. A William Jarvis who died years ago. They worked really hard for this, Boss. Not on our database, one belonging to the National Orphanage Society, William—or Billy as he was known—was an orphan."

That perked me up no end. I grinned and patted Alec on the back. "Find out which of the guys had the crazy idea of looking at orphanage records. I want to thank him. Umm, how long ago was this Billy Jarvis in an orphanage?"

Alec frowned. "I don't know."

"The National DNA database didn't start until 1995. Let's say he was recorded at maybe ten years old, which would put him around twenty-four now?"

Alec did the arithmetic. "Okay. Who are we talking about?"

"Billy Jarvis. Whoever it was that died, we know it wasn't Billy Jarvis."

I walked quickly down to the murder room and scribed a big X across Faulkner's head. I turned around and looked at the few who were there, sipping coffee. "Well done, troops. Bloody well done."

As I was going out, I saw Barbara Patterson looking at her work with very pursed lips. I steered my course past her and bent over her shoulder. I spoke quietly. "Glad you made it to our little outing last night. Now what happened yesterday is strictly between you and me and it'll stay that way, okay?"

She looked up at me with what I can only describe as doe-like eyes. She smiled and turned away and said nothing. Very uncharacteristic, on all counts.

Sergeant Bell was still there in my office when I got back. "Did I forget something, Alec?"

"No, no. You rushed off but there's one further item of news you might be interested in."

"Go on."

"There was an attempted robbery made on a suspected drugs factory yesterday. Your old patch, Birmingham. Nothing proven, nothing reported, nothing admitted. Just made me wonder though, your old friend Richards could have been involved. He's been associated with that Singh feller and Singh was definitely seen driving out of Leicester on the Hinckley road yesterday."

"Right, I'll log that…"

"Ah, Inspector White." Joe Flowers had caught me bang to rights.

"Morning Superintendent, excuse me. I'll check back with you later, sergeant." Then back to Flowers. "What can I do for you, sir?"

Flowers gave me a well-practiced reproachful look. He began his rebuke, the one I had expected since yesterday afternoon. He pointed me to my own chair and sat down on the other side of my desk.

"You ordered two squads, including C19, to conduct a raid. Do you realize the cost involved in that? You must know our budget restraints, I'm sure I've spoken to you about them, at length."

I nodded. "You have sir, I really am conscious of the problems they cause."

"But didn't you think to consult a superior officer to seek approval?"

"Certainly I did, sir. DCI Bellamy left early yesterday. You had left by the time I heard of the incident. I sent a man to your office at once, sir, and you had left."

I looked at the report on the corner of my desk, the one I had worked on until about one a.m. but I decided to save it until after I had finished my reply face to face.

I took a deep breath and continued, "Our practice of restricting the number of individuals with access to the cell phones of senior officers meant I could only contact you or DCI Bellamy over land lines. I tried, without success. I rang you, no answer. I had to make my own decision sir, it needed to be done immediately."

"The Chief Constable?"

"Wednesday, sir. The Chief Constable would have been at his bowls match."

"Yes, well," began Flowers, "surely…"

I used his hesitation to push in some good news, "You might want to hear about the arrests we made, sir."

He nodded. The grim expression smoothed out. I had saved his face.

"The premises were a paper manufacturers, among their products are currency papers, they have watermarks embedded and those silvery stripes, things like that. The paper is usually used by specialist printers in the UK. In fact, there's at least one here in Leeds, Waddington Printers, but it can be shipped anywhere in the world."

"So, it was part-made money?"

"Exactly, last night's consignment would have been moved to Nigeria. They could have made millions of pounds in fake currency."

"I'm surprised we weren't aware of such an important manufacturer here, on our patch."

"That's exactly the point, sir. The less people that know, the fewer leaks there are."

"What about the NICIES? Surely they were aware?"

I pretended to be outraged. "One hopes they are but they had no idea of the job going off, our information came from a private source. We scuppered it with no firearms discharged, no injuries and twenty three hours overtime in total—all with scarcely an hour to prepare."

"That sounds pretty economical actually, Stewart. Convey my congratulations to all involved, will you?"

"Absolutely."

He paused, looking at me for upwards of half a minute.

"The Faulkner murders. What are we doing there?"

"Oh yes, The team have moved heaven and earth. I'd have been along to brief you if you hadn't caught me first. We've proved Faulkner innocent, so that leaves just sixty million suspects."

Flowers knew I was winding him up a little but he couldn't quite see how. "Sixty million?"

"The population of the UK, sir." I leaned my elbows on the desk.

"Ha, ha. Yes, good one, Stewart."

"Not quite as bad as it seems sir. I've got to discuss things with one of my teams and I think we can cut the possibilities down considerably."

"You have the report on the currency paper business?"

I passed it across.

"I'll take this across to the Chief Constable. And, I'll broach the business of cell phone numbers being distributed to, er…" he thought for a moment, "Well, officers of the rank of inspector and above."

I made it home in good time that night. The smell of stew greeted me at the front door.

"Dad!" I called as Pip, all tongue and tail, ran out of the front door.

His voice came from the study, "Through here, son." He was sitting in *my* chair again, looking out of the window down to the river. "Stew should be ready by now." He swiveled the chair around, and nodded to the window. "Now I know why you chose this place to put your chair." He got up and went into the kitchen, he was walking a lot better than when he had first come here; I put it down to his regular walks along the river bank. "You didn't bring anything in did you? Food, I mean."

"No, Dad. I didn't know whether you'd be in or out. I was planning to open a steak pie or something."

"That's good, then. This is your mother's recipe with a few extras provided by my lady friend." He winked. "Pheasant, rabbit and home-grown vegetables. Put some red wine in, should be a heady brew."

Over a wonderful meal, I looked at the old fellow and mused about life, it wasn't all hard work and nasty criminals, sometimes it could be really good. "Your Margaret got a poacher friend?" I asked.

"A poacher?"

"Pheasant and rabbit?"

"Reckon Margaret can take care of that sort of thing by herself."

Later, in my study, I took out a bottle of Dad's favorite cherry brandy.

"Long life, Dad."

"A good life, son, and the love of a good woman."

"Chance'd be a fine thing, Dad. I no sooner meet someone than fate takes her away."

"That's because those weren't the right ones, Stewart. It'll happen."

I went back to clear the table and put the bowls on the floor for Pip to clean up. Mine was still part full of seconds so the dog thought he was in canine heaven.

Dad's final words came back to me as I closed my eyes that night. *It'll happen.*

CHAPTER 20

He landed in Liverpool on his eighteenth birthday and he had already seen more of life—and of death—than most men in their entire lives. He had adopted the name Sean Reilly for his crossing and had his cover story worked out, just in case: he had been taken to London by his parents at two years of age and returned to his roots ten years later. This took care of his lack of an Irish accent but the story wasn't necessary. Sean had found that if he made careful preparations, a story wasn't required.

His accent became Liverpool Scouse in a matter of weeks after working for cash-in-hand at an abattoir. The work was hard and demanding but tough as he was, it hardened him still further. The work also had another effect. Sean had killed other human beings—he recollected three but there might have been others. But the relentless killing at the abattoir, the gallons of blood, the animals shaking from distress caused by the bleating and the lowing, hardened him another way. Death was a constant companion, he became accustomed to its presence, just a part of his life.

The heavy rubber overalls and gloves insulated him from reality. Stripping and spending a few minutes in the showers washed everything away; each time, he imagined he was a new person.

More than a year later, Sean picked up a girl in a bar along the street from where he worked. A drink had loosened him up and the girl looking sideways at him made Sean realize he had never had a girlfriend. There had been occasional visits to brothels, recommended establishments, but a steady girlfriend would have been nice. They started chatting, flirting a little and she went with him to his bedsit behind a baker's shop near Strawberry Fields.

She wanted to kiss and cuddle, Sean had become excited and wanted more than that. He had no condoms, would have fumbled clumsily with them if he had. The girl smacked him across the face and he tried to hold her arms down. She found one of her shoes, it had a sharp stiletto heel, and she hacked at him.

On the bedside table was a pile of folded pillowcases. He grabbed one and forced it over her head expecting her to quiet down but two minutes later, she was still scratching and kicking. "Cut it out, stop it. Just stop it and I'll let you go."

"I'll get a policeman," she screamed at him. "You'll be in jail, you dirty Mick."

The words struck home. *A dirty Mick? He'd go to jail?* He didn't bloody think so. He looked for a weapon and saw a plastic shopping bag full of unwashed clothes. He pulled it up with one hand, letting the contents fall out. He pulled it up and over her head, enclosing the pillow case and pulling the plastic tight around her throat. He planted his knee in the small of her back and pulled. Her struggles weakened as she ran out of air and finally, she was dead.

Sean pushed the limp body onto the floor and lay back, exhausted.

"Damn." He was astounded. His pants were wet and he hadn't even realized there was anything sexual in the final struggle.

At three o'clock in the morning, he put her body over his shoulder, carried her through the trees and dropped the body into a brook of grey water that disappeared into a culvert in the bushes.

That was the first of the *pillow case* murders: her disappearance became a local legend, never connected to the national database.

It had been so easy, once the head was covered and the victim disorientated, so exhilarating too. Before, the murders had been born out of cool calculation, even necessity but now, he had discovered enjoyment, a sexual thrill.

He began to keep a pillowcase already inserted in a sturdy plastic bag in his coat pocket. Anyone who was disrespectful, who shouted at him, who ignored him when he spoke—all of them were looking at potential death. He found himself looking for, even baiting people to get the odd look or off-kilter comment. He was deeply disappointed at opportunity lost. It was an addiction: all the power was his.

With every murder came the need to move and to change his name.

He grew more professional: for the second murder he wore a plastic zip-up boiler suit reminiscent of the work clothes he had worn at the abattoir and a shower cap, plastic overshoes and latex gloves.

He was twenty-two years old, though he looked much older, and far stronger than he had been when he'd worked at the abattoir. The jobs he did all involved heavy manual labor: for a young strong man they were easy to come by. He took work that paid in cash, no tax, and no questions. He was quick to learn and unbelievably intelligent when he wanted or needed to be. Some called it street smart.

A few more killings later and the papers started calling him the "Pillowcase Murderer." He liked that.

The victim looked at him from the corner of his eye and sniffed, wiping his nose on the back of his hand. Sean, now "Colin Petty", left the bar of the Gray Horse in Preston and went to his car. He changed into his killing gear and waited in the shadows as his strange libido rose and flowered along his nerves. He had no idea why he had picked this person out, like the others, he had just looked at him and knew somehow. He had started to think of them as "chosen ones."

The clientele began to leave and he spotted his mark with two others. He followed them as they reeled along the street, laughing and joking as they went. Two of the trio—obviously a couple—disappeared down an alley, leaving Colin's target alone.

His intended victim paused to light a cigarette. The man inhaled, raised his head and closed his eyes. Colin brought down the cotton bag within the plastic one and enveloped the head, smoke, cigarette and all. He put a knee into the other's back, locked into the base of the spine and tugged back on the lank hair within the bag.

A count of twenty and life had gone. Colin tugged him across to a wall and propped the body up with fingers still grasping at the green plastic bag. He unzipped his boiler suit and took out a mini-camcorder. He captured the scene, took off the bag within the bag and recorded it all again.

The start of his collection of chosen ones.

Dad joined me for breakfast; along with getting out of bed a lot earlier, he seemed happier of late.

"Are you enjoying the good Yorkshire air or an Indian summer of love?" I asked lightheartedly.

"I remember you coming home from school and reproaching me for using mixed metaphors," he said around a mouthful of toast and marmalade.

"And you used to lecture me about talking with my mouth full," I retorted.

He ignored me. "I remember one story in particular. You came in and you said Mrs. Price had shouted at you because you'd completed a metaphor incorrectly." He stopped with the last piece of toast held up like a flag. "People who live in glass houses…"

"Shouldn't keep elephants," I said. "And you let me think that was the right quotation for years."

Dad chuckled, and chomped off another piece of toast, "Better than the original, don't you think? Now," his brow furrowed, "what was it your mother used to say? All that glitters, or is it glistens? *All that glitters needs polishing.*"

I laughed and could probably have thought of one or two more but something else occurred to me. "Dad, do you think your new lady friend could be a replacement for mum?"

He didn't hesitate for a second. "Nothing and no one could replace your mother, son. She was my wife for thirty years in the flesh and she lives up here," he tapped his forehead. "She still lives, will do as long as I do."

He smiled at me. "Now, what I've got with Margaret Grimmond is companionship. She certainly reminds me of your mother but she'll never replace her. Understand?"

I nodded and made to get up from the table but he put his hand on my arm. "Don't you begrudge me a little companionship. I don't know how much longer I've got here on this Earth, but it's good to be able to share it with someone."

I muttered something unintelligible which he chose to interpret as he wanted. "That's good, because I've something to propose to you tonight, if you're home early enough, that is."

His proposal travelled with me on the journey into work but faded out as I approached the office. More urgent matters pressed in and I was anxious to get my murder investigation under way again. I realized I was acting as if I was super-human and it could irritate my colleagues. Actually, the truth was that *I* was being irritated—by a splinter or a thorn I'd picked up in the orchard, it was annoying the hell out of me. I rubbed at it now in my left mid-calf area, hoping it wouldn't get worse.

Barbara Patterson was first down the race track that day. I barely had time to get my bottom planted before she stalked into my office. Tall ladies were never my cup of tea—I preferred them neat and petite—but I had to admit that my Sergeant looked stunning. She was dressed in a navy blue suit, with a pencil skirt and a white blouse with a frill edged in red down each side of the buttons. I could imagine her on a photo shoot for Vogue. I must have said something appreciative or maybe it was just my expression.

"A girl has to do what a girl has to do, sir. I think it's time to look for someone to help with life's little troubles. Don't you? I'm officially on the market."

I leaned back. "Barbara, parceled up like that, I don't think you'll be on the market long. And with those legs, you could charm the birds out of the trees."

She laughed. "It's not the birds I'm after, boss."

I grinned back. "So what have you on Billy Jarvis?" And she was back to business.

"Ah, yes. Jarvis. I've tried every resource, even to having a Skype conversation with the head of the orphanage where he was supposed to have died."

"And?"

"He's a *technophile*…"

"A…?"

"Someone who likes technology."

"Yes, I appreciate that—oh, I see. Databases, writing code, hacking, one of those."

"And Billy Jarvis drowned, fell out of a boat on a day trip."

"Anyone else? Anyone else drown?"

She shook her head. "I had the same thought. There was another orphan, a Gabriel Henderson. He was quite badly affected by his friend's death, never said a word and ran away some time later. There are suggestions he might have gone to Cardiff, where he came from, or to London. Can I sit down?"

"Huh? Sure, of course."

"I've emailed the Metropolitan Police, sir, but it was fourteen years ago and they don't consider missing boys all that important—I'm quoting there. How many boys run away from orphanages? Do you know?"

I shook my head.

"A bloody lot."

We sat and looked at each other. "Never mind, Barbara, what's next? Ah, one of the groups was looking into Faulkner's' acquaintances but I had a thought. Might be a bit old fashioned but we haven't looked into his wife's background yet. You know, friends, colleagues, girlfriends. After all, she was the one who got herself murdered and I don't think we know a thing about her."

"I'll get to it, sir. Sheffield should have done that."

"Hope they did."

I turned to the inbox on my desk and spent an hour or so making lists of work I needed to get to—paperwork mostly. It was a relief when Alec Bell appeared at the door. I waved him in and eased my back off the seat.

"Charlie Morgan," he said.

"Charlie Morgan," I replied. "We used to call him Mad Charlie, biggest drug baron in the Midlands, maybe the whole of the UK. Had a run in with him once but my info's out of date. He's got hundreds, if not thousands, working for him but we never got anything drug-related on him."

I thought for a moment, " Ah! Now I remember, my DCI got something—tax evasion? Put him away for eighteen months. It was before I came up here."

"That's the one, boss. Out now, for good behavior. Now I hear he's looking for Leroy Richards. Why do you suppose that is?"

"I don't know the answer to that one but if he is," I grinned, "there's a lot less for me to worry about. If he manages to keep out of Mad Charlie's way, he's going to be lying very, very low."

"Think it's got anything to do with the break-in? In Birmingham?"

"Could be, if Leroy was going to do a job, it could easily have been against a fellow criminal. If he'd been successful, it wouldn't be reported, no comebacks. But if he let the opposition know he was responsible, that was a big slip up."

"I also heard what went off between you and him, boss."

"What? His arrest for drug trading?"

"Well, that too but the real reason he threatened you was because he lost face because of you."

"Oh, come on."

"You jumped in the canal and dragged him out."

"He'd have got away, otherwise."

Alec chuckled. "His boys thought you were saving him from drowning, apparently he wasn't too good at the swimming stuff. Just think what *his* lads would think if a copper had to save his life."

I stroked my lips with a forefinger. "I didn't know that and no wonder he was so upset. He knows what happened but he knows what it looked like too. Hmm."

———

Murder investigations are often slow affairs. Days go by with no progress reported, no new leads to investigate. It does help with the paperwork but certainly doesn't do anything for tempers or spirits. I left the office at four o'clock and because I was early, I detoured to see if Connie was at home. I told myself it was just to check if she was still there or had returned to the US. Since I'd convinced myself she wouldn't be in, I was doubly rewarded when she answered the door.

"Hello Stewart, I can't really believe this, I thought you'd deserted little old me. Well," she stood back, "you'd better come in, I was just fixing myself a drink, like one?"

I suspected that Connie's little old drink would be three fingers of bourbon, I nodded and said, "just a beer for me would be fine. And I came 'round a couple of times but you weren't in."

Connie apologized for her appearance; she was wearing what my mother used to call *slobbing around* clothes, stuff you wouldn't wear to go out but was good enough to wear around the house.

"You look just fine," I said and I meant it. Connie managed to look sexy in a tee shirt and soft, loose pants. Her hair was pinned up in a messy, sexy way. And she smelled good.

I had the beer and was just about to say 'thanks and I'd better go' when she reached out and grabbed my tie. Quite forcefully, she led me into the bedroom and fell back on to the bed. It was an invitation I found hard to resist, and certain bodily parts reacted very strongly in her presence. She pulled off her tee shirt, revealing no bra and delicious breasts. She smiled up at me and winked.

"Y'daddy is emphatically not here, Stewart. You like what you see? You wanna play in *my* yard?"

I was sorely tempted because sex and I had been strangers for quite some time. I had to ask myself why had I stopped by. Something answered—my more primitive self, I guess—*if it's this easy, why not?* But something—call it duty, call it what you like—continued to fight the woman's advances.

Finally, I gave up.

We had a delightful time; afterward Connie brought me another beer and asked me when I'd be by again.

"I'm in the middle of a murder investigation. If you're still here when it's over, or if there's a lull…"

I was lying, I was ready to go at her again, right now. I backed out of the big soft bed and scrambled into my clothes. "Just give me a little more time."

"Whatever you say, honey bun," she drawled.

On the way home I was still bothered by the splinter—or whatever it was—in my calf. I pulled up in the drive and immediately remembered Dad saying he had a proposition to put to me. I wondered if it was something to do with his Margaret. Had she gone to his head? Was he thinking about marrying her?

The cooking smells from the kitchen made my mouth water even though it was nowhere near dinner time. Dad was testing the vegetables with a fork to make sure they were cooked. "Hello son, you're only a half hour earlier than I'd expected."

"Really?" I checked my watch and he was right. I must have been with Connie longer than I'd thought.

"Braised steak and onions, how does that sound? Cauliflower, peas, new potatoes and pureed turnips."

I blanched. I couldn't stand even the smell of turnips. "No turnips for me, Dad. I really don't go for the stuff."

"Oh? Well there's all the more for me and I dare say that Pip will want some, with a bit of gravy on it."

I have to say that sans turnips the meal was excellent and once more, we retired to my study where he plunked himself in my chair without so much as a raised eyebrow. He squirmed a bit and shuffled his feet.

"Merlot, Dad. All the way from…" I squinted at the label, "Chile, in this case. You wanted to tell me something tonight. You'd better spit it out before you wear that chair out. It's to do with Margaret I take it?"

"Err, no." He gave me a puzzled look. "What made you think that?"

Connie had made me think that but I didn't say anything.

"No. I'm just thinking, living down in the Midlands in that big house, I'm rattling around like a pea in a pod…"

"Bucket. One pea in a bucket is what Mum used to say."

"Whatever. It's far too big since you and mum… You know what I mean. Anyway, I've enjoyed this last week or two up here with you and Pip, going for walks, I'm a lot better aren't I? Don't you think so?"

"You are, Dad." I got what he was getting at, even though he was putting off the moment when he had to tell me the big idea. "Now, why don't you just spit it out?"

"Wouldn't it just be wonderful if I could have an extension built on to here?"

I tried to look surprised.

"A sort of granddad flat where I could live independently and still be able to share time with you."

I nodded slowly, thinking about things, how it could be done.

"I guess I'm just bloody lonely down there."

I examined my mind and had to admit I didn't find the idea worrying at all. "Welcome aboard, Dad."

On the way to bed, I noticed that Pip didn't like turnip either. Not even when it was knee-deep in gravy. Before hitting the sack I found a bottle of peroxide in the medicine cupboard and poured a few drops on my leg.

CHAPTER 21

Leroy had lived in Birmingham since he was a young teenager—he had followed his widowed father over from Jamaica. He knew his way around the city without thinking, but the shock of the disaster had taken its toll, and he was dog tired. He found a cab and thought where he might go as they travelled away from Mad Charlie's castle. *Willy Mathews*, he thought, an old acquaintance and not the sort of man the police would ever have an interest in. It was raining but he got the driver to drop him off not far from Perry Bar and walked the rest of the way.

His thoughts revolved around Mad Charlie, how he'd been made to look a fool and how he was going to get his own back. For a moment, he wondered about Asmin but shook his head and walked on. If Asmin wasn't dead... Leroy shuddered. He would come after Leroy, for good or bad. But no, the big thoughtful Sikh was almost certainly dead by now, better to forget the guy.

If he could prevail upon Willy to let him sleep for a few hours he could get back to Leicester in the morning where what little remained of his money was still hidden, he could cool it for a few days and work out how he was going to make Mad Charlie suffer.

Willy lived in a large semi-detached in the suburbs. The driveway was long and had been wide until Willy had put up a row of prefab garages down one side. Willy dealt in cars, old ones, new ones, special ones; if he didn't have what you wanted, he knew where to get hold of one just like it.

The house was at the bottom of a cul-de-sac with trees hanging over his backyard fence, the Forestry land came right up to his boundary. Leroy had fished in those woodlands as a kid, an old, abandoned clay pit filled with murky water held all sorts of fish, very few of which were edible. This had been the young Leroy's adventure playground, where he had learned to defend himself and acquire the leadership qualities that made him a gang leader by the time he was sixteen and had left the orphanage.

Willy was sitting in a recliner with his feet up, watching TV. It was probably the best position because, when Leroy tapped on the French window, Willy nearly had a heart attack. Recognition dawned slowly and he got to his feet and signed that he'd come to the back door.

"Willy! What's up dog?" Leroy beamed good vibrations at the little man.

Willey looked up at him. "What's up yourself? An' what you doin' comin' to my place at this time of night? My missus is upstairs in the bath, what's she goin' ta say?"

"Well," Leroy looked shifty. "Can't come 'round in daylight, There's people huntin' me."

Willy was not best pleased at the news. "Iffen you mean the coppers, they already been here and gone. Week or two back."

"Can I step inside, man? It's wet out here. These police, they come and question you?"

Willy nodded to the first question, stood back and then shook his head to the second question. "They just sat outside number twenty-three for a week or more with binoculars and a camera. Took everybody's picture ten times over."

"But they've gone now?"

"Sure they're gone. I knew they was after someone, knew it wasn't me and my cars."

Leroy nodded, relieved—cars. He abandoned the idea of trying to get Willy to let him sleep on the sofa. "You got a car I can use? Borrow one, maybe? I'll buy one but I'll have to pay you later."

"Where are you planning on taking it?" Willy's voice had grown serious as soon as business was mentioned.

"Hell, not far but it's best you don't know. Less you know, less they can make you say."

"Less than twenty miles?"

Leroy did a mental calculation for the distance to Cannock Chase, where his Jaguar had been left that morning. *Jesus* he thought, it had only been that morning and it seemed like a week already. "Yes, less than twenty."

"Okay, you can use my family car and post the keys and where it's at, to me. A hundred pounds to cover expenses."

They shook hands on the deal and ten minutes later, Leroy was nosing the old Mondeo out of Willy's driveway. The Jaguar was just where they'd left it, under a couple of low branched oak trees. There was no sign of the helicopters except for two pairs of grooves in the woodland grass. Just after two thirty a.m., he was noted on Leicester's CCTV cameras. It was still raining.

And it was still raining as he got out of the car in front of Sammy's and pressed the doorbell. Sammy cursed a bit and dragged himself from his ground floor bedroom. He'd slept downstairs ever since his weight had topped 385 pounds. Stairs were not for Sammy except *in extremis* and he hadn't had one of those since he was twenty-one.

"Leroy! What the fuck're you doin' at this time o' the night?" Leroy had expected more expletives and complaints but Sammy opened the door wide.

"You want a pot of tea?"

"Sammy, sometimes, I think you're my guardian angel." And while Sammy fixed the tea, Leroy went up to his room and took the satchel out from above the false panel in the top of the wardrobe. He checked the contents, counting the bundles of notes still with the bank's seals on them. He took ten of them with him and replaced the rest in the hidey-hole.

Sammy gave him the sugar bowl and Leroy put in three heaped spoonfuls. He gave half of the ten thousand pound bundles to his friend. "A token, mate. Should have been a whole lot more but the job went sour on us."

Sammy nodded his appreciation. "You're a good'en, Leroy. "Asmin and the Asian boys?"

"I don't know, Sammy, don't think they'll be back. And I don't know exactly what went wrong either but those bastards knew we was coming."

"So what're you going to do now? Got plans?"

Leroy shot Sammy a look. "Don't ask." He drank half the pint pot of hot tea. "Ah, that's nice, Sammy. Just how I like it. Don't worry about it, one of these days, we'll both get what we're worth and… what the hell is that?"

That was a heavy and prolonged banging at Sammy's front door. When the banging stopped, there were several voices shouting *police* loud enough to wake everybody in the street.

Sammy pointed to the ceiling. "Get out, Leroy, I'll block the passage way with this lot," he patted his belly, "and my crutches. You'll get five minutes, maybe."

Leroy sadly patted him on the shoulder as Sammy picked up his crutches.

"We'll break this door down if you don't open it now."

"I'm comin.' I don't move too well anymore. Just give me a minute or two." Sammy walked along the hall way slowly scraping his crutches along the floor as Leroy raced upstairs. The enormous black man braced himself ten feet from the door and made sure both crutches were firmly lodged in corners as a doorbreaker was wielded outside.

Several police managed to get in through the doorway at the same time but were halted by the huge figure of Sammy who seemed to be trying to get along the hallway in his great flowing dressing gown.

It took the police seven minutes to get Sammy backed up as far as his bedroom at which point, they swarmed all over the building.

Leroy ran upstairs to the wardrobe, grabbed the satchel of money from its hidey-hole, and was already on the top landing pushing up the hinged cover to the loft entrance before the police got in. As they backed Sammy down the hall, he used the hooked pole to pull down the foldaway ladder and used the banister railing to boost himself into the roof space. The ladder came up, the cover went down and was bolted firmly in place. He felt for the concealed flashlight and walked silently along the boarded walkway across the top of the long row of houses to the end one.

Then, it was more or less the reverse of his climb up, the last staircase led him directly into the garage where a six liter Range Rover awaited. The motor started with a subdued roar, the electric door opened and he exited into the street behind the row of back-to-back houses.

It had been a long night. Two hours after leaving Leicester, shortly after five in the morning, he watched the sky turn a lighter shade of gray in York.

CHAPTER 22

I passed Clive Bellamy on the drag race track—that is, the hall outside my office. He nodded. "Thanks for keeping me in the loop, Stewart. Good to know what you're up to."

"Least I can do, Clive. There's a lot been happening but we aren't too close to catching the devil yet."

"That's police work, though, isn't? Some days, it all happens, some weeks nothing does. Hey, you proved that Faulkner wasn't responsible, one less avenue to go down."

I grinned. At least Clive understood what it was about. It was good to have a boss who wasn't always covering his back about the state of his budget, and didn't appear threatened by his subordinates.

Once Clive had gone, the corridor outside my office was clear. I put the kettle on, pulled the *cafetiere* out of my bottom drawer and brewed a cup of coffee. I went through my mail, tidied my in tray and was halfway through a second cup before Sergeant Patterson breezed in buzzing with keenness and efficiency.

She started without preamble. "You could be right about Faulkner's wife."

"Could I?" I was struggling to remember what I had said.

"Doesn't seem she was well liked—except by the men in her life—and I guess some of those got a bit pissed off."

"A busy lady?"

"Clubs, casinos, that sort of thing. Arriving on her own, leaving with company. I'm told she had a penchant for rather younger men than herself. There's one place in Sheffield where the bouncer swore she had a hideaway, a room, somewhere. He said she was in and out of his place like a fiddler's elbow."

"Hmm. If one of her boyfriends bore a grudge… could you make it a priority to find out where this trysting place might be? I think you could be onto something here, Sergeant. I can turn one of the squads over to you if you want."

She shook her head. "I don't think so, boss. I'd rather run with it alone, that way, I get to talk to all the witnesses and I know I haven't missed any. There's one problem though, I can travel back and forth to Sheffield every day but it would save a lot of time if I could stay over."

There I was thinking nasty thoughts about her using police expenses to see her parents every night and there she was, thinking of using her time better. You can get to expect the worst in people in this job.

I thought some nice thoughts instead. "Take three days and don't book into anywhere too fancy. I'll pay for your meals myself if Flowers grumbles. And..." I stared straight into her eyes and almost tapped her on the chest with my finger. "Be thorough, okay?"

"Absolutely, boss," she stared straight back. "And thanks."

I was at a bit of loss. "What for?"

"Oh, not for this. For being a good boss and... well, for helping. And I'm not the only one to think that, do you know you now have a nickname?"

I was a bit overcome and while I'm not prone to it, I didn't want to color up. I waved my hands at her. "Go on, then. What is it?"

"Well don't forget it's a compliment they now refer to you as 'Stewpot'."

"Go on with you, 'Stewpot'? couldn't they have come up with something better than that? Get yourself off to Sheffield and remember, the clock's ticking."

When she'd gone, I went through the reports from "A" squad who were liaising with Lancashire and Merseyside. I cross-checked the similarities between their murder victims and scenes of crime and ours, and came to the conclusion that I needed to visit all the crime scenes. Well, not me personally, there wasn't time. Running the department meant I'd delegate this task and trust others to do the job.

Turning points in investigations were often the realization that something had been overlooked. The only real lead we had was the blood sample from the carpet that the body had been rolled in. What was I missing?

I was about to turn my attention to "B" squad's reports when the very man knocked on my door. Anthony Levy, "B" squad's sergeant. He was black-haired, around thirty with deep-set brown eyes and a brooding expression.

"Morning, guv. Got a minute?"

"Sure, come in, sit yourself down. Only just picked up your reports so I don't know enough to discuss things."

"No matter." He sat down. "As you know, we've been liaising with the coroners and collating the pathology reports since we cleared Faulkner of involvement."

"That was good work, Anthony, hope your squad got my congratulations."

"We did, thanks. It's nice to make a bit of progress but the job we're doing now is a ball-acher and no mistake. No one's interested in helping us, most of them say it was all too long ago, too much water under the bridge. We're getting a bit despondent."

"Yes, know all about it, we've all been there. Any of your guys have any suggestions—and I don't mean 'Let's go fishing'—ideas outside the box but not harebrained."

He let out a long noisy breath, "Well, we've talked, obviously. The consensus seems to be let's accept what they say 'over the hill' and concentrate on our own patch."

"Okay. Anything specific?"

"Well, the last two murders are the only ones to have hocus-pocus involved. Seems to me too that it's most likely a *he* because I don't know many women who could carry a dead body rolled in a carpet."

"I agree there. A man or just maybe, a woman with help. But there're three cases with hocus-pocus, there's the original Sheffield murder, Mrs. Faulkner, herself."

"Yes, of course, Anyway, I got a bit off-track. I think he's starting to enjoy himself. He's challenging us, doing it for fun, making us look like idiots. Why did he pick Ned Stokes? One of us and well away from the earlier murders—Liverpool, Preston, Cheadle, Leigh."

"Well, if it is the same perp and it's certainly possible," I wrinkled my nose, "then he's simply been travelling to different areas. I'd guess that none are more than thirty minutes from a central point, not with a convenient motorway network out there. The M1, the M62, M63, M56 and so on, they all give him a fast, easy passage to all those places."

"I—we—did think of that but most if not all of the killings took place after ten p.m. Now our boys in blue have their eyes skinned around that time, looking out for drunk drivers and so on. They'd have been most unlucky not to have found a perp in all those people they've pulled over."

"I'm not convinced on that one," something was pulling my memory strings. "Umm, the Yorkshire Ripper, remember that one?"

"Before I was born, boss," he said with a smirk.

"Before my time too," I said, watching the smirk disappear, "But it's a fascinating case, well worth studying. He was a cheeky bugger. I think he was stopped twice while he was out on his spree and neither time was he taken into custody despite matching the description."

"Right, maybe not, then."

"OK. follow up anything you have re the DC Stokes case. Leave the Faulkner aspects alone, Sergeant Patterson's looking into those, right now."

Levy nodded and stood up to go but stopped at the door. "By the way, guv, just with you mentioning Sergeant Patterson… she's really hot, you know."

"Are you implying I'm too old and decrepit to notice?" I asked. That was the second time he had implied I was getting on when I couldn't be more than five years older than him.

He backpedalled a bit, "No sir, but… um… any objection if I asked her out?"

He blushed beet-red and I grinned, "None at all, Anthony. Best of luck."

I got just under an hour of work in before Joe Flowers tapped on the door. I couldn't figure out why he didn't just ring me, have me trot along to his comfortable big office.

"Get your coat, Stewart, bring your keys," he said sharply. He was in uniform, all knife-edge creases and glittery bits. "We've got another murder on our patch while we're kicking our heels here, a chap by the name of Patel, a car park official. The ME's on her way and SOCO won't be far behind us."

"Inside my car, I looked expectantly at Flowers, waiting for instructions but the Super seemed lost in thought. "Where to, Joe?"

"Morley. Valley Parade, it's off the main street, know it?"

"No, but I know a little box that does." I typed the address into my Satnav and followed instructions.

"It's a warehouse that was emptied recently. Bloody recession, couldn't afford to pay their bills and had a fire-sale, sold everything off cheap and got out. Sold greeting cards, been empty for two months."

Pretty succinct. There were two cars with flashing red lights and a half-dozen uniforms milling around. A uniformed inspector led the way with one of the lads holding the yellow and black tape above our heads.

"Very nasty one, this is, sir." Said the inspector to Flowers.

"Hmm, Inspector…?"

"Brown, sir."

"Ha! Meet DI White. All we need now is an Inspector Black and we've got the lot." The Superintendent's little joke. Brown and I raised eyebrows at each other.

Inside the place, there were stacks of empty cardboard boxes, all flattened and never used, there were a dozen or so standing erected and probably filled with cards.

Several of the flat packs had been pulled out to make a rectangular background for the victim who was laid out centrally. He was a male, Asian, lying in what seemed to be gallons of blood although, really there could not have been, the human body only holds about eight pints.

He had been arranged to make a cross—an X shape—and scattered around the body were—I looked carefully to make sure—were severed fingers.

We'd barely taken in the grisly details when the ME arrived and bustled around, expecting us to move out of her way. She was not familiar so probably came from somewhere local or Bradford, maybe. That's the sort of thing that happens in a regional crime squad rather than a city force. Still, wherever she came from, she was extremely professional and did not waste a second.

Ten minutes later, Harrison stood up. "Killed with what I think was a hand-held chain saw. The lacerations are consistent with… sorry?"

It was Flowers who had asked "What the hell is that," not quite under his breath. He repeated himself more politely.

"Think of a cheese wire with serrations. I'll look at some examples tomorrow and let you know. The fingers were severed, I think, when he tried to pull the wire away from his neck."

She stopped and breathed deeply for a few moments. "My God, what will people think of next? I've never seen anything like this before, it's… it's *barbaric*. I shall have to do some research and I'll report tomorrow."

"What time, Dr. Harrison?"

"Twenty-four hours, forty-eight at the most? I'm not promising anything, Inspec… I mean Superintendent."

"And anything significant in the way the body's been laid out?" I asked.

"The cross? My God, if I had a medal for every time I'd seen something like that. well, it's common as old boots. Some experts say it's a way killers offer the bodies to God. Personally, I'm not convinced."

I tried to picture myself with a chain-saw garrote around my throat and trying to remove it with my unprotected fingers, trying to fight against the vicious rasp of the thing. Did the killer slacken his grip to let the victim get his hands in there? Let him gain a little hope for a few heartbeats longer before finishing him off perhaps?

It must have been how it happened.

I turned to Joe Flowers, who was looking pale and sweaty. "This one's serious, sir. I don't know if you'll agree with me but this guy is sick." I rubbed subconsciously at my calf. "We're going to need help if we want to continue to concentrate on the Faulkner business."

Flowers blinked. "It can't be the same killer, Stewart. It has to be a someone with a really twisted mind to use this method. The Chief Constable's going to go ballistic."

I never said anything but as far as I knew, like all of the investigations I was in charge of, details of the weapons used on murder victims were never given to the press. It was standard police procedure.

Over the following year, "Colin Petty" kept his latest name, his flat and his job. He also kept up with his nighttime activities. He had learned his *modus operandi* from the CSI series on television; the programs had taught him to leave nothing to chance—not a single hair, not a flake of skin, not a single thread of cloth must be left for investigation.

Consequently, before killing his latest victim, he had shaved his head and smeared petroleum jelly over his eyebrows, his ears and nostrils. He now dressed in easily washable nylon shirts and underwear, plastic shoes and latex gloves.

Along with the comfort of knowing he was totally invisible to forensics, he gained a feeling of power, a warm glow in knowing that he could slip through crowds without leaving a trace of himself.

That last killing was something totally different to what had gone before. Previously, it had been from necessity—as he saw it—or revenge. Now it was from choice, it was an art form and it still provided that sexual pinnacle of sensation. He liked that his victims were *his* chosen ones.

Colin had become a landscape gardener for a firm owned by a recent widow. Colin had talked to her about his non-existent experience and offered to work for a pittance to make the broken-down firm profitable. He bunged her a thousand pounds suggesting it would help her to put the business on its feet. This coupled with his newly burgeoning personality convinced the lady.

With the widow's backing, Colin took charge of Vista Landscaping. He had a work force of three until he told them all that they still had jobs but would now have to pay their own tax as they were to be offered self-employed positions. One of the workmen left forthwith which suited Colin admirably. There was little else to do apart from repainting a new telephone number on the sides of the white truck and on the sign over the small office on the firm's plot of land. A pay-as-you-go mobile number replaced the land line.

They concentrated on working for the "little man", the kind of man with a small garden that had become a jungle, or trees that were growing roots under the house foundations. They were all quick jobs that were paid cash on the spot for an imaginary discount. No tax, no bookkeeping, and the widow was quietly grateful.

Inspiration struck Colin. They had taken a job to renovate the roadside garden at offices being demolished and rebuilt. Stone abounded, broken wall stone and cracked paving slabs and he got paid for taking it away. Cleaned up and sorted, it was raw material for pathways—crazy paving, raised flower beds and in one case, a goldfish pond.

This became the Vista specialty; there were always houses being knocked down, walls demolished and if he couldn't get paid for carting the stuff away, he could buy it at very low prices.

Not only was the widow-owner pleased, so were his two workmen, who didn't pay tax and claimed state benefit as well. A prime example of how the black economy works.

Colin lived in a house on the outskirts of Burnley, a large, dilapidated Victorian property which he had purchased with the idea of renovating room by room. Now that he had a good income, the work went ahead rather faster—a kitchen, a bathroom, a bedroom and lounge had been carved out of the eight rooms in the house. The other rooms remained uninhabitable. He never had any intention of inviting visitors, and was content with the space he had. He intended to make this a permanent home, one he could keep separate from his evening activities.

The lounge was floored with inch-thick oak boards; he installed a safe here to take his collection of videos, the murder by murder story of his hobby. Later, he installed home video equipment so he could watch his collection in comfort.

Steadily, he worked on his house, bringing all the rooms up to an acceptable standard and then beginning work on the garden. He frequented the same shops, pubs and cafes. Even the local park became a home from home to him, he walked there at all hours and he was becoming well known, something that had never happened before. No more was he a loner, he became friends with two local councilors who suggested he might stand at the next elections himself. He went ahead and successfully contested the area which included his house.

Council meetings varied from subdued to lively but brought him contacts and opportunities to expand the business over a drink at a local pub after council work was completed. Eventually, and because he was now a respectable pillar of local society, Colin employed a bookkeeper and purchased two more small trucks. Everything became legal and above board.

A new employee took him for a drink after work and explained an idea he had: make resin models of garden gnomes, bird baths and gargoyles. The man had already started a spare time project but found that demand outstripped his capability, would Colin be amenable to joining him? Colin would, and did. He went to see a demonstration of the secret process and this was followed by a partnership.

His interests had grown and widened so quickly that Colin rarely thought of killings and victims until invitations through the council activities took him to social events.

Her name was Valerie, and she was to be another chosen one, a waitress at The Grove Restaurant. The council had selected The Grove for the first anniversary of the Cross-Pennines League celebration—an organization set up to heal the four hundred years old friction left by the Wars of the Roses.

By the end of the five-course meal, Valerie had given him her telephone number and an invitation to visit. Colin was a little nervous; there was no possibility of his making all the usual preparations in advance. He opened the passenger door and Valerie, very impressed, got into the Vauxhall Insignia he had hired to match the car he used from the council pool.

Their planned destination was a country pub with a fine restaurant. But: "I think, I'll just top up with gas here." Colin said as he turned in at a filling station. He got out, put fuel in and went to the shop to pay. He was slightly longer than

Valerie expected having gone to the rest room and changed the clothes he wore beneath his light overcoat.

"Sorry, took a little while to find these for you." And the box of chocolates relieved any curiosity she might have had about the delay.

A few miles further on, he slowed down, looking uncertainly. "Ever seen the waterfall at Mary's Leap?"

Valerie shook her head and then replied, "No, I've never heard of that one."

"Just back there." He stopped and looked at the dashboard clock. "I think we've got time for a side trip before it's too dark, what do you think?" Before she had time to question, Colin was out of the door.

He took off his coat and left it in the car, then walked hand in hand with the young woman along a just-discernible pathway. The narrow bridge over a small stream was heaven-sent, as he held back a second to let her go ahead in the gloom, he pulled the pillow case and plastic bag combination over Valerie's head with practiced ease. The knee to the small of her back kept her away from the bridge and the drop beneath it.

The high as he felt her struggle and fail was like pure cocaine flooding through his veins.

Colin propped her, crucifix style, in the low branches of a Douglas Fir, fully clothed and seemingly asleep; before he left, he combed her hair—only the post mortem would prove the violent end. Colin returned to the car for the camcorder and floodlight to make a record of the girl's end. He drove home with his trousers uncomfortably damp and put them straight in the washer.

Later, when he viewed the resulting video, he thought of it as his greatest work.

CHAPTER 23

Asmin woke up to absolute blackness. He remembered the two blows that had laid him out and wondered if his sight had been damaged. Every bone in his body hurt and clamored for attention. His ankles hurt the most and he tried to bend enough to massage them. Nothing happened, the will was there but he couldn't move because he was strung up by his feet and his hands were tied to something below him.

He was also cold—very cold. And naked.

He realized that he must be a prisoner of Mad Charlie's: he would have been better off dead. Just when he thought that he was going to die of pain or of cold or blood pooling in his brain, bank after bank of bright fluorescent lights were switched on: too much brightness to see properly.

At least he knew he wasn't blind.

Three men surrounded him and administered such a kicking that he didn't have time to scream with pain before the next shock hit him.

"Who are you?" One of them shouted at him.

Asmin answered without thought. "Jasminder Singh."

"Who do you work for?"

No need to lie, Asmin thought, and replied, "I'm a driver and bodyguard for Leroy Richards."

There was another kick so severe that his entire right arm was numbed. "You're a liar. You're a Leeds pimp. Now, answer the question, piss-head."

That was a slightly longer sentence, it gave Asmin just a second or two to think. It didn't seem to make any difference what he said but he replied anyway. "I'm not a pimp, never have been. Told you, I worked for Leroy Richards. I worked for Tevi Lars as a frightener but I didn't collect money for him."

One of the three knelt down and turned his head sideways. It was enough to let Asmin make out that it was Mad Charlie. He took a measure of satisfaction from the swollen lips and the plaster over one eye and the ear.

"If you was a driver-bodyguard, like you say, why did you come here to rob me?"

"Leroy said he had a job for me, said it would pay well. He showed me the building, said all I had to do was turn up and look tough." Asmin licked his lips. "I didn't know who was involved. I work to put food in front of my family."

There was a long silence, long enough to suggest that Mad Charlie was thinking hard. Where's Leroy now?"

"How should I…"

"Okay, where's he likely to be?"

Asmin was silent for longer than he needed to put an answer for that one together. "He's been laying low in a house in Leicester."

"Yeah, Uppingham Road but the police already been there, they didn't find him. Where else?"

This was a tough one, he didn't know Leroy well enough. It was news that the black man had got away but where to was another question.

"I don't know. He's talked about other places and maybe I can remember some of them if I had the time and I was right way up."

"See, he's playing for time," said one of the other two. "Give me a few minutes with a pair of pliers." he punched Asmin in the stomach but the Asian saw it coming and took the blow. The man hesitated when Asmin didn't react to the punch, then he chortled, "I'll have him singin' like a turkey bird."

"Shut up, Jools. Cut him down, let him put his clothes on an' give him some warm water an' a towel."

"Boss, I think…"

"No Jools. That's what you don't do an' turkey birds don' sing, they gobble."

They let him down, feet first but none too gently. He got dressed and hobbled painfully into the warmth of Mad Charlie's office.

Charlie himself was sitting behind a desk big enough to support a small elephant. He pointed to a coffee machine. "He'p yourself big man and have a biscuit, you're prob'ly hungry."

Asmin did as the other suggested. "Now sit there and we'll continue our li'l chat." Mad Charlie grinned and held his jaw. "You throw a mean right, man. Never saw it comin' but I felt it." There was grudging admiration in his words.

Asmin shook his head and winced. "You are the first man I ever hit that didn't go down. What have you got in there? Concrete?"

"Six years a pro. That's what it does for you, now let's talk."

Charlie sat back and said, "Jasminder Singh, you came over here from the Punjab when you was fourteen. Never went to school, as far as I can make out, probably because you were big enough to pass as a grown up. You worked for your uncle in the textile business—a factory full of cast-off clothes which were sold to market traders and party plan operators."

Asmin put his hand up as the other paused for breath. "All right, enough. You know a lot about me, you've made your point."

"A lot?" Charlie smiled without humor. "Everything. I know everything except what you did for Leroy Richards. He never said a word about you when we was in prison together. Not a word. Now Leroy, there is a big waste of space. He tried to milk me for information, thought he'd learned all my secrets by the time he left us."

"But he only knew what you wanted him to?" Asmin leaned down and rubbed his ankles, noticing the absence of the tag but said nothing. "Leroy arranged for someone to drive him the night he escaped from that prison. I happened to be the one who got picked. He wanted me to take him to see Winston Umbok, a bloke who…"

"Sold drugs for him. Come on, this is old news, I want new stuff. An' stop rubbing your ankle. I have a boy who removes tags if that is what you'm worrying about. We don't want you tellin' ever'body where you're at."

"Did you know that Leroy forced him to swim a river? Not a good swimmer, I have a feeling he never got to the other side."

"Oh. No. I didn't know that. I thought he'd gone back to the Caribbean. He used to buy from me when Leroy was inside. Now that's more like it, what else do you know that's interestin'?"

Asmin looked straight into Mad Charlie's eyes. "What I can tell you, is this. Jasminder Singh works for the man who pays his wage. Now Leroy didn't do that. At least, not enough and not often enough. Is that interesting?"

"Go on, Jasminder."

"If you've got wheels and pay expenses up front, I'll get him for you. I'll bring him back in one piece if that's what you want. How much is that worth?"

Mad Charlie Morgan sat and stared at Asmin for a long time, weighing up possibilities and probabilities. "You'd better not be playing me for a fool, Jasminder. If I help you out and you let me down, I'll go after your family first of all and when I finally deal with you…"

Asmin nodded slowly. "Try me. Pay me and pay me well. I'm not going to put a time limit on this job but I'll find him."

"How is it, Jasminder," Charlie asked, "that you speak better than a British Army Officer?"

"Because, Charles, that was how the British Army taught us in the Punjab."

CHAPTER 24

Dad peered at me over breakfast, "You were late in last night, son. Was that the job or your social life?"

I laughed out loud. "Social life? Whatever gave you the idea I had a social life, Dad? No, it was work and a particularly nasty crime that you really don't want to hear about."

"You could try me."

"Not a chance, put you off your breakfast, and I'm not joking."

"Sorry to hear that. Does it mean more late nights or was it just a one off?"

"I'm not sure at the moment. Hope not, though I shan't know until I get to the office."

Dad made sympathetic noises.

"So, what about you? How's Margaret and what did you do yesterday?"

"Margaret's fine thanks, we enjoyed a nice chili-con-carne for tea. Pip and I got back about nine or maybe a little earlier, just before it got dark."

Dad finished his eggs and bacon and reached for the toast.

"You know that neighbor of yours?"

"Not if I can help it. Nasty piece of work."

"Well, I came up from the river and reached the fence and he was watching me. We neither of us spoke but he was standing there trying to look ugly and menacing."

I was a bit concerned, I didn't think Dad had spoken like that about anybody since he'd put away his war uniform. "Hmm. What was he like? About your height, do you think? Ruddy complexion, red nose? Usually wears a tweed hat."

He shook his head. "No, no. This fellow was taller than you are, heavier too. Long face, big nose but it wasn't red. Hmm." Dad ruminated for a minute and spread marmalade. "Had a flat cap, I think. And… he was holding a gun of sorts, that's why I didn't stop to speak."

"Well, don't know who that might be. I only know the farmer—the one who shot Pip. God, I could've willingly strangled the bugger but I didn't. If he's another of the same sort, you'd best just ignore him."

———

I got to work and sat down, subconsciously scratching my calf—it felt numb, not sore anymore. I could hear footsteps outside my door. Not high heels, Alec Bell, then. He didn't give me a moment to draw breath.

"Have you heard the Leicestershire police raided the house that Leroy Richards has been hiding out in?"

"No. Good morning, Alec. No, I didn't hear that but, at least, he'll be back behind bars for a bit."

Alec ignored my attempt at pleasantries, "They didn't catch him. It seems he had a clever escape route planned for just such an event."

"Loose again then and, this time, we don't know where the hell he's gone."

"Pretty much, guv. There's news on the grapevine Mad Charlie's put a price on his head."

I grinned. "Now, I can't think of two nicer people who need to get together and chat. I'm sure that worrying about Mad Charlie will take his mind off me."

The phone rang and I picked it up. "Inspector…" It was "high heels Barbara", as I had started to think of her.

I waved Alec goodbye and when he'd gone I spoke. "Hi, Sergeant."

"I'm in Sheffield…"

"That's good, that's where I expected you to be." There was a silence in which puzzlement was quite loud. "Sorry, a joke, not a good one. What have you got?"

"Just bringing you up to date, Boss. Gwen Faulkner. Unlike her husband, did not sit on the Sheffield Council but she certainly attended most of the social functions. Quite a party animal. Liked mixing up her sex life not always with her husband. *Swingers*. You know…"

"Oh, I know all about it though not from personal experience, you understand?"

"I wouldn't suggest such…"

"Have you been able to get any names and dates from around the time of her death?"

"I'm doing that, boss. Nothing yet, no details but in another day, who knows? I'm giving it all I've got."

"Hey, I know that. Just do your best."

A little while later, Sergeant Levy poked his nose around the edge of the door. I waved him in and looked at him with raised eyebrows.

"Maybe a little bit of a break, guv. The boat where DC Stokes was discovered was built at Peter Keys Boatyard, that's in Rotherham. It had been back there for some work recently and they said the name had been changed. It had been *Belle* but when it went in, it had been painted over, with a new name: *Abra*."

"As in Abracadabra, someone thinks he's got a sense of humor. Why didn't that appear in the case notes?"

Levy shrugged. "Don't know but guess who that someone is, or was?"

"You tell me, I'm not guessing."

"Our friend Faulkner. They said at the yard that it was a really rough, do-it-yourself job. The old name had just been painted over, not even sanded down or anything."

I nodded. "Wanted us to find out, didn't he? Or else he wanted us to think we'd found out."

Levy nodded. "Exactly."

"And where are we now, then?"

"We thought it made sense to establish who bought the boat and sold it to whom. One of the chaps at the boat yard remembered the work done on it when he told me about the name—not Faulkner's name, changing the boat name. Some long gone character named Pike did it."

"Yes, I've got that."

"But the guy I was talking to did do some work on the front wall of the cabin."

"The forward bulkhead, we call it."

Sergeant Levy didn't look impressed and I began to wonder if his expression ever changed. Then I put the thought aside, Alec Bell had once looked like that, maybe Barbara would improve him. "Okay, I'll change it in my report. The thing is, the boatyard proprietor died recently so we can't trace the ownership any further back."

"Suspicious death?"

"Not unless you count old age. He was eighty-two."

Clive Bellamy interrupted things by simply walking in on our conversation. He did apologize. "Sorry chaps, this is important, I need to discuss the Patel murder with Inspector White."

Levy nodded and backed out as he passed another officer I heard him say, "…*might look soft but he's as hard as conkers soaked in vinegar…*"

"Patel?" I queried, my mind still on Levy.

"Ah, didn't you know the guy's name?"

"Are we talking about last night's little outing? The chain saw killing? No, sorry, if I did hear the name I must have forgotten. My mind was full of the details: murder weapon, severed fingers, and things."

"Understandable but it doesn't matter, come to think of it I had to look it up again myself. Spoke to the medical examiner this morning and she tells me it was—probably—a thing called a 'commando wire saw', part of an elite soldier's survival kit."

"And now we have to interview everyone at the local barracks?"

"Hardly. Anyone can buy one off the internet for a fiver, Dr. Harrison gave me a link. It's a thin serrated steel cord; it's looped at each end and fastened to webbing straps that go around the wrist." He pushed a note toward me. "There you are, the link. Have a look."

I grimaced. "You know, I wonder if we'll—mankind, I mean—will ever stop thinking up new ways to kill each other. Still, that's not why you're here."

"No. You're right. I just thought the Faulkner business and the other jobs you've got on your plate are enough. We can take this one on, the Thannet and Squires murders have just been closed so we've got a little bit of space."

"Thannet and Squires, that's..."

"Turned out to be a jealous sister."

"Oh yes, on the TV news, crying her eyes out and imploring the public to help..."

"The very same, Stewart. We don't need new ways to kill, she used a bread knife."

"Okay Clive. Thanks but if you need help..."

"I know where to ask. Cheers."

Clive left me and I tried to remember the last time I had had a superior officer I had liked as much. One of these days, I was going to throw a party, celebrate the closing of the Faulkner case, maybe. Clive would be high on the invitation list. Tentatively, I reached down to my calf but it appeared to have settled down, it didn't make me wince every time I touched it as it had done a day or so ago.

The rest of the day passed without incident. I worked through my lunch hour, knocked off at four and took the opportunity to stop by Connie's place.

Glass in hand, she saw me through the window and waved me to come inside. I guess that whatever was in the glass was alcohol though I had never seen her even a little bit tipsy. She raised her eyebrows and a bottle of amber liquid but I shook my head. "No thanks, Connie. Coffee would be good, though, if you've got some bubbling."

"Never switch the machine off, Stewart. I know Columbia's the center of the world's dope problems but if they ever stopped growing coffee beans, I'd likely die. Hand me that mug, will you?"

I passed her a dark blue china mug with a dice emblem on the side and she filled it with wickedly black coffee. "Milk and sugar?"

"Milk, yes. Sugar, no. Thanks. I don't have a sweet tooth. And coffee is grown in Sumatra, Africa—lots of other places besides Columbia."

"Smarty pants," Connie said and brushed off her dress. She was wearing a wrap-around sarong sort of dress, brightly colored with yellows and oranges and sheer enough to show off her bra and panties beneath. Is this what she wore every day? Or did she see me drive up and change?

She put the mug on a tray with a small jug of milk and a long silver spoon. I wondered which of us was the devil. We sat on stools at the counter, she even made serving coffee a sexy business. I added a swirl of milk and stirred gently. "Now, that's the best cup of coffee I've had all week."

"You probably tell that to all your girls."

I said it because it was true but to Connie, I said: "You're right. Every single one of them and you're the first."

I sipped some more, and then a little more. There didn't seem any reason to stretch the conversation out any further, she made me feel very much at ease. Eventually, I had to say something, "I... um..."

She raised her little finger. "Shush, there's nothing to say. I'm the kinda gal who goes for the gusto, you know what I mean?"

I nodded.

"But maybe I'm too bold for you English fellows. Next time, you take the lead."

Next time. "Hmm." I had a sudden vision of carrying her off to the bedroom and kissing her all over.

Maybe Connie read my thoughts, because she raised an eyebrow.

I contained myself and asked, "How long have you got before you have to go back home?"

"There's still another eighty days on my visa, around that anyway, but there's always the possibility that I'll be needed earlier."

"We all have responsibilities, I guess. I've got a murder case to solve." I finished my coffee. "Thanks, that was really good. I don't think I'll keep you waiting eighty days, though. In fact, that's a promise."

I caught my leg against the couch as I moved and pain lanced through me. Connie noticed and asked what was wrong. "I think I have a splinter in my calf. I've had one or two looks but can't see anything."

"Let me take a look." She moved to my side and sat on the floor in front of me. "Looks nasty. Can you stand a little pain?"

How could I say no?

She squeezed in one spot and held her thumbs together as I tried to contain a moan.

"There you go, wasn't that bad was it?" she lifted her thumbs up and parted them revealing a thin white object covered in blood.

"What is it?"

"It looks like a sliver of glass. Stay still, I have some antiseptic spray and that wound needs some. Quite a bit of pus came out with the glass."

I heard her words but I was lost in thought trying to remember where I had come into contact with broken glass. Then it came to me, as I had climbed the stairs to Faulkner's office, I had kicked a bottle in the dark. It had exploded into a million pieces, one of them must have found its way into my leg.

Connie came back with the spray and a Band-Aid and professionally tidied me up. "Now if that gives you anymore pain, promise me you'll see a doctor." She moved toward me and said. "A goodnight kiss from my fella?"

I hadn't ever been her 'fella,' as I recall. Still, if I forget everything else about that night, I shall always remember the kiss. It was bittersweet, filled with poignant promises, sad sensuality. We didn't even say goodbye in words. And this was the woman I had been having doubts about.

CHAPTER 25

It had been another posh do held in the equally posh Regal Ballroom in Bolton with guests from the Cross Pennines League—all black ties and tuxedos with full-length satin and silk gowns, just a few pantsuits here and there.

Colin had attended not just for the cordon bleu five-course meals that were the hallmark of these council-funded conventions but also for the entertainment which would last well into the evening. Entertainments included singers, dancers, stand-up comedy and magic acts; tonight's magic act was a well-respected amateur who was a familiar figure on the council.

The get-together was as good as ever, the food first-class and so tempting that Colin was well into the main course of rib of beef before he noticed the woman's eyes turning ever and again in his direction. She was sitting on the opposite side of the table and about six places further up. Her expression was one he'd not encountered before—her tongue flickered out, licked her sensuous lips, retreated, the eyes regarded him from beneath heavy, half-closed lids. There was a definite sense of the lascivious. She stood up, brushed an imaginary crumb from her shimmering dress and walked out, glancing back at him. A tempting invitation.

Colin swallowed, wiped his mouth and stood, making his way to the restrooms. They were situated down a long passageway at the end of which was one of the exits to the parking lot. He wandered slowly along toward the exit.

The voice matched what he had seen: rich, sensual. "Looking for a way out?"

Colin moved into a patch of darkness and reached out. Without a further word being spoken, she was close, in his arms, kissing, her mouth open and inviting his tongue inside. He cupped her breast while his other hand searched lower, caressing. The woman echoed his movement, stroking until they were pressed together.

"My God," she said, her voice thick with excitement. "I want you so badly. Not yet, though. Later, when the cars have gone, when I've watched you in front of the others and they don't know what's to come."

Colin could only guess at what she was talking about. He nodded and tried to make a reply but she kissed him again. "My car's over there." She pointed. "The Rolls, it's the Ghost, the silver one."

And she was gone.

Colin returned inside, stopping at the washroom to splash water on his face and use paper towels to remove the crimson lipstick smeared across his mouth. His jacket was awash with her perfume, there was nothing he could do about that.

Back at the table, he turned down the dessert, not wishing to eat too much, considering what he hoped was to come.

There was coffee, sharp-tasting chocolate mints, and spirits as the entertainment began. The female singer was good, performing the hit songs of several of the latest stars. The man, her partner, did not sing as well as far as Colin was concerned although the feminine half of the audience appeared to appreciate the routine.

He was really only partly paying attention to the singers in any case; most of his awareness was concentrated on the woman who had approached him.

Finally the last of the entertainers was introduced. "Ladies and gentlemen. An illusionist of the finest caliber, one of your very own, from a neighboring county. I give you the man with the magic touch. El Supremo, ladies and gentlemen."

The illusionist, who was either a councilor or an officer from the upper echelons of council staff, seemed vaguely familiar. Perhaps someone he had seen during the course of his work but had never had cause to speak to.

He wore a black suit over a black shirt with white buttons and a white bow tie. He had a constant superior smile, an expression that told everyone just how exceptional, exclusive and much more wonderful than anyone else, he really was.

Colin hated the man, not least because he felt himself to embody these qualities. However, the man was entertaining and clever. The entertainer started with common-place card tricks, asking for cards to be nominated by the audience and cutting the pack to show the requested card or making it rise from the deck by itself. Then he took a long piece of rope, requested a card to be chosen. He wrapped the rope around his hand and the deck of cards; then unwrapped it, and cut it into two pieces.

A member of the audience selected one piece which the magician discarded; the process was repeated until there were only two six inch lengths left. One was placed in a wine glass on the end of the diners' table. The other was unraveled to expose a small cylinder at its core; he unrolled the cylinder: the card which had been selected at the start. The spectators gave the illusionist a long ovation which he had to quell with calming gestures.

It was not the grand finale, this was still to come.

Colin leaned back and looked at the woman. Her glowing eyes were already on him, she smiled, licked her lips with the very tip of her tongue, and pouted a fleeting kiss in his direction before turning back to the entertainment.

The man with the magic touch descended from the stage and walked down the far side, his hand actually touched the shoulder of the woman that so fascinated Colin. He moved on, around the end of the table and back up Colin's side.

"You, sir." The voice came from directly behind him and Colin realized the other had paused. "Have you a note, sir? Something I could borrow? A five pound note, a tenner, something more?"

Colin pursed his lips, unwilling to be the center of attention. He opened his wallet and gave the other a ten pound note.

"Perhaps you would sign it please?" The illusionist proffered a pen.

Back on the stage, the magician tucked the ten-pound note in the waist-band of a near-naked and very nubile female assistant. A swirl of a black cloak, the girl had disappeared completely until he directed attention to a three-cornered glass box where she stood—sans bank note.

Hardly believing that he'd been the victim of a con trick for ten pounds, Colin felt hot beneath his collar and uncomfortable as his fellow diners glanced at him.

Finally, the magician, looking puzzled, felt in every pocket, looked under everything on his table and then remembered the piece of rope in the glass, which everyone had forgotten about. He unraveled it slowly. there, in the center, was a roll of paper. "Would the gentleman I borrowed this from, come to the stage."

Colin obliged uncomfortably. The roll was unrolled, the paper was a ten pound note, and the ten pound note bore his signature. To thunderous applause, Colin returned to his seat, his face a deep pinkish red, the same color as the ten pound note.

The silver Rolls Royce was almost the last car in the lot. As Colin came abreast of it, the rear door opened and he peered into the dark interior—not even the courtesy light was on. She seized hold of his lapels and pulled him roughly inside. He kissed her as urgently and needingly as she kissed him.

He closed the door and moved to lie on top of her but with surprising strength, she pushed him away.

"Oh no, not like that my lad, this is my party and we'll play the games I want to play."

That suited Colin's somewhat neglected sexual education. They were very quickly naked and now, she climbed on top of Colin and the leather upholstery squeaked and groaned and smelled as good as good leather should.

Later on, exhausted, they lay back against the leather and held each other as the parking lot lights went out. Colin's few real sexual encounters had been rather casual. He had never realized that a woman could be so insatiable. "You know," he said at last, "Tonight would have been perfect but for that idiotic illusionist interfering like that. Out of all the men in the audience, he had to pick me."

Colin's companion broke into peals of laughter. "Why? If he hadn't been there, neither would I. You do know who he is don't you?"

Colin shook his head, then spoke into the darkness. "No."

"That's Travis Faulkner, head of finance at Sheffield. And he's my husband. I watched him watching me watching you. You were no chance pick-up, he picked you because I did."

"You mean you select his audience participants?"

"Sometimes."

"And does he pick whatever man you give the eye to?"

"Of course."

"And you're the reward?"

"Not always. We keep a very open relationship, it keeps things fresh for us. Now, would you like to take this to the next level?"

Colin wanted to answer *yes* but with his desires blunted for the moment, he had no intention of admitting it. "What's the next level?"

"To start with, more nights like this one? More wining and dining like tonight? Maybe I'll take you to my little hideaway if we really take to each other."

"And do I continue to shill for the great Travis Faulkner?"

"A plant in the audience? No, Travis doesn't do that."

"All right, let's see where this goes. What's your name?"

"Gwen."

"Colin. So, the great Travis Faulkner is an illusionist, a stage magician. How did he get to be as good as he is?"

"It's his hobby. You know, I can see you're really taken with magic—illusions—aren't you? He started with books and watching others and lots and lots of practice. He's paid for one or two of the more amazing tricks, The one with your tenner ending up inside the rope—which it didn't by the way—cost him a thousand pounds to learn."

"Hmm." He began to dress. "Yes, let's see about the next level, as you call it. I'll give you my phone number."

Gwen was going to be something he could really look forward to, and the magic, as Gwen had said, had caught his imagination. From today, he had two new purposes in his life.

CHAPTER 26

Leroy's Satnav found the house for him, delivering him from the A64 bypass to the Edwardian-style building with pinpoint accuracy. He left the Land Rover in the huge parking lot of a nearby pub and walked back. The front garden held roses: red, white, and pink with a single purple lupine.

He opened the small wooden gate, closed it quietly behind him and at the front door, knocked on the glazed panel. Belatedly, he noticed a bell push and pressed this too.

Evangeline Kinti was a Jamaican-born woman with skin so beautifully black that it glowed. She was proud of her heritage, she stood proud and straight and glared at anyone who dared look down on her. She was considered beautiful by some, angelic by others and downright evil by those who knew her best. Those who also knew that she practiced *Obeah*—Jamaican Voodoo—smiled sweetly at her and feared her, protecting themselves with charms and counter-curses.

She opened her door and glared down from the top step at Leroy. For a long moment, she hovered on the edge of recognition then she smiled, a smile filled with pearly white teeth.

"Leroy? King Dick himself! My man, you come to give this lady some sugar?"

Leroy was yet another type of person, someone who considered Evangeline beautiful, angelic, and wholly lovely. Occasionally, he remembered to be frightened.

"Eva, I would not have thought it possible." He clasped the woman in a huge embrace and lifted her off the ground. "I am sure you've grown even more beautiful since we were last together." He put her down gently, like replacing a china figurine on its pedestal.

Evangeline backed inside and closed the door behind her visitor, shutting out any onlookers, especially the bitch across the road who flicked her curtains at her. "You always did say the most wonderful things, Leroy. Even when we was kids playing marbles in the dirt back in Kingston."

She pushed the curtain aside and looked this way and that through the front door window.

"I also did some of the cutest things to you when I was fourteen and again on that holiday we shared when I was eighteen. You remember, Sugar?" Leroy had been back to the Caribbean for occasional holidays and sometimes, had looked Evangeline up.

"Why di'n you tell me when you was comin' to England?"

"All in good time, Leroy. Now come on." She pulled him through to the kitchen and reached for bottles. "I'm just gonna show you I haven't lost any skills at making *Cuba Libras* but you're goin' to have to get outta here. The police have been 'round here a lot of times. They sit out there in a black Astra, just up the street, just watchin'."

"How they know 'bout you? Hmm? I never told no one 'bout our connection."

Evangeline twisted her lips. "Oh I don' know Leroy, but they come here a while ago and asked if I'd seen you. I couldn't deny I knew you, they seen it in my eyes, they'd have known I was lyin'."

Leroy shivered, the thought of being returned to Barlinnie Prison was overwhelming. He never, ever wanted to hear another Glasgow accent as long as he lived.

Eva could see him thinking. "It's no use worrying, man. That'll do you no good at all." She poured coke over the white rum and ice. "What we need is somewhere you can go into hidin.' Somewhere where they won't think to look."

Leroy took the drink and almost finished it in a single long swallow. It was a thoughtless action, like taking a beer so fast you didn't taste it.

"Well, what do you think?"

"About where to go?"

"About the drink, you *e-d-at*."

"Thanks Eva, done me a power of good. You not lost your touch."

"Don' lie to me. You never tasted a thing, di'n' touch the sides on the way down. Now think where you can go and *then* I'll make you another. Maybe."

"You got any friends we can ask?"

Eva shook her head emphatically. "None that I'd trust for that." Her forehead furrowed. "You gotta be 'way from people for a while."

Leroy's forehead creased as well. This was not what he had in mind. He was a social animal who had already been cut off from the bright lights for long enough. He had been looking forward to getting out, strutting his stuff; clubbing, wine, women, restaurants. He shook his head. "Don't think about me going out into the countryside, Eva. I lived in Kingston and Birmingham. If I was ever outside of a city, it was because I was coming from one and goin' to another. Put me out of the city, girl, an' it'd be like planting a sapling in a cellar. They tried to put me in a prison and I couldn't stand it, had to get away. I need the stink of city air, Eva; need to be ridin' out wi' my homeboys."

Eva lifted an eyebrow. "There're precious few o' your homeboys 'round here, Leroy, but I just had a thought." She closed her eyes, and rubbed her temples. "Suppose we find some rental in the city but not in the city."

"You talking noise, Sugar."

"Oh you'll un'erstand, Leroy. 'Cause I gonna show ya."

Evangeline spent five minutes going through handbags before she found what she wanted—a pair of rose-colored shades and a beanie hat. "Now don' turn your nose up. We don't wan' you spotted so these a' goin' to change the way you look. Like totally."

Leroy wore the accessories without comment. They were far from his taste but, looking in a shop window, he had to admit, even he would not have recognized himself. In fact, by the time he had inspected his appearance in two more windows, he was sold.

"Y'know. I am such a handsome boy, I could go with these."

The pair walked across to Coney Street, one of York's up-market shopping areas and just as Leroy's eyes lit up at the prospect of buying a new outfit entirely, she dragged him into an alleyway which led down to the river, less than a hundred yards away.

"This is a big river, Eva. Bigger'n I've seen for a long time."

"Been a lot of rain lately. It swells up an' it slides down. Now this is one o' the Snickelways of York."

"An' what's a sniggleway?"

"Snickelway. They criss-cross the old city, they go 'cross roads, go through some of the big stores and run for miles. I want to find somewhere to rent along here. There's often a few that's empty but you gotta search 'em out, they don't get in the papers."

"Sniggleways. Like it."

Eva corrected him one last time, "Snickelway, man, sn-ick-el-way. Like a rabbit warren, hide out in full sight here, long as you got your disguise on."

Eva tried three places she knew of by rumor but none was vacant. She walked him through a hardware store and out the back into the Shambles—a street of butchers in medieval times—and then along another with tall buildings to both sides, around the corner and at the end…

Leroy loved it. Off King's Square with an entrance in constant shadow and a back exit so narrow that only Leroy or a fox could have made it through. He paid two months in advance, in cash; the owner was off to Saudi on a temporary job so Leroy had it fully furnished, food in the freezer and even half a dozen cold beers in the fridge door.

"King's Square, just the spot for King Richards, eh?"

"Can't move in for three days," said Eva. "I can't put you up at my place, it'd be asking for trouble, I've…"

"Don't worry woman, you done well for me, real well. I can sleep in the back of ma Land Rover for three nights, be just like sleeping inna bed."

"What about the number on your car, they might see it and check…"

"The man who lent it me is all clued up, no one knows anything bad about this car."

Sammy opened his door to find Asmin smiling at him. "Asmin, my friend, come in. Fancy some chicken? I'm just cooking up another batch for the freezer."

"That would be nice, Sammy. I see the police didn't put you away, then."

Sammy led the Sikh back to his kitchen where the usual aroma of fried chicken was thick in the air. "Nah. What could they do me for, eh? I showed them the rent book I kept for him, his name was Elijah Wood. Did you know that?" asked Sammy in the most innocent of tones. "They showed me a photo and I said yes, that was the man I rented a room to. Escaped prisoner, would you believe it?"

"Ah well," Asmin commiserated, winking. "How could you know?"

"You're right. 'To Let' sign in the window, could be anybody."

"Absolutely, Sammy. Did he get away in the Land Rover?"

"Course he did. Easy as you like. Don't know where he's got to, but he showed the police a clean pair o' heels."

"Best you don't know exactly, Sammy. But we've gone down to the smoke, we've both got friends there, lots of places to lose yourself down there. Look, we wondered if you've got the registration papers? Just in case we need to re-tax it while we're there."

Sammy passed him a plate of fries and chicken. "You get your face around that, my friend. I'll look for the car papers."

"Thanks. I'll make sure you get some compensation for the car."

Sammy waved his hands. "Don't worry about that. Leroy'll get that seen to. May not look like it with that face he puts on but that guy has a heart of gold."

A short time later, and while he was alone, Asmin replaced the tag on his ankle, then took his leave and walked down the road to the car Charlie had arranged for him. He sat in behind the wheel and took out his cell. He dialed and looked in the mirror at Charley's West Indian minder slouched in the back seat as his call was answered. "Asmin here. Leroy left in a Land Rover, black. Registration," he read from the registration document, "H04 EUK. Now I need to know where it is, can you help?" he switched the phone off and turned on the radio.

"Could be a while," he told the other man. "We'll wait until they get back to me."

His cell rang ten minutes later. "Hi. Been clocked on the M1? Oh, that stretch of cameras, yes." He listened some more and put the phone on its dashboard holder. "Going north on the M1, and there was a partial recognition eastbound on the M62," he told the silent watcher. "We'll assume the partial's right for the moment and hope for some corroboration as we go. Hope Charlie's as generous as he wanted me to believe. Won't be long now."

There was a pause, a long one.

"Don't you ever speak?"

Still no answer.

CHAPTER 27

Sunday and I had planned to sleep late. I had been working at home until nearly 2:00 a.m. going over the reports I had brought home and trying to get as much as I could fixed in my brain. I woke and checked the bedside clock—7:00 a.m.—some lie-in! Something had woken me and it took several seconds to figure out what it was. I was halfway out of the bed before I fully realized it had been a shotgun.

"Dad!" There was no immediate reply. I slipped into a pair of old jeans and a tee-shirt, rushed downstairs, found a pair of wellingtons, and went out into the backyard. "Dad," I shouted again, "where are you?" Then, "Pip!" There was no answering yelp. I heard something from the direction of the river bank, perhaps a faint cough. I ran through the orchard and came out at the side of the river. I found him lying on the ground covered in leaves and twigs.

"Dad, for God's sake. What's happened?"

He stirred and sat up, shook his head. "Pip asked to go out, must have left his dog flap bolted. I brought him down here. There was this gunshot and part of that bloody apple tree fell on me."

"Okay." I helped him up and he staggered a couple of times before he found his feet. "You're not hurt are you?"

"Bit shaken. Don't think there's anything else. Give me a second or two."

Bang! Another gunshot. Loud. Closer than before. More leaves rained down from another of my trees.

"You stay here, Dad. I'll be back in a moment."

I walked quickly to the boundary fence between my land and my neighbor's. There was the man my dad had described He carried a shotgun, broken open over his arm. I leaped the fence and ran at him while he was trying to load a cartridge. I caught him by surprise and backed him up against the fence, he dropped the cartridge and I wrenched the gun from his hand and flung it away.

"What the devil do you think you're doing? You've half-killed my father from shock, why in hell are you shooting at apple trees on *my* property?"

He must have outweighed me by thirty pounds and they weren't all fat. If I hadn't caught him by surprise, he could have retaliated and maybe hurt me. As it was, he just stood there, saying nothing.

"Come on," I continued, "cat got your tongue? Just what do you think you're doing? You fancy being up on a manslaughter charge?"

That got through to him.

"Manslaughter? For shooting wood pigeons?" I detected an Irish accent.

"No, not wood pigeons. For spraying shot around the area where other people are walking and minding their own business. My father's over there, he's pushing eighty and he's got heart palpitations from being shot at."

The man's face betrayed every emotion that passed behind it. Concern, fleetingly, then worry, anxiety and cunning. "I didn't shoot at anybody. I was after those buggers," he stopped as two more pigeons flew noisily overhead. "They been pinching our corn. Only way to keep 'em off is to shoot 'em but they go an' hide in your trees." He tapped me on the chest. "Need to be cut down, see—not left there for birds to nest in."

I knocked his fingers away. "I happen to like birds—and apple trees! It's not illegal to shoot pigeons, but it *is* illegal to shoot on other people's land without permission. And it's illegal to discharge a firearm that could endanger someone's life."

"You a lawyer, then? We don't have that problem over the water. Shooting over the land, that is. Vermin needs to be got rid of wherever it is."

"No, I'm a policeman—and we are *not* over the water. If you do fire over my property again, I'll arrest you. It's that simple."

I turned and climbed back into my own backyard and went for my dad, to support him conspicuously back to the house. Problem was, he wasn't there. When I did find him, he must have realized he had worried me.

He was carrying Pip. "Poor little feller was hiding in a hole down near the water. Must have frightened him quite badly. Look how he's shaking."

"Not surprising. If someone's taken your leg off with a shotgun, you're going to be a bit anxious next time you hear one." I scratched his head behind the ears and spoke to him gently. "If he comes near you with a gun again, I'm going to shoot him myself. Okay?" He seemed better.

We went back home and cooked ourselves a full English breakfast. Not healthy—but then, neither was being shot at. Pip had his version of the meal; he liked black pudding and was partial to a nice piece of bacon. Tomato, beans, and hash browns, on the other hand, he was not so fond of.

Dad, replete, sat in my armchair and went to sleep. Pip curled up in his basket and also went to sleep. I considered taking a nap too, but switched on the computer and began a search. I'd realized that Dad being here was a major part of my life and his suggestion of building an extension to the house had crystallized my feelings. I really couldn't let him go back to Birmingham. I was plowing through prefabricated extensions and mobile home advertisements when the phone rang.

"Stewart White."

"Barbara Patterson, boss."

"Hello Barbara, how's Sheffield treating you?"

"Can't wait to get back. Working away from home is fine for a day or even two but I'm feeling really sympathetic for anyone who has to do it permanently. Anyway, I've finished here, I think. I'm planning on driving back up this afternoon. Just wanted to share some observations with you."

"Fine, go ahead."

"Right. Point one. Gwen Faulkner frequented the Madhouse Club. The manager has been quite helpful, actually, I think he rather fancies me..."

"Tall guy?"

"Not really, not as tall as you, actually, why?"

"Nothing really, just wondered if I knew him."

"Anyway, Mrs. Faulkner sometimes booked a bedroom. She'd occasionally drink too much to drive and there was often a guest. And you'll never guess..."

"He put a video camera in."

"How *did* you guess? Sure you don't know the manager?"

"No, But I know the type. Most of them do in these circumstances and most of them keep copies—personal entertainment."

"And sometimes, blackmail."

"That too."

"Very good, boss. But here's something you don't know. She was here the night before she died though she didn't use the room, the manager lost his bet with a punter. She was with a man though, bald-headed guy and he reckons he could ID the man, says he seemed to be too young to be naturally bald."

"Well, that's something. Any video?"

"No, they didn't use the room."

"I meant from the general CCTV, could we identify him?"

"Nope. The bar tapes get overwritten usually once a month."

"Tapes? Video cassettes? Thought those went out with the ark."

"Apparently not here. If the Sheffield people had asked to look at them at the time, they'd have got him."

"Oh well, spilt milk and all that. Not necessarily our man, anyhow."

"Well, a final tidbit from the manager. The chap had been in before—the bald one—with Gwen Faulkner, but not since."

"And the vids from the bedroom? The ones he keeps for 'home entertainment'?"

"He's going through them now. His cataloguing skills, apart from 'this is a good one', are pretty non-existent. I'll bring back what he can find."

"Right, Barbara. That's a job well done, thanks. Safe journey."

I went to bed, it had been a long day and a short night and I was asleep as my head hit the pillow. I was still asleep at 5:50 a.m. and did my best to switch the alarm off only it wasn't the alarm clock, it was my cell.

"Do you know who this is?" Asked the voice.

"Faulkner." I replied.

"Well done, Inspector. Faulkner calling from somewhere on the high seas."

I didn't want him knowing that I could tell exactly where he was so I said nothing.

"Just wondering if you've caught the bloke who killed my wife, yet."

"No. We haven't. The good news for you, though, is that we know it wasn't you. You can come home anytime."

"No more jail time?"

"You may have to spend a night or two in a police cell while we clear some stuff up but not a long stay." I got out of bed and struggled one-handed into my dressing-gown and went downstairs. "You're probably aware that your wife had a number of liaisons."

"Of course. Both of us did. Put a bit of spice back into our marriage."

"Did you ever see any of these… shall we call them partners?"

"Oh yes. We videoed them so we could view them later. It's what we did."

"Your choice, sir, your prerogative, but tell me, did you see any of them just before she was murdered? In particular, was there a bald headed man? Was there anyone like that on the videos?"

He was silent for some time. "Not on the videos, no, but I know who you mean. He started coming to my shows—my conjuring shows?"

"Yes?"

"Actually, I thought he was coming to see my wife, I know he met her in the parking lot once but I fancy he was coming to see me too, maybe even more so. I thought he had alopecia, much too young to be losing his hair naturally. You think he was the one?"

"We don't know that. He's just a possibility at the moment." Faulkner didn't reply.

"Sir? Are you still there?"

"Yes. Were you aware that my wife had a suite of rooms on the floor below the office where she was murdered?"

Interesting, Faulkner thought she had been murdered in the office, I wasn't so sure.

"I didn't know that." I said. "Why do you say that? Something relevant?"

"Well, she might have taken him back there. She must also have had a camcorder hidden there. I don't know, it was her place, she didn't discuss it. We just shared the end product on occasions."

"Hmm," I said and thought, *whatever turns you on.* "Who has the keys?"

"My solicitor. He has keys to the whole building. I own it from the retail units at street level to the storerooms on the fourth floor." There was another longish pause. "You are going to get him, aren't you?"

I smiled into the early morning sunlight. "Oh yes."

Friday night. Colin had agreed to drive over to Sheffield to meet Gwen. It was a two-hour drive but he considered it worth the effort. Apart from her sheer animal qualities, the woman excited him.

There was so much that was new, so much that he had never tried before, never even knew to try before. Last time, she had come to him as a dark-haired siren in a see-through dress that just tantalized him all the way though the preparatory meal; she had covered essential parts of their bodies in chocolate sauce and they had spent an hour licking it off. The time before that, Gwen had been a short-haired blond with six inch heels and legs that just went on and on.

What would it be tonight, he wondered and his imagination answered him. A redhead with a Russian accent and a whip—not too big a whip, maybe she would want handcuffing, maybe…

Colin had just left Glossop on the A57; he was on the lonely stretch passing the Hurst Reservoir with the Snake Pass through the Pennine Mountains ahead of him. The car gave a lurch and began to pull more and more strongly to the left. He fought the wheel which had developed its own ideas, reduced speed and brought the car to a stop on the grass.

When he investigated with a flashlight, he found a nail right though the passenger-side tire. He got the spare from the trunk, rolled it around to the front and then went back for the jack. Except there wasn't one.

He groaned in frustration; no jack, no tire change, Colin was going to have to call her. And here again, fate dealt him another blow. Out here in the wild, he could not raise a signal on his cell phone.

He had passed a call box four or five minutes before the puncture, he was certain he had seen it, at a junction. Three miles or so; a forty-five minute walk minimum and it had started to rain.

His watch told him that he was already late when he arrived at the call box, she had probably left the pub at which they were meeting by now, probably switched her phone off too. Instead of calling Gwen, he contacted the Automobile Association and waited at the box for them to arrive.

Two and half hours after the time of their meeting, he had a tire fitted and he turned back toward Lancashire and stopped, cold and wet, at the welcoming sign of the Green Man.

It was a food pub and not interested in a meal, he sat in a corner of the waiting area and drank his whiskey without tasting it.

There was really only one thing on his mind—so much so that when a girl's voice said in his ear, "buy us a drink, eh?" he turned, expecting to see Gwen there. But it wasn't, of course. It was a much younger woman with coarse hair and too much lipstick and a face too old for her years.

Perhaps it was Gwen, in an excellent disguise? No, definitely not.

Sadly, Colin bought her a plate of quiche with a baked potato and a half pint of beer. She sat down next to him. "Thanks." She said. "Name's Mary."

"You look hungry, Mary."

"First thing I've eaten in two days."

Her arms were bare and there was no sign of track marks but it was obvious that this was her lifestyle, if such it could be called: picking up strangers and trading a quickie for a pork pie or, occasionally, a full meal for a night in one of the hotel rooms, perhaps.

"Something else? A hot pudding?"

"I'll have a chicken pie, if you don't mind. More protein." It was the only time she showed any animation and she ate the pie as quickly as she had eaten the quiche, as though Colin might change his mind and take it away.

Mary followed him out of the pub and tried to kiss him as they reached a shadowed part of the wall.

"No," he said. "No, I…"

But she persisted, as though she felt a bargain had been struck.

"Well, let's go somewhere quiet. I'll drive you back here afterwards."

The first lane they turned up led out onto open moorland and he stopped the car as soon as the background light had died away. Once he turned the headlights off, Mary reached for him again, anxious to repay him for what he had done. Again, Colin demurred. "I'm really hot," he said. "Let's go for a walk."

Perhaps Mary was a little alarmed because she tried to hang back but the path they trod was a narrow one and he ushered her ahead.

"Pick a nice spot, I'll get a blanket out of the car." It seemed an inane thing to suggest in the darkness but Mary did her best to comply while Colin went back and opened the trunk.

Mary smoothed some rough heather down and reached for the expected blanket. Instead, Colin's bag and pillow case combination enveloped her head. She struggled, even when she was on her stomach with his knee digging into her back. Mary was a strong girl, she took quite a long time to die but it was no less satisfying.

Colin laid her out with her arms and legs making a cruciform, her head pillowed on a tuft of heather. He went back for his camcorder and carefully recorded the outcome, even feeling a little virtuous for putting an end to such an unhappy life. Another *chosen one*.

The evening hadn't been a total waste, after all.

Leroy spent every daylight hour exploring his new neighborhood, the York warren of lanes known locally as the "Snickelways." It was such a change from the somewhat run-down Midland city areas he had known for so long. The almost heaped-together jumble of modern housing and twisting alley ways and literally ancient houses and shops was something quite beyond his experience.

Once a resident truly knew their way around, it was possible to traverse the center of York in minutes, unobserved, swapping time zones from the early fourteenth century of Our Lady's Row to twenty-first century stores.

The area was home to the lantern tower of St Michael's church which used to guide travelers across the marshes, the small carving of the printer's Devil above a corner shop, the Hole in the Wall pub. A random walk would take Leroy from the Hole in the Wall to the Precenter's Court lined with elegant old—and expensive—houses furnished with old street lamps and the most stunning view of York Minster imaginable.

As he walked, he noticed the blue plaques with dates and the names of famous occupants. The oldest date he saw that afternoon was 1610 and the most notorious name he recognized was Dick Turpin, a feared highwayman of the eighteenth century. He was disappointed to see that he was not the dashing thief of legend but the lowest of villains.

Virtually lost by now, Leroy jumped as a car horn brought him back to the present day and looking around, he knew somehow, that he was close to his current home off Bedern Path.

He found his front door and slid the key into the lock only to find that it was already unlocked and as he opened it, so there came the smell of liver, bacon and onions. He paced quickly along the hallway and put his head around the kitchen door to see Eva dancing in front of the window.

She was wearing headphones and quite unaware that she was being watched. Leroy crept up behind her and slid his arms under hers, and cupped her breasts. She stiffened, he felt her draw air into her lungs ready to scream to high heaven. Quickly he pulled off one of the headphones with his teeth and whispered "takes me back to those nights on the beach, honey child. We loved each other then; what went wrong with it all?"

Eva stood still. "Oh, I remember, Leroy. I remember what went wrong back then. What went wrong was Latitia Hall."

"Oh, come on, sugar lips."

"Don't you sugar lips me! I don't know whether Latitia was trying to swallow that black mamba of yours or just biting it to death."

CHAPTER 28

I knew there was something happening the moment I got into work. Normally, I was the first or second arrival but this morning, half the room was already full. I passed quickly by the noisy incident room and went on to my office. I'd spent a year in this job and had never become enamored with the idea of coming into the office every day. I had been used to being out in the field, getting on with the investigation and, in fact, I could see Barbara Patterson felt the same way. Solving crimes was my forte, organizing others to do the solving was not nearly as much fun.

A young, fresh-faced constable was lurking uncomfortably close to my door as I approached. He seemed relieved to see me.

"Good morning, sir. Chief Constable's compliments, he'd like to see you in his office at nine a.m. sharp."

"Thanks, Constable." I looked at my watch. "I'll be there."

I went in and sat down, seventeen minutes early. I was feeling weary already. A movement caught my eye, Alec Bell was grinning through the glass door and I signaled him in.

"What joyful news are you bringing me this morning, Alec? And why's everybody in so early?"

"Grapevine is buzzing, boss. The Chief's on the warpath. Even Joe Flowers has been catching it."

"So why are you looking so cheerful, then?"

"I've seen three chiefs here in my time and I guess I'll see two or three more. Every now and then each one has this little ritual, bang their fists on desks, make threatening noises. Seems to work for those who aren't accustomed to it."

"Well, that's as may be but *our* work has to go on. What have you got for me?"

"Couple of things. On good authority, I hear that Jasminder Singh has jumped ship—he's now working for Mad Charlie and is looking for the vanishing act, Leroy Richards."

"Poacher turned gamekeeper, eh?"

"Well, hardly. Poacher turned even bigger poacher."

I nodded. Alec at his sunniest could be a bit wearing. "I also heard—from a totally different direction—that there had been a blood sample left at the scene."

"Scene? Which one's that, then?"

"Patel's. At Morley."

"Some sample. Couple of bucketfuls."

"No, no, different from that, another one, tiny, just a couple of drops. We can assume it's the murderer's, must have cut himself without realizing, it's been identified."

I looked quizzically at Alec. I wished he wouldn't be quite so theatrical.

"Ready for this? Belongs to a Billy Jarvis. A man we already know is dead but, here's the thing, do the Chief and Clive Bellamy?"

"Alec, I love you. If you were Barbara Patterson, I'd probably marry you."

I phoned Clive Bellamy as a very self-satisfied Alec Bell left. Clive wasn't there, his secretary said he was probably already with the Chief Constable which is where I should have been. I scrawled a note for Clive and stuck it to my folder.

I passed Barbara Patterson just coming in and said, "Hello." She could see I was in a rush and just nodded.

Clive Bellamy seemed rather full of himself when I got there. He'd obviously been in conversation with Joe Flowers en route to the Chief's office and I had to wait as they did an "After you, no after you" dance at the door.

While everyone was settling down, I slipped the note to Clive: *Might not be in your file yet, the Patel murderer was identified as Billy Jarvis. Jarvis was supposed to have died years ago, as a boy, blood DNA recorded at orphanage.*

"Morning, gentleman." The Chief Constable looked at each one us. I watched Clive suddenly stiffen as he finished my note. He stuck it in his case file as the Chief singled him out to start with. "Chief Inspector Bellamy? Hope you've got something for us?"

"The Patel case, sir? It's only been thirty-six hours but we do have enough for a probable ID on the murderer."

"That's welcome news, Inspector… there's something more?"

"We've got a match on an oldish blood bank record, a Billy Jarvis. Unfortunately, Billy Jarvis was recorded as dead when he was at an orphanage. Years ago?" Clive looked at me and I nodded infinitesimally.

"Inspector White, have you any further information on this?" He asked, passing the buck.

"We have, but oddly enough, not to do with this case. At the scene of DC Stokes's murder, we found a similar small amount of blood which was also identified as Jarvis's. We're still waiting for information from the Metropolitan Police Authority but we haven't been able to shake anything loose yet."

The Chief's eyes bored into mine. "You mean two quite separate murders were carried out by the same perpetrator?"

"It's more than a possibility, unless the sample was planted. Until we learned about this from the Morley killing, we had no real evidence that the blood sample actually belonged to the murderer. We haven't followed through on the implications yet because we've only had this last information for a short time. Plus the MO is different."

"And you were aware of this, Clive?"

I nipped in quickly. "The report on Jarvis was submitted before the Chief Inspector was asked to take over."

Joe Flowers, a past master at armor-plating his own back, joined the conversation to show that, at least, he was up to the minute. "This William Jarvis who supposedly drowned, didn't you suggest in your report that he might have exchanged identities with another boy?"

"I did suggest it sir, but only as something we should look at when the intel from London comes in. The other lad," I frowned, trying to recollect, "Gabriel Henderson, I queried his name with London too but if no one noticed the switch, it speaks volumes for the state of our child care facilities."

The Chief Constable *harrumphed*. "It was years ago, Inspector. No doubt they've improved. However, I'll take up the matter with the London Authority and see if we can't expedite matters. Let me have the name of the individual you wrote to."

The Chief leaned back in his chair and looked at us all. This was what the meeting was *really* about, I could tell. He started, "I know it's part of my job to handle the demands—the increasing demands, I might add—of the media. And I'll tell you this, I find it bizarre to have to fight our corner against not one but five MPs."

Another round of hurt looks.

"We need a break and we need a break soon. The hounds are baying and I don't like being the fox."

Clive Bellamy caught up with me on my way back. "Thanks for the breaking news, Stewart."

"No problem, Clive. It was only minutes old, thought it would keep us out of the mire. I have to say, I like you as my boss, you don't deserve to be dumped on."

"Nevertheless, I won't forget."

We walked on. I was smiling to myself, knowing that that was a favor I could call in at some future time.

"He's right though," I said, "we do need a break."

"We may have one if we can figure out exactly how blood samples from two different sites belong to a dead man."

"They don't help much unless we can get our hands on this Gabriel Henderson—we've no leads to him at all."

Clive went his way, I went mine and winked at Barbara who was standing in the doorway of the incident room.

She was clutching a DVD. "The proprietor of the Mad House has sent you this with his compliments."

"Keen to help the police, is he?"

"Absolutely. *Help*—spelled: i-n-g-r-a-t-i-a-t-e. And it's dated two months ago."

"I presume it's Gwen Faulkner?"

"Oh, yes." We reached my office; Barbara gave me the disc and closed the door. "I'd prefer us not to be caught watching this by any of our colleagues, you get to see quite a lot of Gwen. She's a very…"

"Forthcoming?"

"Adventurous lady."

"I slid the disc into the machine and saw exactly what Barbara had meant. A naked woman with remarkable—attributes—bouncing up and down on a man whose face was turned away from the camera. Long black hair swirled and cascaded around her, a wig, I imagined, since the woman in the morgue had short black hair according to the report. I'd not had the time to visit the pathologist's lair yet. And she was… had been pretty athletic judging by the contortions her body went through. I switched it off. "Oh, do we see the guy's face if we keep it going?"

Barbara shook her head. "Pity we couldn't see if it's our bald-headed guy.

"Great stuff all the same, Barbara. Anything else to add?"

"One thing, guv. I interviewed a councilor, a Ms. Partridge, she wouldn't tell me her given name. I don't know why, *Partridge* isn't that common. She told me that Gwen attended all the council's social functions. Used them to pick up men in full view of her husband. She'd meet them later, or so the gossip goes, for naughty stuff. Travis Faulkner was quite frequently in the entertainments as a magician and she went to his other shows and did the same. The Partridge woman had overheard her, Gwen that is, boasting about it."

I gave myself a mental kick, Travis—that was the first time I could recall hearing his first name, somehow it hadn't seemed to matter. "Okay, at least we know her lifestyle."

"Not finished yet, guv. The best is yet to come. Ms. Partridge has an aversion to bald-headed men."

I almost smoothed my own hair down, just to make sure it was still there.

"At least, that's what her tone of voice said. The last two occasions, she's seen Gwen, there was this—these are her words—'*bald-headed man she went off with—can you imagine?*'"

"Does the council use this Mad House place for all their functions?"

"Mostly, I think, At least for the moment, could be a contract?"

"Yes, it could. I think we want to have a look at the general CCTV discs for the past two months."

"They have tape cassettes, boss. Remember?"

"Damn. Yes I do. Well, get everything they *have* got."

"I've requested a list of recent events and venues from the council secretary."

"That's good. Get the Mad House guy to send you the CCTV stuff, will you? Or get the local police to pick them up—that would be best, actually, seeing someone in uniform usually quickens things up."

"Well that's it, so far."

"Um, Barbara…"

"Guv?"

"If you're interested, Sergeant Levy mentioned that he likes you."

She grinned, and leaned forward. "I hear that you'd marry me if I looked more like Alec Bell."

I dissolved into laughter and when I'd wiped the tears away, she had gone.

On the way home, I took a call from Forest Homes. I pulled over and took the phone off the dashboard holder. It was interesting and rewarding news that required me to get Dad out of the way for a little more than forty-eight hours. I would get Margaret in on the scheme. I made a note to call and see her. My calf was feeling much better now that Connie had removed the sliver of glass; hadn't had a twinge out of it all day. I drove home feeling much better.

After the car mishap, Colin contacted Gwen and apologized. It took him almost half an hour to go through the whole story from nail-in-tire to freezing-rain to no-phone-signal before she was satisfied and then there was the humiliation of telling her how he was missing her and asking how could he manage until next week without her company?

Eventually, he was forgiven. "Don't you ever do that again," she told him. "Get another phone provider, a signal booster. I thought you'd stood me up and I've been extremely angry. No one does that to me, no one."

"When can we meet?" he asked in what he hoped was a suitably submissive voice, though secretly he was annoyed at her superior attitude. "Tonight wouldn't be too soon for me."

"Oh no, Colin. I have a normal life to lead as well, you know. It has to be at a time when my husband is at a function, otherwise it would be just too difficult for me."

Colin wondered what a normal life would be for this woman. It was irritating in a way. He had never needed anyone before but she was like a drug, the more he had, the more he wanted.

"Friday, you can come Friday. Travis is doing his magic act at the Civic Center."

"In Sheffield?"

"Of course. Be there no later than seven and go to the booking office. I'll arrange a ticket, it will be there waiting for you."

"And later?" he asked, eyebrows raised, though she couldn't see them.

"And later, if you please me, I'll take you to my flat. It needs work, the floor's a disgrace but it's handy. It'll have to do."

At six-fifty on Friday, Colin ran up the steps and claimed his ticket. The room was magnificent, with a small stage and dining tables set out herringbone fashion. Two minutes of searching brought him to the seat reserved for him with a small card on the table. He picked up the card and pocketed it.

By seven-thirty the room was full, and the first course was being served.

Gwen, he discovered, was seated between two rather handsome men a little older than herself. She appeared to be listening to both men; her expression was vivacious and interested. She didn't look at Colin.

Curtains were drawn back from the stage and drinks were served as the preparations for the magic act were made. Faulkner, dressed in a capacious cape of black satin, white kid gloves and a top hat, bowed to the audience. He removed the top hat and placed it on a small table, perhaps a foot square. One by one, the gloves came off and were dropped into the hat.

Faulkner began by asking various couples to think of numbers while he was writing on a series of small slates. When he had half a dozen, he showed each slate in turn with the correct number as it was called out.

His next act required a window, fully glazed, to be brought in by two stage hands and propped up at the front of the stage. Faulkner descended the steps and began by throwing playing cards at it. Each card hit the glass and slid to the bottom. While he was doing this, he told a story about a crow laying a duck's egg and the duck... he stopped and threw the rest of the pack at the window in a single cast. The audience forgot about the story, a single card was lodged in the window, half way through the glass. One half protruding from the back, the other from the front and verified by a member of the audience who simply couldn't pull the card one way or the other.

During the applause, Colin felt a light touch on his shoulder. Gwen had just walked past. He rose to follow her. Her husband's eyes seemed to burn holes in his back as he followed her from the dining room to a deserted ballroom.

Behind velvet drapes across a huge window, Gwen's hands plucked at his shirt and tore it open. She kissed him so sensually that it was difficult to stop himself engaging with her there and then. He felt an overpowering need to show her who was really in charge. *Later,* he thought.

"That's just a foretaste. See me in my car afterwards and if my husband wants to make you a part of his act, you go along with it. He gets his kicks from that, you know how I get mine."

Colin did up his shirt though one button had come off. He re-tied his tie in the dim light and made his way back to the dining room.

He had only just sat down when Faulkner once more approached him. "I'd be obliged if you'd help me with one of my illusions, sir. Would you mind telling all the ladies and gentlemen that we don't know one another."

Colin shook his head. "No, we *certainly* don't know each other." And he felt and looked sufficiently discomforted for everyone to believe it to be true.

"This way," the conjuror led the way to the stage. "Of course, we may both know other people, friends we have in common." They reached the stage and Faulkner, who had been drinking from a pint sized beer glass finished it and put it on the minuscule table. "Do you have a pound coin, sir?"

Colin looked through his change and passed a coin across.

Faulkner took it and held it between his palms for a few seconds before passing it back.

Colin took the coin and immediately dropped it. "Bloody thing's red hot!"

Faulkner moved like a flash of light and caught the pound coin before it reached the floor. He thrust it against the empty glass where it stuck to the surface as smoke poured from the glass.

Colin was still spitting on his fingers and massaging the low-level burn.

"Many things turn out to be too hot to handle, don't they?" Faulkner asked and held the pint glass up above his head. "I'll pass this around so everyone can see the power I have in my hands."

The glass went along one table after another and awed voices exclaimed over the imprint of the Queen's head in the glass.

Faulkner offered the pound coin back to Colin with a wicked smile and whispered, "Don't worry, it won't burn you now though other things belonging to me just might."

Gwen took the Rolls around the city to the street where she had her flat. As they ascended the staircase, she gestured to encompass the whole building. "We own the place, all of it. The second floor is mine and Travis has the third floor, mostly offices and bedrooms though he's got a lot of work to do on it yet."

In the kitchen, she rubbed soap onto his burn. "Clever isn't he? You'll have a nice scar now to show to your friends."

"How does he do that heat thing?"

"You'll have to ask him," she said then asked. "What do you do for a living?"

"I finish buildings, make gardens," he said. "Convert buildings like this one. Would you like me to work on this building?"

"Never mind, that's not what we're here for. I may tell you about that later." She backed him out of the kitchen with a firm grip on his lapels and into the bedroom.

CHAPTER 29

After many attempts at conversation, Asmin had at least found out the name of his minder: Floyd. One or two other snippets had emerged: Floyd had worked for Mad Charlie for fifteen years and was mindlessly loyal.

Looking at his passenger in the rear view mirror, Asmin guessed that Floyd had been about eighteen when he had joined Charlie's organization. Asmin liked to judge other people's qualities and character, it was a game he played although he had no way of knowing how close he came to the truth.

Despite having spent his early years in the Punjab, his most formative time was the first few years in the UK. He had not travelled a great deal but everywhere, he watched, listened and learned.

He had made the intersection with the M62 and was travelling relatively slowly when the call came from Mad Charlie's contacts in Traffic. Sammy's Land Rover had been spotted in St. George's Field parking area in central York.

"Ready to go?" he asked the face in the mirror. "We're only thirty, forty miles away."

Floyd nodded and turned his attention back to his copy of *Postponing Armageddon*. That was something that Asmin wondered about, his minder's addiction to the bizarre world of fantasy. Weren't their everyday lives fantastic enough? It wasn't like they were shopkeepers or office workers.

The Satnav unit turned them off the motorway on to the A65 trunk road and then into the heart of York. Taking slightly longer than the forty-five minutes Asmin had reckoned on, they reached the area and because the Land Rover stood out quite well, they found it in minutes.

"Finding the car's one thing," Asmin grumbled, "finding Leroy's a different matter. Might have dumped it here and taken a train somewhere else."

"Best thing to do," Floyd spoke slowly, as if it was a test, "is to wait here. He will come back eventually."

"We could be here days at that rate."

Floyd patted his pocket. "Charlie will let us know if he don't like it."

"Still going to need food and toilets."

Floyd tapped the window and pointed. Just outside was a sign—PUBLIC TOILETS. "Over there," again he pointed and chose his word carefully, "is a food shop. You can fetch us something to eat while I keep watch. There is no problem, fool-fool."

Asmin scowled and thought, *Fine it's still daytime, but what about later? Don't think we can sleep here.*

"Have you got another book?"

Floyd handed over a dog-eared copy of *Steampunk Magazine* and Asmin leafed through the first few pages with a distasteful expression. "What *is* this?"

"Steampunk. It's funny, try it."

"Anything else?"

Asmin used the washroom and then went to get sandwiches and two cardboard cups of coffee. They spent two hours parked near to the Land Rover and the light was beginning to fade when Asmin's objections suddenly became academic. Not that Asmin noticed, it was Floyd who saw activity. "Hey, we're in business."

"This is quite good." Asmin tore the end flap of a packet of cigars to make a bookmark. "This part is written by a woman, you know."

"I know that. Look over there."

A pretty black woman had opened the doors of the car. They watched as she brought out a couple of plastic shopping bags and carried them across to another car, a silver VW Golf.

Asmin started the engine and followed the Golf out onto the road. Floyd protested. "What you doin' man? We should be watchin' the Land Rover."

Asmin turned briefly to look at Floyd. "This woman's a solid lead. She's taking some stuff to Richards, he's probably hiding out somewhere. Now you can call your boss if you want to but just wait and see what happens first, 'cause I reckon this is the quickest way to find him."

The journey was not long, three minutes at most. The VW pulled up outside a house in Fulford Road. The woman took her bags and carried them through the front door.

Floyd watched the door close after her. "Are you going in after her?"

"Not me, you. Leroy might have told her about me so it's better for you to go. Just say you're an old friend."

"How'm I supposed to know he's there?"

"Leroy asked you to say hello if you were ever in York. If he's not there, she'll maybe give you his address."

Floyd sat and thought over Asmin's suggestion.

"Go on then. What're you waiting for?"

Floyd got out and walked back to the house. He climbed the steps and was about to ring the doorbell when he saw the little rope figure nailed to the door frame. Floyd had been born in Birmingham, but his neighborhood was—multicultural. He knew a voodoo symbol when he saw one.

The decision on whether to stay or go was taken from him. The door opened and he was confronted by the black woman. *Had she seen him approach? Through the curtain?* Floyd shivered.

"What you doin' hanging 'round my doorway with your mouth gawpin' like a milk calf waiting on being fed?" With hardly a pause to draw breath, she continued. "Come on, man. What you want an' where you from?"

Rattled by the verbal onslaught, Floyd babbled away without a sound coming out of his mouth. He wet his lips and started again. "Leroy... Leroy told me to call by, say hello."

It cut him no slack. "Don' you go lyin' to me, *bwoy*. I can *smell* lies. Leroy Richards would do no such thing so what is it you after? Eh? Who sent you?"

Floyd was easily twice the size of the tiny woman at the door yet he'd never felt so frightened of anyone in his entire life. He pulled himself together and pushed his way across the threshold.

"Oh no you don't." An amazingly strong push put him back on the steps. "Who you think you dealin' with? Huh? Some café dancer, some *loosaz*?"

Floyd stuttered. "Ma *mudda*, she warned me about such as you, a... a *mambo*."

Eva sneered. "So little you know, *nah nuh head*. I'm not some priestess you mom hear 'bout. I'm *Kongo*. I call an' the *Angels o' Petro Loa*, they listen me—an' they answer. I ain't no *mambo* neither, they kiss my feet."

Without realizing it, Floyd was slowly backing down the steps.

"I'm Queen Evangeline, I practice the true *Vodou*. Yo wan' a buy spells, you go Professor Alba. I order the spells—now, g'way."

Floyd didn't go away. He stood like an immovable stone. Eva seized hold of a bottle she kept just inside her door. She tilted back her head and poured a great gulp of the contents into her mouth. She pursed her lips and sprayed the fluid over Floyd and muttered half formed words.

The cant was senseless, even to Floyd, who heard the cadence of the Jamaican patois of his youth. But the words—sounds—once *had* held meaning and their power remained. Floyd stood there and shook as though in an epileptic fit. Eva put out her foot and pushed him in the chest until he backed off the last step and she watched him stagger into the road before she closed the door.

Asmin saw all that happened, and understood none of it. He opened the door, ran the ten yards to where Floyd was acting like a twelve-pint drunk and wrestled him back to the car. He drove away, hung a U-turn and drove back to the parking lot.

Floyd was in a trance-like state for four hours, twitching and jumping and seeing all manner of nightmares behind his closed eyelids. The two of them sat there, Floyd hardly conscious; Asmin mystified by the whole thing. Eventually, Floyd fell into a deep sleep.

CHAPTER 30

This morning, I felt unusually satisfied with myself. I had talked Margaret into suggesting to Dad that they go away for a break and—what was more important, Dad had agreed. In fact, he considered it a good idea and was quite touched at Margaret's thoughtfulness. The manager at Forest Homes noted the times and dates and we were all set.

Barbara Patterson practically jumped me as I reached the office door. She was wearing a form-hugging blue dress. "My, you're looking good this morning, Sergeant Patterson."

"Thanks, Boss," she gave me a great smile. "Thought I'd look my best. Anthony asked me out; got a date straight after work tonight."

"Hey, I'm really pleased for you both. That why you collared me so fast today?"

"No. I got a video cassette from the security man at the Seven Bells Conference Center in Rochdale. There was a function there a few weeks ago, one that was on a list I got from Sheffield for out-of-town bashes with our friend Faulkner on the entertainments list. Now... well, see for yourself. You may have to borrow the equipment."

"A VCR? Hmm, they're not *that* out of date. When Joe had moved out of here, before I moved in, he had left a cupboard filled with stuff he didn't want to take with him. "Yes, somewhere in here." I rummaged through the boxes and files and came out with an old TV with a built-in VCR. "Cross your fingers. This is *not* going to be like the last recording you showed me, is it?"

I plugged it into a wall socket without waiting for a reply and, shaking her head, Barbara handed over the cassette. It still worked. It was not a good picture but Faulkner was recognizable from his stage outfit: the top hat and white gloves. Barbara pointed to another man, only just in the shot; he had a dress jacket on and a demonstrably bald head.

"Can we get that enhanced, do you think?" asked Barbara.

"Convert tape to digital format, maybe. But this could be our mystery man. I wonder if that's Mrs. Faulkner there." I rewound the tape and started it again.

"Could be her," Barbara agreed, tapping a long silver nail on the screen some way from the bald man.

As she said, it could have been, but the likeness was not good enough to be sure. I looked again at the man as the picture moved. Something made me think I'd seen the man before but I said nothing beyond, "We'll get some photos made up, if the tech guys *can* sharpen the image up a bit, so much the better."

"Actually, I might give Sheffield a visit and see if anyone recognizes him."

"Do that. In fact, I'll go with you, but I'll follow you in my car."

She looked a question at me.

"I have to be back on the dot tonight."

"More reports to get up to date?"

"Something like that. I know they're important but I've been cooped up in here for days. I think if I'd been put on this earth to fill in paperwork, I'd have been born with a pen up my bum."

She grinned. "See you in the garage."

"Give me five to do a bit of delegation and I'll be with you."

I rang the technology whiz-kids and explained the problems with the tape cassette. As I hoped, they were able to capture the images and improve them while we waited. The results were better than we'd seen on the TV screen; still a little grainy, but greater contrast.

In the garage, Barbara was parked two spaces away from me. I shouted across to her. "Let's try that Rochdale place first."

"You'll be pushing your luck to do that and Sheffield, too—and still get some work done tonight."

"So be it. I'll leave the Sheffield end to you, then."

At Rochdale, we discovered the Seven Bells Center was a mainly daytime venue for business training. It rarely opened its function room in the evenings except for large events. We were directed to a booking clerk, an alert young woman who understood our requirements as soon as we explained our purpose. She was able to print out a list of names, addresses and phone numbers for the part-time personnel who would be called in for evening events and, with a little cajoling, she looked up the Sheffield city function and gave us a list of attendees. "I'm going to have to ask for a signed receipt for this," she said, very seriously. "And please add your rank and identification."

We were happy to comply and even had a quick drink in the bar while we scanned the list hoping that something might strike us as significant. The only item that did was the entry: *Mrs. G. Faulkner and guest* which did not advance our knowledge, one iota.

Some of the staff who had worked at the evening function were there. We showed them the picture we had. Two of them, a waiter and the barman on duty, recognized the face and head of our bald friend, but neither knew his name, which was understandable. "Magician pulled him out of the audience," the barman said. "Maybe he works for him, a plant or some such."

I returned to Leeds.

Scot Meredew, head of "C" squad, came to see me. They had been charged with collecting and collating evidence from the various murder scenes and victims. It was hard, meticulous work, and could tie up men for weeks.

"I acknowledged the grinding work they had put in. "Next time, I'll land 'B' squad with this stuff."

Meredew smiled broadly, an array of teeth that were too even and too white to be real. "It's okay, guv. My sort of work actually—methodical sort of brain, I guess."

"So what has your methodical brain turned up? I take it this isn't a social call?"

"Well, no, it isn't. There's only one new thing cropped up in the last day or so. I got a call from Professor Mandors at Leeds University. You remember the carpet we assume DC Stokes was wrapped in?"

I nodded.

"I may have told you I sent him samples of the animal blood from the carpet—they have much more advanced staining techniques than our path lab— and they've identified the so-called chicken blood as a pigeon's."

I laughed. "A pigeon's. Been having pigeon pie for supper?"

Meredew threw open his hands. "Sounds a bit incongruous and I don't know what it tells us, but there you are."

A thought tickled the back of my mind: *Pigeon... dove... magician?*

I called my home phone number to make sure Dad had left on his trip with Margaret—a two-night stay at the Windermere Hotel. There was no reply which I took as positive evidence that he had gone. While I was in a telephoning mood, I called Connie and her pronounced southern accent was music to my ears."

"Hi. Connie here but not for long."

"Hello, Connie. It's Stewart."

"Why, hello there, Stew. How you doin'?"

"I'm fine, and you?"

"Good. I'm doin' good. Thought you'd forgotten about little ol' me."

"Now, how could I do that? I've been awfully busy the last few days but I'm trying to put that right. How about dinner at my place, tonight. Say about eight?"

She cleared her throat. "Now, would your father be invited?"

I laughed at the joke—hoped it was a joke. "He's away for a couple of days."

"Then I guess the answer's yes. You want me to bring my own bourbon?"

"Only if that's what you prefer. I have gin and scotch, wine..."

"Oh, I'm a sour mash girl through an' through. See you at eight."

I drove home, parked, and walked around to the backyard. A wide expanse of concrete had been laid today out among the fruit trees. I went over and tested the edge to make sure it was reasonably hard. I didn't want Pip leaving any paw prints on the pristine surface.

I let Pip out and put the salmon under a low grill to cook slowly while I prepared lemon cream sauce. There were also sweet potatoes with butter and cinnamon and tiny sugar snap peas. I was so absorbed that I never heard Connie arrive, only Pip's bark as he rushed out of the dog-door made me look up. There was Connie, watching me through the kitchen window.

I drew a deep breath as I crossed to let her in as "too-late" thoughts flooded into my mind. Was this the right thing to do? Was it real attraction or just lust? Pip shot back through his little door before I got the main door unlatched.

Briefly, I fussed over the dog and then stood up to look at Connie properly. "Wow."

She was wearing a knitted dress that varied from a light plum through damson to black at the hem. "Wow, Connie. You look amazing."

"Takes your breath away?" she sort of sang from the song.

"Damn right."

"Can you turn the food down a little? Kinda like to work up an appetite first. Maybe you would too?"

I turned off the stove and let her lead me upstairs and into the bedroom. We fitted together like two halves of one of those agate bookends. All ideas my mind may have been holding—like her hiding a knife under the pillows because of her brother Robert—were dispelled that night.

We sat back against propped up pillows and as Connie enjoyed a bourbon I summoned up the courage to tell her what had been on my mind. I began, "Connie my dear, I'd like to be truthful with you. I have had my doubts as to why you wanted this relationship, especially as I assume you think I killed your brother."

Damn, I sounded like a stuffy old professor, even to me.

Connie smiled devilishly. "Have you never heard of instant attraction?"

"I have, of course I have, but how could you like me at all if...?"

"Well I..."

I cut her short. "Let me tell you this, then you can say what you wish; I didn't kill him. A sheriff from Florida shot at him, he fell into a fast moving underground stream and disappeared. It was my duty to apprehend him because he had killed people but I never harmed him."

Connie reached across and held me. "I have to admit that before we met I had this half-baked idea of gettin' back at you, some kinda half-assed revenge.

Just how I was goin' to do that I don't know because it's not in me to hurt anyone. But you treated me with the utmost respect, you were a gentleman, and that quickly changed my mind. That and I had a long phone chat with Sheriff John Merrick in Sebring the day after I collected those suitcases from you. He told me he was entirely responsible for what happened to Robert. So shut up and give me some more of that lovin'."

I gave a relieved sigh and reached for her.

Some months had passed since—as Colin preferred to think of them—the last "incident" had taken place. He assumed that this was because of his relationship with Gwen Faulkner. She had steadied him down, poured oil on the troubled waters of his psyche. During the time he had known Gwen, Colin had expanded his business interests by taking over an ailing floor and tiling firm complete with six employees and a book full of orders. The firm had been run by a working boss of nearly seventy whose knees had given out on him, the result of years of kneeling on cold concrete.

His own foreman, Nick Grandly, was bright enough to listen to new ideas and to implement them if they made sense. He had worked out an idea to give a metallic sheen to the garden ornaments they made by treating the rubber molds they used with a low-temperature metallic powder in the release wax.

Colin had just finished a contract with Gwen Faulkner, remodeling the office block in Sheffield. While Mick and his hands had been busy laying floors there, Colin had been viewing apartments in Chesterfield, a town only a half-hour away from Sheffield.

He chose one and settled in, moved his furniture from Preston and got to know the neighborhood. The location pleased him for many reasons. The proximity to Gwen was fantastic, but Chesterfield and Sheffield had active branches of the Association of Conjurors where members could both teach and be taught. Colin's interest had been sparked off by Travis Faulkner's stage act and he had built his own ideas of what could be done with conjuring skills. He wanted to put them into practice, to become a magician in his own right.

Colin had tackled everything which had caught his interest with a considerable degree of success. There were 'how-to' books which he studied before joining both branches and mastered the three card trick, the rabbit from a hat deception and the disappearing bird illusion, all rather basic. The very first night, he had bought a magic clock from a retiring magician and spent hours examining the hidden compartments and the illusions that could be performed with it.

There was an old man who seemed to live at the Chesterfield branch, a former strip club still complete with stage. He always sat close to the bar, drinks in hand, and regaled anyone prepared to listen with tales of his life on the magic circuit.

Colin sat next to him, the old man winked and introduced himself: "Jack, stage name was *Guacamole, the Iti' Wizard*. Short for Italian, tha' knows? Can you believe it? Me, as Yorkshire as they come."

"He bought that clock of Larry's," someone said.

Jack looked at his glass, which had only a few drops in the bottom. "Could tell you about Larry if'n I had summat to wet me whistle."

Knowing he had been hoodwinked, Colin bought Jack a pint of strong cider. He didn't tell him he knew that guacamole was Mexican. Those around the pair leaned forward and pricked up their ears.

"Used to tour with the Great Lorenzo or as we knew him, Larry the Dip. Had a marvelous act, he would invite a mark to join him, he could remove his watch, his wallet and his belt or braces before he'd reached the stage, all with what seemed like little touches to guide him up the steps. 'Course, the audience could see all this happening, they'd watch spellbound as his pants fell around his ankles while Larry waved the belt or what-not over the feller's head. He'd ask the mark for the time or for a fiver to do some trick with, and they'd find the watch or the wallet gone."

Jack sank a quarter of his glass. "Brilliant. Seen him pull a guy's shirt off without taking his jacket off. Bloody brilliant."

"What happened to him?"

"Seven year stretch in Brixham was what happened to Larry. Grand larceny, for the umpteenth time."

"What did he do that for?" Colin asked. "There was no need to thieve if he was that good."

"You're right, of course. Oh, he was good, never ever got caught in the act. Done for possession, his last mark was a policeman wearing a shit-load of bling. A set-up. There was a team watching with a slow-motion camera, only way to catch him."

"Still doesn't explain why."

"Just couldn't stop hisself. It was a game."

Colin nodded. "Funny you should say that. I'm kind of interested in getting people to think they're seeing one thing while really, something else is happening."

"That's the start of most magic, innit? There's only two ways you can do it: speed or props. Watch this." Jack opened a hand to fan a pack of cards that had not been there a moment before. Closing the pack, he put it face down and turned the top card face up and drew Colin's attention to it. Using his right hand, Jack took a red handkerchief to wipe the cider froth off his lips.

Colin watched both movements and then looked back at the pack to see that the face-up card had gone. "Damn me, I was watching that card, how did you do it?"

"You wasn't watching close enough. Soon as I lifted the hanky, your eyes moved. Split second, it's all it takes, and practice of course, lots of practice. Most magicians can do something similar, is it card tricks you want to go for?"

"I'd sooner know about escaping from a locked room."

Jack grinned again and looked pointedly into his glass. Colin obliged.

"Classic. Comes under props. Nothing terribly clever, takes a deal of thought and careful planning or construction. You've got to know about it and your audience don't. That's it."

"No sleight of hand?"

"Nah. Just like the magic box—there's a girl in a box. The box is closed and locked, the box is opened and she's disappeared. Years ago, she'd reappear in the same box, nowadays, she might reappear in the audience. The magician knows what happens, the girl does, the stage hands do, but not the audience."

"Ingenuity, not years of practice?"

"The practice is in misdirecting the watchers."

Colin bought innumerable drinks over a month of evenings and learned all about magic boxes, sliding partitions, false sides, quick release catches and floating boxes above angled mirrors.

When it came time to meet up with Gwen at another of her husband's performances, Colin was, of course, the dupe.

This time, Faulkner came to stand behind him while he sat and watched the table in front of him.

He could see Faulkner's hands making passes to either side and gradually he grew aware of birds flying around his head, the breeze of their passing cold on his scalp. A white blob appeared on his jacket cuff, another further up his arm, then more all over his jacket.

Faulkner leaned forward. "I'm going to have you, son. Going to shit all over you like these birds." A bird alighted on his shoulder, another on the far side and bird lime slid down his lapels. "Enjoy my wife's company do you? Not for much longer…"

Back at the flat, he grumbled to Gwen, "I'm not putting up with this. He's getting to be beyond a joke. Look at this bloody suit. It's ruined, bloody ruined."

"Well, lover," she laughed at him and stripped his jacket off, "it's all part of the show. You have me, my husband has you and I won't have it any other way. Now shut up complaining and get those clothes off. I think I might beat you tonight, Ever been beaten?"

Not since the orphanage… Christ! Where had that thought, that memory, come from?

He let her drag his clothes off, but his mind was busy; his actions were automatic. He had thought himself to be in control but he wasn't. His perceptions moved through ninety degrees, he saw things quite differently. This woman was using him… he was just meat… and that was not how it worked in Colin's world. He needed to change some things, assert himself maybe?

Later, after the caning, while they were relaxing as far as he was able to, he asked: "Suppose I asked you to come away with me. Hmm? A new city? A new place and a new life? I could give you more than he gives you. Plenty of time for sex, just think about it."

"Sex? You think this is just about sex? Come on. I could go to any city in the country and get sex, any kind of sex I want." She pushed herself up, leaning on an elbow and began pulling his chest hairs one by one. "This is a game I play with my husband. He watches me go off to have sex with other men and he doesn't complain. Why would he? He knows I'm never going to leave him. I thought you knew that too."

Colin laid back and nodded. "Maybe you should think about leaving? Maybe it's time for *me* to find someone else, do you think?" Colin was quite serious.

She laughed, stood up and got herself a drink from the sideboard, brandishing the glass, spilling as much as she drank.

A splash hit Colin's face, stinging him in the eye. "Goddamn, it woman! That hurts."

"I like hurting men. I can do what I like with them. And remember this, lover, there'll always be another along in a minute. Like city buses, an inexhaustible supply."

It had been a long time, months, since he'd last lost it. He watched Gwen staggering around the room, now she had the bottle and was splashing the contents across the bed. It might not have been much but it was enough, he snapped. He got up and pushed the door open to the adjoining room.

"That's it then?" she called. "All done?"

Colin ignored her and changed into overalls and found the jar of Vaseline: they were never far away. He took the plastic bag out of the waste basket under the dressing table and shook the pillow out of its case onto the bed.

Gwen was well on the way to falling-down drunk when he returned. She looked at Colin and sniggered before collapsing back into a sofa. "Very sexy, a railroad navvy? Come as…" She thought the phrase was absolutely hilarious.

Colin walked behind her, brought the cotton case down over her head and followed immediately with the plastic bag, grabbing hold of her hair as she tried to scream. He pulled her head back across the back of the settee and counted—*five, six, seven*—and then waited to be certain.

As always, a nice neat job, not exactly a "chosen one" but still satisfying. He found the keys in her handbag and carried her upstairs to the next floor and laid her out on her husband's desk. She was the first in a while he hadn't specifically targeted to kill. But damn, she had gotten annoying. And—yes—it gave him an opportunity to try out a little conjuring of his own.

Colin went downstairs and mixed a bucket of precisely measured floor sealant. Back upstairs again, he locked the office door, slid the interior bolt across and then poured the bucket's contents near the small trap door in the floor. Moments later, he left quickly by the secret exit.

Finally, he changed back into the bird-lime stained clothes and made a big parcel of overalls, pillow cases, and bed sheets from the lower floor. Gwen had a cleaning cupboard in the kitchen which included a vacuum cleaner. Colin used it to clean everywhere he had been, changed the dust bag, and put the used bag into his parcel. He searched her bedroom drawers and removed DVD's and a rather heavy revolver he hadn't known she had, placing them in the same plastic bag he had used to kill her. Finally, he wiped everywhere that a hand could reach with bleach and dropped the almost empty bleach bottle, the bag and the cleaning cloths in with the soiled linen.

Colin couldn't help laughing as he left the building with the bundle under his arm. *Who'll have the last laugh now, El Supremo?* The timing was weird. No sooner had he got behind the wheel of the Rolls Royce when his cell phone rang. He pulled over and lifted the phone. "Enjoy it while it lasts, sonny." It was Faulkner's voice. "I know your every move, everything about you, even where you live."

"Actually," Colin said, his voice deliberately low, "you don't."

Colin left the Rolls at the back of the club, cleaned the wheel, gear lever, door handles, transferred the bundle from the flat to his trunk, locked up, and dropped the keys into a drain filled with muddy water.

He motored back to Chesterfield in his own car and packed everything up in the apartment. He cleaned up thoroughly and put all of his possessions and clothes into the car. Aware that he couldn't fool a forensic examination if it came to it, he left a fictitious forwarding address in Spain on a slip of paper on the counter and put the keys on top—like magic acts, a little misdirection never hurt.

Goodbye Chesterfield, goodbye Faulkner, goodbye Colin Petty, he thought.

The following morning, from a payphone in Sheffield's main post office, he rang the police. He suggested that they look at Faulkner's office.

CHAPTER 31

I was awakened by the sound of a trailer vehicle trying to back up the driveway. The driver went up and down through the gearbox like a yo-yo before he had the thing off the quite narrow road and into my gateway. At least, the double gates meant we didn't need to knock the garden wall down.

The racket didn't wake Connie up. I got up showered, dressed and left a small breakfast: muesli in a bowl, fresh fruit on a plate and a loaf of bread next to the toaster with bread knife, coffee machine primed to go and a short note—*Connie, enjoy your breakfast and slam the door when you leave. I'll call when you've had time to get home. That was a fabulous evening, thank you.*

A nicer note than the one on my desk which told me to see Joe Flowers as soon as I got in. I lost no time getting to his office.

"You wanted to see me, Joe?"

"Ah, yes. Morning Stewart." He pointed to a chair. "Bring that across and come around to this side of the desk."

Not the sort of tête-à-tête I expected.

"We've got a response out of the Met, not from the enlisted boys but from the top brass. This is a Skype message from the Assistant Commissioner and if I record it—as I have—I have to delete it as soon as I've finished with it. Clear?"

I nodded. "Pretty clear."

The man on the screen was resplendent in a uniform that must have come straight from the dry-cleaners and all the chrome badges of rank and other doo-dahs these types festoon themselves with. A dress hat perched close to his left elbow.

"The Commissioner has asked me to look into your query regarding a Gabriel Henderson. This is what we know.

"Henderson came to London around ten years ago and the reason the Inspector your man spoke to…"

"That's you," Flowers interjected quickly.

"…was reluctant to provide you with information was because there are unclosed murder cases—his—that Henderson is linked to."

The Assistant Commissioner lifted a cut glass tumbler and took a long swallow.

"Henderson was pimping in Norwood but had ideas of improving himself by moving into Soho. He was considered an upstart and forcefully discouraged. Henderson was not amused, he got hold of an old car and ran down the man he blamed. The man, the club owner, was rammed through a plate glass window. I'm telling you this," he took another drink of water, or whatever it was and went on, "…telling you this because you need to know how violent this man is, he was in his teens when this incident occurred.

"He's been traced to Stamford in Rutland, to a group of itinerant workers in Somerset and to Southern Ireland- though the Garda have no record of him except a possible incident in a Dublin pub. He has left a trail of death and injury behind him. It's all we know. He's used the names Ali Malek, Art Lemic, and Harpal Kumar—that one is a probable, from the Irish Republic "

The Assistant Commissioner combed his fingers through his rather elegant silver hair. "I'm sorry, there's no more because we'd very much like to close the book on his crimes in the capital."

Joe Flowers closed the file. "Does it help you?"

"Not really, I don't think. It's a pity they didn't have a picture, that might help quite a…"

"Aha, forgot to mention…" He looked for an email, found it and clicked on the attachment. "This came with the Skype notification. "It's a bit grainy but may be of some use."

I saw a shot of a dark-haired young man in a dimly lit passage. It might have been identifiable by someone who actually knew the person.

"It was on the security video at the club where he supposedly killed the owner. It's old, obviously, but it's all we've got."

"Have you got a memory stick handy to put it on, Joe? I've got an idea."

"I'll just forward this to you. Bet it beats you back to your office." Joe Flowers was in his easygoing mode.

"Barbara? Stewart here, where are you?" I called her as soon as I got back to my office.

"On the M1. Just passed the M62 interchange." She didn't ask why I wanted to know which pleased me.

"Put your foot down, sweetie. I want you here, I've just had an idea."

"Sounds fun."

I got a cup of coffee by way of a brain boost and marched along to the incident room. There were, maybe, seven officers there. "Anyone know where the rest of the crowd is?"

"Around, most of them." Sergeant Levy looked at his watch. "Probably getting bacon sandwiches from the canteen."

"Can someone do me a favor? Go and roust them, get them back here. Been a development and I have an idea I'd like to pitch."

Someone went. I perched on the corner of Levy's desk and sipped my coffee. Minutes later, I had eleven of my sixteen guys. Twelve, because Barbara came in at that moment. I handed out the prints I'd made on my computer.

"I've just sent the original of this picture down to our pet geeks and asked them to run it through their ageing software, see what he might look like now. Also, I've suggested they try putting glasses on him, a beard, different hair colorings, no hair, any variations they can think of. This," I looked around, "could be the face of our killer."

There was a long silence, then a range of imaginative expletives. Encouraged, I hit them with my follow-up.

"Now this changes everything. This is the face of Gabriel—Gabe— Henderson and almost certainly of William—Billy—Jarvis because we think they were one and the same person."

"Jarvis!" Barbara blurted out. She and her team had been working with the blood samples, perhaps she already suspected that Henderson and Jarvis were the same person.

I nodded. "We also believe he's used several aliases over the years." I wrote those that the Met had given us on the wall.

Archie our tech wizard came in and thrust a handful of prints at me. "I used FARS—Facial Aging and Recognition Software—to get these, Inspector." He pushed his glasses up to the bridge of his nose and scratched at the leather patches on his jacket elbows. "They're rough but we'll refine them over the next hour or two."

"That's good, Archie. Just give me a moment." I shuffled through the prints, young, older, dark, fair, red hair, bald, like a pack of cards and stopped. I went back one shot, the bald one, and peered closer. I knew the face but I could not recall from where. Where, where, where? And then it hit me like a punch in the stomach: he'd been standing on the pavement when I'd met DC Stokes with Shelly. He'd been standing next to Ned when we first went to Sheffield, the bald guy.

I thumped Archie on the back, "That's one very clever bit of software, Archie. This is the guy." I turned around, looking. Sergeant Beech, get Archie to shoot you an electronic copy of this and send it off to Faulkner, see if he can identify him."

Faulkner was in for a double surprise because we had never told him we knew where he was.

"Barbara—sorry, Sergeant Patterson, you've seen that other shot we have of a bald feller—is this the same one?"

When she confirmed it, as I was sure she would, I informed them all that Barbara would be coordinating this phase of the operation.

I felt a rather welcome sense of satisfaction as I motored out to my house that evening. I pulled the car up on to the hard standing part of the drive and walked through to the backyard. The huge truck had left big wheel ruts in the compacted surface but I wasn't too upset, especially when I saw the result of all the planning and not a little subterfuge.

"Bloody marvelous," I said to the night air and as Pip heard my voice, he bulleted though his dog flap and ran circles around my feet.

Inside, on the counter, there was a note from Connie. "Enjoyed last night, too. Next time I'll cook, southern style."

CHAPTER 32

Asmin called Mad Charlie after he'd found the number on Floyd's cell. "Found the car where it was supposed to be and kept watch on it. An attractive black lady took some stuff out of it and we followed her home."

Charlie asked if they had seen Leroy.

"No. But your boy Floyd went to this woman's door and she spat a stream of something into his face, smelled like rum when I got him back in the car but he's been in like a trance ever since. Can't get any sense or anything out of him."

Asmin listened.

"As a matter of fact, I did slap his face a time or two. Nothing. Should I take him to hospital?"

Charlie was silent for some time. "Sounds like Voodoo to me. Keep Floyd quiet, cover him up—lay him out on the back seat—and cover him up. Floyd was a believer in this stuff, I've seen it before. He'll be all right in a day or so but stay with him, I'm on my way."

"You're coming?"

"Bet your ass. Where you at?"

They were all over. He had just returned from buying some smokes when he saw them standing in Goodramgate, peering around the corner into King's Square. They were wearing body armor and tooled up like they meant business—and Leroy knew instinctively they had come for him. He turned back on his tracks and entered the first snickelway he came to and at once he felt at home. It took ten minutes to navigate his way to his tiny back entrance but he was elated. Once he had his money it didn't matter. He could soon find another place.

At the last corner he paused and pretended to be lighting up a smoke while he looked around; at first he thought it was all clear until some sixth sense made him look up, there were various buildings overlooking the grassed area leading to his narrow rear entry. From one of these, and that was all it needed, a police peaked cap was pointing across to his home.

They were everywhere. Leroy had no idea who had told them, or how they could have found out about his back entrance, but they had.

He made tracks back to the main street and allowed himself to be swept along in the tide of humanity, a feature of York in the tourist season. He stopped in the King's Head for a quick short to calm his nerves and started with surprise when he saw the face of an old acquaintance staring down at him from the TV over the bar. A subtitle read "Baldielocks sought for Lancs/Yorks murders." *Billie Jarvis* he thought, *always reckoned you were funky weird*. He left the pub and had reached the banks of the River Ouse when his cell rang.

It was Eva calling to tell him about Floyd's visitation. "I went to your car, Leroy, to get your bags like you ask' me. They must have taken me for a fool, I saw them watchin' me, a black guy and a big man with a scarf around his head. They followed me home so I cast a spell on the black boy. It'll keep him away for a time then he'll be too scared to come back but what about the other? What if there are more of them?"

Leroy thought long and hard. What with the police all around his own pad and now this, what on earth had happened? For the first time in a long time he could feel imaginary handcuffs gripping and squeezing his skin. He didn't want to admit it but it sounded as though Sammy had given out some information. Maybe they had cut him up, maybe cut off his supply of fried chicken. Maybe six of Charlie's boys had jumped up and down on his stomach… though Sammy didn't know where he'd gone; Sammy knew about the car, that was all.

Charlie must have far-reaching contacts, maybe just the traffic police, maybe higher than that.

For the first time since he'd broken out of that kindergarten jail, Leroy felt vulnerable. For once, he was not on top of the situation.

"What do you think we should do, Sugar?"

And that was an admission of the way he felt, no mistake, thought Evangeline.

"Well, for a start, I'm goin' to pack ma things. I can drop a load of stuff at a friend's along from here and then I'm coming to you. Nobody knows of that place. We get some bottles of wine in an' we sit it out. They're goin' to get fed up in a week or so."

Leroy grimaced. "Can't do that, tell you all about it later. Give me an hour or so and I'm coming for you, better pack a bag and get the car warmed up."

But still Leroy tried to think of other ways out of his predicament. Rather like a smoker who imagines he can give up the habit, Leroy's need for socializing, to be continually in the limelight and on the move meant there were other things to do first.

He paid a lightning visit to a sports shop for a hunting knife, that made him feel a whole lot safer and then an hour in the Swan for a few more; just long enough for him to chill. The pub was in Goodramgate and from there into

Hornpot Lane, across Low Petergate and Mad Alice Lane… through and up and along the maze of lanes and snickelways he had grown used to… to stand in the parking lot where he'd left his Land Rover.

Leroy's eyes popped when he spied Asmin propped up, asleep, behind the wheel of a Ford Galaxy only two parking spaces away from his own car. In a flash he knew; the big Sikh had changed sides. He didn't blame him, he'd gotten out while Asmin and Mad Charlie were hammering the hell out of each other. No doubt Asmin felt like he'd been hung out to dry. Briefly, he thought about killing his erstwhile driver and fingered the brand new knife and then put the idea from his mind, cold-blooded hands-on killing was not something he could manage. It was not the kind of guy he was.

He was still pondering his next move five minutes later when several cars, fender to fender, sped into St. George's Field and bracketed the Galaxy front and back and side to side.

Leroy watched with open-mouthed disbelief as Asmin was pulled out of the front seat and frog-marched to the window of a big Bentley. Harsh words must have been spoken from behind the smoked-glass windows, angry words punctuated with short, hard punches from those who held Asmin. There was a glint of metal which Leroy took to be a gun; he shrank into the background as the altercation continued.

There was one number on Leroy Richards's cell that he never thought he would ever use, that of the Northern Regional Crime Squad. He thumbed the icon.

"Northern Regional Crime." The voice was young, female and definitely Yorkshire.

"Can you connect me with Inspector Stewart White, please?"

"Who's calling please?"

"I'm his old friend Leroy Richards and believe me, he will want to speak to me."

"One moment, please, sir." She was back on the line in considerably less than one moment, sounding very apologetic. "I'm sorry, sir, Inspector White is not in at the moment. Will another officer be able to help you?"

"Can you tell me his cell number?"

"We're unable to give those numbers out."

Leroy looked across the parking area to where Mad Charlie's hard boys were forcing Asmin into one of the cars.

"Can you get a message to the most senior officer there? Tell them that Mad Charlie Morgan is in York threatening to kill people. If they don't know the name, tell them to check with the Birmingham Police. He's heading for Fulford Road, number 142."

He thumbed the phone off and started sprinting toward Eva's house.

"Ugh!" Asmin buckled from a vicious blow to the kidneys and stayed down, huddled on the ground. They bundled him into the passenger side with his head pressed against the window by the cold muzzle of a handgun. "Where to?"

"Where to what?" he asked, his lips leaving a blood stain on the glass.

"The black woman, idiot. Where she lives, show us."

Asmin's immediate thought was to direct them to the city center where they might get themselves lost but that would only hasten his own demise. He complied, there was no other option. The powerful car surged forward toward the exit and he directed them toward the Fulford Road with the flotilla of cars trailing behind them.

It was only minutes away and on the opposite side of the road so Asmin had no direct view of Eva's home. He slowed the driver down when he judged they had come far enough and pointed across the road. Since Asmin still had his face squashed against the window glass, it was some seconds before he was able to sit up and point uncertainly across the road where, to his great surprise, Leroy was pulling the black girl down the steps.

He acted without thought, leaning across the seats and wrenching the steering wheel around to send the car careering into oncoming traffic, the driver stamped on the brake and Asmin almost plunged into the empty passenger seat.

As they broadsided Eva's car, which virtually fell apart, Asmin reached for the driver's door catch and got it open. The driver was hanging out of the car while the man in the back with the gun was climbing out of the floor space between the front and backseats.

A click of the fastener and the seat belt came free, the driver sprawled out into the road. Asmin clambered across, floored the throttle which brought the door swinging back and screeched off down the suburban road.

"You're dead, you effing rag head."

"And so are you," grunted Asmin, flinging the car from side to side. He did a U-turn, braking so savagely that one of Mad Charlie's pursuit cars crashed into the rear as they skidded and turned 180 degrees before accelerating back the other way.

Asmin slid to a halt where Leroy and Eva were watching the car-rodeo. He heaved himself around and snapped the other's gun down across the back of the seat, breaking both bones in the gunman's forearm.

Leroy reacted quickly, wrenched the back door open, dragged the screaming man out and pushed Eva inside before getting in himself. "Go."

Asmin went.

Bullets streamed after them, clipping the bodywork and shattering a side window. Oblivious to the hail of lead, Asmin gunned the motor and deliberately drove along on the wrong side of the road as police sirens filled the air and squad cars strobed red and blue ahead of them. One turned out to block the lane but Asmin simply continued on the wrong side of the road, mounted the sidewalk and drove past.

The fast-thinking police officer who had blocked his way was now effectively blocking his fellow squad cars as two attempted to reverse and follow.

The several other squad cars, braked and blocked Charlie's army. Armed police were scrambling all over the place as a reporter from the local paper began taking pictures for a late edition.

Asmin re-crossed the river. "Where does this go?" he asked.

"Hang a right around this roundabout," Eva shouted. "…. and… next exit."

She gazed ahead. "Now, right here." They took Hull road like an express train until it split into a two lane highway. "Now right again and you can slow down and pretend we're a nice family just going back from the shops. Phew!"

Asmin did as she suggested, and drove for fifteen minutes. "Does this go anywhere special?"

"I don' want to get on a busy road just now. Take any of these side streets and park up. I'll call a friend and see if we can get a hidey-hole. He's got holiday cottages he lets out, maybe has one this side of the river."

CHAPTER 33

Confirmation came back from Faulkner that the picture the technical bods had cooked up was the bald guy his wife had been having a fling with. Faulkner didn't comment on the fact that we knew his location. There was also a note on my desk that raised my eyebrows; it said Leroy Richardson had called from York. I assumed they meant Richards. I'd been pretty tired the night before and hadn't listened to or watched any news; didn't hear a thing until I flicked on the car radio: a full-fledged gun battle had been fought in the streets of York late the previous afternoon, I did fleetingly wonder if there was a connection with Richards. I trudged along to the incident room and got a bit of a scowl from Sergeant Patterson which told me she was snowed under. I crossed to Alec Bells' desk. "Got a paper, Alec?"

He obliged and I looked at the front page story of York's historic armed skirmish. The battle had been between the police, of course, and a gang run by a Charles Morgan. Two of them and Morgan himself had been injured, they were being treated, under guard, in York General Hospital.

"Hell's bells." The name had only just filtered through my brain. Charles Morgan was Mad Charlie, from Birmingham and—wasn't he connected with…

Damn but my brain was sleepy that morning. The note about Leroy Richards had mentioned Mad Charlie which made the business mine. I grinned and put the paper down. Leroy was definitely connected with the murder and mayhem which made a refreshing change but, reluctantly, I decided the Faulkner thing had to come first.

"Alec, are you up for a ride out this morning?"

"Me? I'm not the one that gets to go out."

"Do you want to or not? There are plenty of others who'd jump at the chance."

"Did ah say ah didn't want tae?" The Scots brogue was suddenly strong.

I grinned. "Come on then." We buckled in, I switched on, waited for the computer to baby me through the oil check and so on.

"Where are we going, then, guv?"

"Sheffield. I want to put that analytical mind of yours to work on a real crime scene for a change. Any objections?" Alec shook his head as we emerged from the parking garage and the door folded down behind us. The next forty miles passed without comment apart from an almost whispered rendition of *Scotland the Brave.*

I drew up outside the building, still with its black and yellow tape seals. "This is the Faulkner place," he said as we got out. Since it wasn't a question, I didn't reply, just flashed my ID card at the uniformed officer standing outside.

He saluted and handed me a set of brand new keys from his pocket. "The chief says to keep them as long as you like. They open all the doors on the top three floors and the entrances down here, on the ground floor, sir."

"Thanks, that's fine officer. I'll contact your chief later and thank him. Oh—this is Sergeant Bell, like me, he's from Regional Crime squad in Leeds. We'll probably be here for a while. There's no point in your hanging around unless you have to. Why not grab a coffee? We'll be here at least an hour."

I initially headed for the second floor because I still had a clear mental image of the murder scene up on the third. The second floor had not been cleared out.

We wandered around a bit. It was a woman's boudoir, something out of nineteenth century literature maybe: red velvet curtains, bright pink and red regency striped wallpaper, a four-poster bed, but no bed linen or night wear. A sort of cloying scent clung to everything, even the atmosphere was redolent with the perfume.

"Don't think we need to guess at what went on here, Alec."

Alec was looking in the en-suite bathroom. He turned and shook his head. "There's enough perfume in here to float a battleship. The cost of this stuff would keep my old lady in clothes for years. I buy her a nice perfume every year, her favorite is this one, Chanel No. 5." He picked up a square bottle with a lozenge-shaped top. "Seventy-five pounds for a quarter-ounce. And this one's Givenchy, and that's only two…oh… Pi by Givenchy, says it's for men."

"Expect she wanted her men to smell good too. Stinks of opulence, doesn't it? And there's something else… what else strikes you, Alec?"

The Scot came back into the main room and breathed in a lungful of atmosphere. "Hmm. Seems to me, maybe what you mean, smells sort of unused, as though there hasn't been a cleaner through here for weeks."

I nodded. "Like someone came here occasionally and never opened a window to let the breeze blow through."

"I'm minded of a holiday I had with my mum and dad, years ago in Ayr. A holiday cottage that'd been closed all winter. It's the same smell we had there the first day—if you discount the perfume."

I sighed. "Terrible waste, isn't it? I'd expected something simpler than this but we can't choose what we want. Alec, I'm putting you in charge of a thorough inspection, fingerprints, anything in the water traps under the bath and basin…"

"It's a shower, boss."

"Shower, then. Vacuum clean the place and see what you pick up. Come down and start in the morning, box up everything that's not nailed down once the finger printing's done. Find me something, Alec."

"Right." Alec had been pacing around the floor as I spoke and now he pointed to an upper corner of the bedroom. "Wonder where that goes, guv." The building was quite old, the ceiling around nine feet high. He had noticed a trapdoor— what looked like a loft entrance except that there were another two floors above; not a loft space.

"Hmm. See if you can find a ladder, will you?"

Alec left and I struck lucky: I found a long pair of step ladders in a hall cupboard along with an ironing board still in its plastic covering and a box of tools, cleaning chemicals and a bag of dusters, none of which had ever been opened. I propped the ladder in the corner and climbed up. As I got up there, I saw that whereas a trapdoor to a loft is normally fitted to push up into the space above, this one had hinges and a bolt and was made to fold down. I withdrew the bolt expecting the cover to fall but that wasn't the case, it remained firmly shut.

Alec came back in. "Alec. In the cupboard in the hall where the steps came from, there's a box of tools. See if there's a good hefty screwdriver there, maybe a hammer, wanna see if I can release this thing."

A minute later he came back with an ugly looking screwdriver that might do the job. He tossed it up to me and I began to work it into the crevice at the side of the trap. I turned it and levered it and was eventually rewarded with some movement. A little more persistence and a large piece of wood fell off the edge. Now that I had a space large enough to get my fingers into I began to pull until the trapdoor opened suddenly and I was forced to skip down the ladder to avoid a fall.

Looking up, we saw a brownish colored surface apparently flush with the door frame. Alec shook his head. "No space there for anything."

"You're right," I agreed climbing up again. There were two wires, thin, light enough to be loud-speaker connections. Nothing ventured, nothing gained: I used the screwdriver and hammer to break through the surface above. I made a small hole and, removing the screwdriver I had used as a chisel, I put an eye close to the gap. What I could see was a plaster ceiling rose, a Victorian design and in its center a five bulb light fitting. I backed down with a big grin on my face.

"Well guv? What have you found?"

"I think we've found the way the rabbit jumps back into the top hat. Let's go up to the next floor. Oh, and by the way, there are two wires in that little recess. I want to know where they go to."

"You'll be wanting to know the secrets of the universe next, boss."

"No, this'll do me for now." I stood in the room where Gwen Faulkner's body had been found, oriented myself, and walked across to the corner above the trapdoor down below. There was a hole in the floor, no bigger than my thumb and the piece of flooring I had knocked through.

"Have a look here, Alec. I thought the whole floor was just polished linoleum when I came here before. I thought the skirting board had been fitted over the top of the lino so I never thought of fetching it up. Neither did SOCO, of course."

"Well, it certainly looks that way."

I passed him the lump of flooring I had knocked through. "We'll have to get it to the lab but I think that's hardened resin. You can use it to make all sorts of things—chess pieces, wall plaques and so on, even seen it used for garden ornaments. In a place like this, you could pour it on and it would fill every little nook and cranny and make a real smooth surface."

"And you think…"

"I think Baldielocks went through and poured resin all over to hide the trapdoor."

"Who?"

"The bald-headed guy we're hunting for. He came into this room with the murdered woman's body. There was probably a chair in this corner, something to hide the unevenness, and then he left through here after he'd bolted the door over there."

"Sounds complicated."

"Not really. He mixed the resin up, he must have calculated exactly how much he needed, I'm sure he's clever enough to have done that, poured it out and closed the trap door quickly enough that it didn't drip through."

"He would have to have been fast, though."

"Damn right. I reckon he could have done some practice runs first."

"Looks like you're right after all, guv. You have found the secret of the universe."

I clapped him lightly on the shoulder, glad that I'd brought him with me, it would cement the bond that had sometimes seemed a little shaky over the months I'd known him. "We'll be grandmasters in a month or two. We could join the Magic Circle."

———————

I reached home at least an hour before Dad was due and went around the back to examine the work I had had done. *I* was pleased, I hoped Dad would be too. Margaret brought him home at precisely six o'clock, just a she had promised. I gave her a hug and said thank you.

"He's been as good as gold, bless him."

"You had a good time, both of you?"

"We had a wonderful time, didn't we, Ted? All that paddling about in mineral water and herbal body massage with those scented oils, made him feel like a new man. And yes, Stewart, I enjoyed it all too. Thank *you*."

Dad had been getting his case out of the trunk of Margaret's car but I think his ears had been flapping. "Well, since you're both feeling in a good mood, come around the back and see this."

I led them around to the back. Margaret's smile grew wider; so did Dad's eyes.

"What... is it?" he asked although it was obvious. "Is that for me?"

"Absolutely, Dad. It was faster having this put up than going through planning permission and this, that and the other for an extension."

The builders had laid a paved pathway beneath the cherry trees which bore masses of red fruit at the moment. I gave him the keys and a gentle shove.

Inside, the smell of fresh paint greeted us. The fitted kitchen, the modern bathroom with a shaver point, the soft-feel vinyl floor, everywhere got his rapt attention and in the lounge area was *my own* favorite recliner chair. Mind you, I did get myself a brand new one for the house.

I could see the start of tears in his eyes so I turned away and spoke to Margaret. "Marvelous what a few men who know what they're doing can manage in two days, isn't it?"

Dad was too filled up with emotion to say anything but the hug I got was the best I'd ever had.

"Just wish," he mumbled, "'your mum could see this. No offense, Margaret."

The night Colin Petty had stopped to speak to Ned Stokes outside Faulkner's office block, he had hoped to acquire some information. Four weeks had passed since he had killed Gwen and placed her body on her husband's desk. Only belated thoughts of Gwen's predilection for recording the encounters with her lovers had brought him back here. He had grown rather partial to the idea himself, a consequence of the more macabre recordings of his posed victims.

They had spent any amount of time together, watching Gwen's library and he'd taken her box of DVDs as a keepsake. But, suddenly, he had wondered about the video recorder itself and the DVD player that should have been attached to the big TV monitor. He had never seen them, never given a thought to where they might be. Come to think of it, Gwen had always kept him busy. Loose ends had made him return, loose ends that needed tying off.

As it happened. DC Stokes was standing at the side of the road, waiting. Colin recognized *police* immediately and stopped to engage him in conversation.

Colin nodded to the yellow police tape still around the door. "What's happening, chum? You've still got tape up there, I'd been thinking of trying to get a job at one of the shops…"

A car came up from the main road end and drew to a halt a few feet away. He recognized the passenger, not just as a policeman but as a quasi-celebrity. It was Detective Inspector White, Stewart White, who had caught that American tourist, the one who'd come to Britain chasing—someone, had it been his brother? No. No, it had been his brother's wife and everywhere he went, there was a dead body.

And here he was, now. Colin stepped back and walked across to the multistory entrance, watched from the shadows as White and an attractive black woman got out to talk to Stokes and then went to the Faulkner building. He climbed to the third floor of the parking building from where he could see into the Faulkner offices. They were looking at the scene of his "incident."

Eventually, they left and Stokes remained standing outside, like a club bouncer on a bad night.

Colin spent the hour or more they were inside remembering what he could about White. Part of the Regional Crime Force, based in… it took a bit of thought but he eventually ran it to ground, in Leeds, just up the road.

This was the guy who was investigating *his* business. He'd certainly given him enough to think about, enough to make it obvious to a fool that Faulkner had done it. Stage magic was his hobby, stage magic killed his wife: a locked room that only a magician could escape from. Maybe if he rubbed White's nose in it he might start joining the dots.

The lights came on in the parking building and he realized it was time to go and search Gwen's flat. There was only a single door at the rear of the building and this led into a dark, concrete lined stairwell and an elevator. He still had keys to this door but not to any of the other external doors.

Colin had checked to see that he had his pillowcase and plastic bag but he could only find a plastic bag. He cursed. "Shit!" Then he remembered the pillow cases and sheets he had stripped from the bed were still in the trunk, would he have time? Well, he would just have to make it. His fingers located something else and he pulled it out. It was a survival saw used by campers and soldiers—he had used it on jobs to clear tree branches over the paths they laid. He opened it, tested the serrations, and nicked himself. He cursed again as for one fleeting second he considered using the tool but no, he felt more in control with the pillowcase. He flexed and twisted the tool then stepped back toward the car.

Fully equipped he returned, telling himself he would aim for the side road down past the building just on the chance that the policeman would not challenge him. It was a forlorn hope, but—you never could tell. He made the turn and reached the darker pavement beyond the main lighting.

"Hoy." That would be Stokes, couldn't keep his nose out of other people's business.

Colin turned, walked back, contriving a drunk stagger and moved toward Stokes with a friendly grin.

"Where're you going down there?"

"Live there, don' I?" He moved to the policeman's side and put out a friendly hand.

"No one lives down there, just back streets."

Colin peered blearily along the road and stumbled into the entry, out of sight of anyone looking down the street. "Where is it, then? Compton Road?"

"No Compton's around here, son." Stokes turned to point toward the main road and it was enough. With Stokes's back turned, Colin dropped the bag over the man's head and assumed his normal position, knee in the back and pulled. The result was exhilarating, he felt the life draining out of the man. Sensing when it was done, Colin counted to seven and let go. He dragged the body over the waxed floor and jammed its feet against the wall. He then lifted and carried the body into the ground floor of the parking lot, opened the trunk and dropped it onto the carpet he kept there to protect the lining. There were cleaning tools in the trunk, from work. He cleaned the floor and the stairwell before leaping up the stairs two at a time and entering Gwen's bedroom, using the bunch of keys he'd taken on the day she died. Ten minutes and he found no camcorder or DVD player and if he couldn't find them, no one else could.

Stokes's relief hadn't shown up when Colin left the building and walked circumspectly around to the front. With a dead body in the trunk, Colin's thoughts worked overtime. His mind swung between disposing of the body and Inspector White. The papers—as he remembered—had painted him as a brilliant police officer. Maybe he should do something about that.

He never thought he would be caught. He was the man who left no fingerprints, no DNA, no clues of any kind. He was the invisible slayer, a man with no identity. The original Billie Jarvis had died in a lake, Colin sometimes had difficulty remembering what his name had been. He sucked absent-mindedly on his forefinger.

Some miles had passed beneath his wheels before the idea struck him. Why not leave the brilliant Inspector White an obvious clue? Yes, another clue leading him to Faulkner. Why not use the boat? Brilliant! Faulkner's magic prop. The boat he'd bought *could now be used against Faulkner. Sheer genius.*

CHAPTER 34

Raindrops hit me as I locked the car outside the office building. I smiled a little, it was almost summer and the pelting rain of gentle April and the savage winds of playful March were flooding the streets of our cities and blowing roofs off houses.

English weather!

Barbara Patterson clattered up to me just as I was about to run up the three double flights of stairs. I put thoughts of keep-fit to the back of my mind and hit the elevator button. The cage trundled down to the ground floor.

Sergeant Patterson shook her magnificent mane of red hair and showered me anew with rain water. "Morning, guv."

"Morning, Sergeant, Going my way?" She grinned and reached across in front of me to press the button, I could smell roses and cinnamon both at the same time. Good enough to eat. A heady brew that should make Sergeant Levy sit up and take notice.

"Um, got something for you, guv. Shall I mention it now?"

"Please do."

"Oh, first there's something else. Everyone in the office is calling him Baldielocks now, your nickname's caught on. I hear even *The Sun* has got hold of it." The lift dinged and stopped, we got out. "Where was I? Yes. I have confirmations from several sources that this guy Baldielocks was the one escorting Gwen Faulkner around and, this is the good one, including the night she was killed."

"My initial reaction should have been elation but I was puzzled. "It's almost as if he wants to be identified, as if he wants us to know it's him."

Barbara nodded. "You could be right. It hadn't struck me before but we can't prove anything even if he admitted it all. If we do find him, we need to be able to go the full ten yards. On the other hand, perhaps he's so cock-sure of himself, he thinks he's invulnerable."

Barbara carried on walking as I answered my cell at the door of my office. "See you later." It was Alec Bell, from his guest house in Sheffield. "We've got him!" He launched straight into what he wanted to say. "Those two wires you mentioned... they went behind the wallpaper. I had to rip them out. There's a tiny pickup inserted into the picture rail and the other end's under the floor, between the joists."

"The recorder?"

Yep, the floor's beach blocks in a herringbone pattern, a section lifts up and there it was. Without the wires, we wouldn't have noticed a thing."

"Great. Brilliant, brilliant."

"One more thing. There's a full disc. It's got our man in some very active scenes."

"Brilliant again. Get it couriered up here will you?"

"Will do. Also…" I could almost hear him grinning. "I think, perhaps, they'd been acting some fantasy out. There's a mirror next to the bed, a huge one, remember? It's clean, except for one place at around head height: big smudge of greasy sweat. I'm guessing it's lover boy's head. Just a thought…"

"Well?"

"There was a big TV set in the corner. Presumably they watched this stuff on there. No wires?"

"WiFi. The DVD player had a router connected."

I went straight in to see Joe Flowers and brought him up to date. Joe reacted just as I expected. He held up his clenched fist and extended his index finger.

"So, we know he was with her on the night she died." Up went his middle finger. "We can prove he's not who he says he is. We can even infer but not prove he's Billie Jarvis." Third finger. "But there's not enough to prosecute. No DNA." The pinky. "Nothing that would tie him into other crime scenes."

"Those blood samples."

"We'd have to catch him and get him to volunteer a DNA sample."

"Well, how about this for an idea. I bring the squads up to date then we call a press conference."

"So?"

I told him my idea.

Flowers grimaced, not too happy. "I'd have to get the Chief onside and you know your neck's going to be on the line?"

"I know all that but without a very lucky break, we're not going to force him out of his hole, are we?"

I broke the news to the troops first; the cheers could have been heard along the road at the Town Hall. The investigation had been a long one with very few breaks along the way, now they could smell blood.

We held a well-attended news conference. The two local area TV channels, the Leeds and York papers and the local Sheffield evening one were there. We had reporters from over the Pennines—Rochdale and Preston, even a woman from Manchester. Several of the red-top papers were also represented. They were firing questions and leaving no space to actually say anything. Eventually, they realized that their voice recorders were only picking up each other's noise and they stopped.

I told them that I was only prepared to give them a statement and no questions would be answered. There were some unhappy journalists but it was better than nothing at all. "Ladies and Gentlemen," I gave them the benefit of the doubt, "I'm able to give you some details of the progress we've made on the Faulkner killing and some related murders."

"Aha, the Lancashire Choker," said Vic Lamont from the Mail, *sotto voce.*

"Wasn't a question, was it, Vic?"

"Who? Me? Never."

"It's bloody Baldielocks isn't it, Inspector?"

I looked across at the man from *The Sun* and hoped my look said it all. "We've identified the man we wish to interview in connection with a number of murders—including that of Gwen Faulkner. His real name is William Jarvis though, under that name, he has been pretending to be dead for almost two decades. We now know he has been living under an extensive list of aliases, but this is what he looks like now."

I held up the largest clear print we had from the doctored image Archie had prepared for us and started a clamor.

"Settle down ladies and gentlemen, please. We'll let each of you have one of these plus some background info on the suspect. I expect this will please your readers, especially when I tell you that I, personally, can identify this man. I can state quite definitely that I saw him at the scene of the Faulkner murder talking to DC Ned Stokes, who was murdered the same day."

Pandemonium broke out. The reporters had their cell phones out, texting or calling their editors. But I needed to add something... I shouted: "One more thing. I'm not going to rest until I have this man in custody."

TV cameras focused on me, a couple of dozen recorders caught my words.

"Until then, please call this number," I pointed to the contact number in big black letters on the board behind me, "All calls will be treated in confidence and under no circumstance approach him, this man is dangerous."

"This is going to make you a marked man, Inspector. You realize that, don't you?"

I had no idea who made that observation but that, of course, was the general idea. I made no reply.

When our friends from the media had gone, one of the guys went to the vending machines and filled two trays with cardboard cups of coffee. Barbara Patterson handed me one.

"Milk, no sugar, guv."

"Thanks, Barbara."

"That fellow was right, you know."

"Right?"

"About you being a marked man. Now Baldielocks is going to come gunning for *you*."

"It's like this, Barbara," I said. "It's the only way I can think of to get him to come out in the open." There were more than twenty officers present and every one of them must have heard me. The mutter of conversation stopped. Someone clapped and then all of them joined in.

A movement at the door caught my attention. Joe Flowers was standing beyond the glazed panel signaling me. I waved to my guys and went outside.

Joe patted me on the back. "Wasn't sure you were actually going to go through with that, Stewart. Bloody brave thing to do. We'd best go and see 'Archie the Geek.' He's got some clever friends down there in the Goblin's Cave."

When I arrived home, Dad had been busy in the kitchen. Chili-con-carne extra strong and bread-and-butter pudding.

Once I'd sat down in my new recliner, I couldn't have moved an inch if Baldielocks had suddenly materialized brandishing a blunderbuss. "By the 'eck, Dad, as they say up here, that pudding was right out of Mum's cookbook."

He put a hand on his hip and struck a haughty pose. "By the 'eck, lad, who do you think taught her to make it?"

He returned to normal and sat down opposite me. "Hope you've done the right thing. Maybe I'll sleep in the old spare room for a bit longer."

"Why? Something wrong with your new bed?"

"Certainly not. It's perfect, best I ever had."

"Then what's on your mind?"

"Saw you on that news conference you had. That guy at the end was absolutely right. This killer is going to come after you."

I made a dismissive gesture. "Stop worrying, I'll be fine."

He nodded thoughtfully. "We'll see." He came across and gave me a hug, we did hugs pretty good in our house. I loved the old feller.

CHAPTER 35

ordan Holmes—Colin Petty until a week ago—relaxed on the couch and watched the news. There were no ties to his old persona left. He had sold his businesses at a knock-down, cash price to his employees, principally Nick Grandly, who became the company's new managing director. His car went in an auction and, at the very same auction (but under his new name), he purchased a sleek black Audi TT. He had noticed an elegant Chinese lady inspecting it earlier; it was very different from the metallic red Mercedes he had been using.

His apparent taste in clothes had changed too. The three-piece suits he wore during the working day and the dark slacks and blue check shirts for evening wear went into the dustbin to be replaced by a range of light-colored jeans and black or dark grey short sleeve shirts with leather jackets and white-trimmed loafers. He had let his hair start to grow out and there was now a just-discernible fuzz all over his skull; at a millimeter a day, he reckoned, he'd have a half-inch crew-cut inside two weeks.

Jordan had rented an apartment in a newly-converted mill building on the edge of Wetherby. It was a furnished let with modern furniture that he felt went with his new character. And a huge new TV, great for music, film, sport, drama and now, news. Fighting in Syria, Soldiers dead in Afghanistan, floods in Australia, murders in the UK—and his own face!

"Christ," he murmured and sat up. A recent photo, his head as bald as an egg and now they were calling him "Baldielocks." Where in hell had they got that from? He tried to record the transmission but, unfamiliar with the new controls, the news item had finished by the time he had it figured out. He sat there, his mind almost blank as he waited for the piece to be repeated fifteen minutes later.

He snapped the button on the remote so that he could go over it in detail later. For now, he just took in the main points. The list of recent incidents, his first name, Billie Jarvis, and a list of his other aliases. There were shots of the police spokesman with his threat to put him away.

Jordan poured himself a drink and reviewed the recording. It was all there, in far more detail than he had imagined possible and that Inspector who he'd last seen the day he had killed Stokes. White—Inspector White, the nerve of the man threatening him. Identify him could he? Well he would see about that.

His breathing began to subside toward normal. He no longer looked like the photo, not a lot, anyway. And the more time passed, the less resemblance it would bear him.

Jordan recovered and went to the spare bedroom where several of his cases remained to be unpacked. Some were filled with the apparatus used in magic tricks: a folding bird cage with the sharp corner he had cut himself on, a top hat with a secret compartment and another which collapsed to a disc and dozens of packs of playing cards. All of those had come from a magician in the Chesterfield organization along with stuff he had never had time to examine in detail.

But among the things, yes—a bag of wigs. Jordan sorted through them, discarding those which were too long, the wrong color or too obviously false. He found two which might serve his purpose. He tried them on in front of a mirror, nothing that a comb and a pair of scissors couldn't fix. He looked at his barbering in the mirror, not bad, with the addition of a cap it would pass muster.

Now, all that was needed was to find White and get him alone.

Eva's friend had provided them with a studio apartment next to the boatyard in Acaster Malbis. It would have been ideal if they had been able to have a grocery order delivered. It was empty of everything but the barest of necessities: two armchairs, a bed, and a fourteen-inch TV.

No matter how amorous they may have felt, only so much sex is possible without food and drink other than tap water but at least they had the bed, Asmin would have to sleep on the floor.

Two days of such privation and Leroy was climbing the walls. "Might as well be back in that prison," he grumbled. "At least I got fed."

Eva tried to understand but the frightening gun battle she had gone through a day or so before had shaken her badly. "Look, my man, we know they got Mad Charlie so they goin' to know 'bout you. They just waitin' for us to step out so they can get their claws into you. You really wanna get caught again?"

"I could just pop in the club house over at the boatyard or something. Nobody knows me there."

"The club house is for members and members own boats. You got a boat? You know the first thing about boats? And dammit, you're probably the only black man around for miles."

Leroy opened his mouth to say something and closed it again.

"I'm goin' ta go to that little supermarket at the boat yard to get us something to eat. Maybe I'll pick up a newspaper and a couple of DVDs and Asmin, you goin' ta get fuelled up."

"I'll do that," said Leroy, "Asmin's asleep."

"I'm not asleep, Leroy. I'll take Eva, I can carry her bags."

Eva leaned over and smacked Leroy. "It's you they is lookin' for, you just gotta keep outta sight for a week. 'Til the heat dies down."

After Eva and Asmin had left, Leroy stood up and walked aimlessly around the apartment. He opened cupboards, looked in tins and boxes in the kitchen and finally made a rude, exasperated noise. He pulled on a hoody and went out, pulling the door shut behind him. The river bank was a nice, relaxing place to be. Boats passed in both directions, their wakes lapping stealthily along the shore.

He passed an old fisherman sitting on a folding stool.

"What you after?" asked Leroy stopping and looking in the man's keep net.

"I want a chub, a big one. A record one."

"Well good luck to you." Leroy's crankiness had passed now he was no longer penned in.

A boatful of passengers went by, back toward York. Children waved and he waved back at them, a few half naked women in holiday gear waved as well.

"Hmm," added Leroy. "I like fish, man, but I ain't no cook. My girlfriend, she the one has the way with the frying pan. Aw man, fryin' fish, bacon an' onions." For the first time in two days, Leroy thought he just might survive.

"Sounds good, young man. You take care of your girlfriend, now."

Alec brought me the video from Gwen Faulkner's apartment and we played part of it on my desktop computer. I'll be honest, Gwen Faulkner may have been a mature woman but she was attractive and athletic. Her lack of inhibitions made concentrating on Baldielock's face a difficult job There were, thankfully, several frames we could freeze and make up images of the man for further distribution, better than those we had pretty well 'manufactured' from the age-enhanced teen photo provided by Archie.

Peggy Allerdice brought me an email fresh in from the York Police, they had located Leroy Richards. Later, an Inspector Thomas made a courtesy call, asking if I wanted in.

I asked how they had managed to find him and was told that six people at least, had phoned in to say they had seen him strolling the banks of the Ouse as if he had not a care in the world. His girlfriend too, had been spotted visiting a local shop.

"Leroy's girlfriend?" I asked.

He laughed and said. "There're not that many Rastas in Acaster Malbis, especially carrying voodoo dolls and threatening the guy behind the counter with dire spells if he wouldn't take a fifty pound note!"

"Cast iron, I'd say. Got them both bang to rights. No, Inspector Thomas, you go ahead with my best wishes. Just keep me in the loop when you have the time."

Well, Leroy was really the least of my worries and when Barbara told me that Billie Jarvis was now known as Colin Petty, I pretty well forgot my self-appointed Nemesis. "So, how did you come up with that?"

"Two sources, Boss. I have a council clerk who handed out an invitation to a Colin Petty some weeks ago and she connected the name with his picture. The clincher was the firm who carried out the recent work in Faulkner's building. Vista Landscaping, owned and managed by a Nick Grandly but previously by Colin Petty and identified by his ex-employees.

The police came in force to pick Leroy up. They had occupied a two-story holiday home with views of the small bungalow where Leroy, Asmin and Eva were holed up. They had spent some time with binoculars before they were certain that Leroy, who seemed a little shy of windows, was there.

They were certain that he *was* there and confident that they could apprehend him—after all, he was one man against ten and not even the boyfriend of a voodoo lady could walk on water.

Six o'clock, ten minutes short of high tide. A whistle sounded, the police moved in.

The whistle also alerted their quarry, an early riser. He abandoned his newly-brewed pot of tea, the two crisp slices of toast, and Eva. His reaction was magnificent, not a thought for his girlfriend or for Asmin, both still asleep. He left by the back door, through the rose beds and the honeysuckle which obscured the view of his flight and reached the edge of the water unseen. He crept, doubled-up, along to the boat yard as the police closed in carefully on the house. Most of the boats were too big for him to handle but another early-riser was already painting the topsides of a forty-footer and he was standing in exactly what Leroy wanted: a motorized rubber pontoon-style motor boat.

Leroy jumped up onto the cruiser's deck and came to a halt above the busy owner. Leroy was not given to forethought. He jumped down onto the rubber floor, the shock knocked the man with the brush over; half in and half out of the boat. Leroy helped him all the way out and into the water and cursed as some of the red paint slopped over his sneakers. His knife cut through the mooring lines and he pulled the starter cord.

He congratulated himself. The motor was still warm and started on the instant. He sped for the open water and dived for cover as an armed policeman arrived on the bank and began firing but the bullets hit the water—mostly—well-short of his speeding craft and there was simply no way they could catch him now.

Five miles downriver, at the confluence with the river Wharfe, still in flood after the recent rains, the water surged along. The brown muddy water took hold of Leroy's boat and carried it along like a cork in a barrel.

He kept it broadly in line with the current until, with a couple of derisive snorts, the engine died. No amount of pulling the starter cord would get it going again and Leroy looked around, in vain, for a fuel can.

Spinning, as often broadside on to the current as facing both downstream and upstream, he reached Cawood and was swept under the bridge just as he became aware of the amount of water around his feet, a state of affairs that simply got worse. He cursed. At least one of those bullets must have found him and vibration and the stresses of the flood were making the leak worse.

Further down the river was Selby, a sizeable market town now bustling with early starters. As the rubber boat finally lost all buoyancy, Leroy stood knee-deep and saluted.

A final heroic gesture.

Barbara Patterson's phone was ringing. She lifted it and frowned. "Who?"

"Ted White," said the voice. "This is Sergeant Barbara Patterson, isn't it?"

"That's correct."

"Good, you're the one he talks about."

"Me? Um, Who are we talking about, Mr. White."

"Stewart, of course. My son. Look. I've got this idea…"

I called Connie from the office and told her that my dad had moved into his new home. I neglected to tell her that his new home was situated in my garden, fifty yards from my house. I had considered this carefully and I concluded that what she didn't know wouldn't hurt her.

Initially, she wanted me to come to her place; I had cooked for her on the last occasion and it was only fair…

"I'd really prefer you to come to me, Connie, if you wouldn't mind. I may still be called from work and I don't want to embroil you in any problems that might bring up."

She capitulated and agreed providing she could bring the wine and the desert.

"Well, that's really very nice of you, Connie. I really would look forward to that."

"You'd better. There're folks who've tasted my key lime pie who simply can't eat ordinary food for weeks afterwards."

"Marvelous Connie, simply marvelous. Look, there are two men standing in my doorway making urgent signals, really have to go." I turned to look at the door.

"Okay, Alec. You've just pissed my girlfriend off, what can I do for you?"

Alec was not contrite. "Morning, guv. I want to introduce Ranjit Patiala to you." He turned, gestured toward his companion. "Ranjit, this is my governor, Inspector Stewart White. Guv, Ranjit Patiala of the National Crime Squad. You may have heard of him as Jasminder Singh."

I felt as though I'd been knocked sideways. My eyebrows must have shot up to the top of my head because the big Sikh just gave me a huge white grin.

I managed to ask, "Leroy's henchman?"

"Most recently." He held out his hand and I shook it tensing up for a crushing grip, he was surprisingly gentle. "Yes, I've also been a henchman—I like the word—or confidant, driver, bodyguard and so on and so forth to many other villains who simply put Leroy in the shade. It's been my specialty for almost six years."

"Please, sit down," I invited belatedly. Both Ranjit and Alec took seats. "And to what purpose?"

"Recovery of the proceeds of crime, mostly. Locating the hiding places of money and goods used by men who prey upon the law-abiding and the weak."

"So that is how you came to be associated with Leroy Richards, I guess."

"Exactly."

"I've just heard that they've fished what was left of his boat out of the river at Selby, that's about twenty five miles from here. He'd been running away from York police in a boat. No sign of a body."

"Ah." Ranjit was silent for a few seconds. "Ah," he said again, "As for the money, I don't think he owes us too much. We managed to convince him that his one-time associate, Winston Umbok, had moved six million pounds to an offshore address. We have that money now."

"I did hear about that but I wasn't sure how true it was. Do you think that was connected with Umbok's death?"

Ranjit shook his head. "I was in character, of course. Leroy told Winston to go for a swim and me to fire into the water to speed him on his way. I didn't fire at him, not that it would've mattered if I had, my gun rarely fires anything except blanks. Neither of us realized he couldn't swim."

I nodded. "You reckon Leroy will surface again, somewhere though?"

"I would think so, Stewart. Leroy is a social animal who needs to be with people."

"Any chance of the money you recovered finding its way back into our budget?"

Ranjit pursed his lips, a serious expression on his face until he realized I was joking.

"I think I've been responsible for recovering something like twenty million pounds in cash and goodness knows how much in goods: stolen paintings, sculptures, antiques and quite a few Rolls and Bentleys and suchlike. I would doubt that the Police Force benefitted from any of that."

"Well, it's nice to meet you Ranjit." I spoke the name carefully, I was still thinking of him as Jasminder.

"You too. I'm on my way south now but I just wanted to tell you something you won't have realized."

"Oh?"

"You meant a lot to Leroy."

"Me?" I was astonished.

"Oh yes, you. Certainly he was a bit…" Ranjit was searching for a suitable word, "… a bit hacked off about being saved from drowning by a policeman but once he'd come to terms with that, he never shut up about you. He respected you, Stewart. Opposite sides of course but he genuinely admired you."

"Well, that's kind of weird but thanks for telling me."

"And, we must remember, without Leroy, we wouldn't have got to Mad Charlie. What we recover from him will be astronomical."

Ranjit left, leaving me with mixed thoughts but I put Leroy onto the back burner and returned to the job at hand. Despite knowing the alias that Billie Jarvis was now operating under and despite having a good picture of him, the case had slowed right down again. Where did we go from here?

Home, that's where. I decided to leave early. Before I went I emptied d my inbox, possibly for the first time since Christmas.

I stopped by the incident room and said, "Cheers, guys."

The people looked up at me, everyone looked a bit guilty.

"I'm away early for a change."

They looked relieved, "Great, sir. Enjoy."

Ted, Stewart's father, walked along the path and knocked on his own front door. "He's got his girlfriend with him," he said by way of explanation to the lady. "Probably stay the night."

She closed the door behind him. "I'll sleep on the sofa."

"Don't be silly. You need a proper bed."

At home, I started preparing the meal I intended to put before Connie. Foods that might be unfamiliar to her: parsnips, fresh asparagus, baby new potatoes, and Barnsley chops—a sort of double lamb chop that I had only come to appreciate since moving to Yorkshire. And with that was mint sauce and gravy made from the meat residues after cooking. Then I wondered exactly what she usually ate. Fried chicken? That was a cliché.

Unexpectedly, Connie came exactly on time. I sensed something different about her; a change, no longer the flirty, southern girl with the pronounced drawl. Not a happy Connie.

What had caused this? I wondered.

"I know you like this, Stewart." She handed me a wrapped bottle which I found to be a nice rich Shiraz. "I got a good one, I think. And..." Just the suggestion of a smile at the corners of her lips," I've got a half bottle of Jack in my bag, just in case."

I took her wrap and pointed her to the sofa in my lounge. "Make yourself comfortable. You seem a little distracted, unhappy news?"

Connie turned those great big eyes on me. "Might as well get this off my chest, I guess." She sat down, hands flat on the seat, feet and knees together like a little schoolgirl.

"I came over here, to England, to collect my brother's things. Just a job to do, didn't expect to meet anyone I'd like and most of all, I didn't expect to meet up with the guy who had been chasing him." She took a tissue from her handbag and dabbed at the corners of her eyes.

"Well, that's..."

She put her hand up to stop me.

"Now, don't you stop me. You already know that initially I was trying to get a little payback. I hadn't really thought it through: I really played the ol' party girl and eventually succeeded in getting you into my bed." She laughed a little sadly. "You put up quite a fight, Stewart, thought it wasn't going to work but it did and here's the kicker, I ended up liking you, for real, not just pretend."

Connie heaved a huge sigh and was silent for a minute or more. I sat down across from her. "Not just liking you. I admire you, darn it. You're polite, like pulling out my chair when I sit down. Opening doors. Like even picking up my clothes and folding them. You're gentle and you're a gentleman."

Another sigh. "But I've reached the point where I'm asking myself: where do we go from here?"

I could have drowned in those huge blue eyes.

"I guess it's time for a decision, perhaps a conclusion. I'm quite well off, you know. My first husband's alimony and Alan's insurance has seen to that and there's his house on Lake Kissimmee..."

I was willing her to get to the point of all this. I nodded. "And?"

"And I thought maybe you'd quite like to leave England with its funny weather that's different every day. Come and live with me in the sun."

"Wow." I considered the possibility for a moment.

"But I realize that it's not going to work. You're committed to your work, and there's your father. I know whatever I can offer isn't going to be enough. So I'm admitting defeat, I'm flying home on Sunday. I'm leaving before I fall for you even more."

I got up and went into the kitchen to give me time to think, I saw to finishing the meal and set it out on the table there.

"Come and get it."

I served it out onto the plates and we ate it and neither of us tasted a single bite.

Obviously, I didn't want her to go but she was right in all she'd said. When we'd finished eating, I pushed my chair back and cleared the table on automatic while I tried to think of something to say. I put the plates next to the sink, ready to go in the dishwasher and said something incongruous. "They have a phrase for this in Yorkshire. They call it *siding the pots.*"

Connie smiled slightly.

I sat down again before adding, "You're right, of course. I mean we hardly know each other... although I was looking forward to the getting-to-know-you-better bit. I actually have quite a good holiday allowance from my job. And, I hardly ever take it all so it's mounted up a bit this year. You can stay here for three months at a time with a visitor's visa and I could drive you over to see The Lakes or scoot on up to Scotland. We could still see a lot of each other. If that's something you'd like to do. Though I guess you'd need to think about it, obviously."

Connie looked thoughtful, "A long distance-relationship? Me here three months... and then what?"

I started feeling maudlin and I could feel myself filling up. "Let's go through to the sitting room. Got that Jack Daniels? I feel I'm going to need it."

Jordan, Petty's new incarnation, had been sitting on the broad bough of an aged apple tree for some time when Stewart's father had returned to his home in the orchard. The dusk had become darkness and he had a clear view into the lounge where White was entertaining a woman.

He had followed the policeman home and watched as he spent time in the kitchen and when the woman had arrived, he had smiled at the prospect of playing Peeping Tom when he realized what was going on. The smile had gradually become a scowl as it became plain that nothing did appear to be going on.

Time passed and the night became a little windy, rain pattered down. Jordan was bored, stiff and uncomfortable and there was no point in waiting all night to

198 — JACK EVERETT & DAVID COLES

act. He shoved the Smith and Wesson .38 firmly into his pants, lowered himself to the ground and went around to the front door.

He prepared himself, checked he had the combat chain in his right coat pocket, knocked at the door and backed around the corner to be out of sight. White was almost certain to come out and look around, exposing himself to attack. A cell-phone rang inside the house and there was a murmured conversation.

At the same time, there was the sound of steps on the pathway, they came to the corner, paused. White's figure came into view, he was wearing a police rain coat and stopped there, looking around uncertainly. He turned around, ready to go back when Jordan pounced.

Split seconds was all it took. The combat chain was around the other's neck before a breath could be taken or a cry made. He pulled it tight, felt the serrated edge bite. He twisted the chain, felt it tighten into the flesh.

"Done with your fucking meddling now, haven't I, White."

"I don't think so, Mr. Magician." It was a woman's voice, it came from between his hands.

"Evening, Mr. Jarvis. Or is it still Mr. Petty? That's not me over there, I'm over here. Or should I say *Abracadabra*?" This voice came from behind him.

The words startled him; the growl of a small dog alarmed him and small teeth fastened into his ankle. It may have taken six or seven seconds to react, long enough to throttle someone, handcuffs went *snap* around one wrist. He was pulled back and the cuffs came toward the other wrist but he wrenched away, drew the gun and blindly struck out with it. He was off around the corner of the house leaving the dog and whoever had fooled him behind. A shape came at him out of the dark and he made to hit out at it just as the moon chose to come out from behind a cloud. He stopped himself and grabbed the woman in front of him, turned and ran dragging her behind him.

In the backyard, he forced his captive over a fence. The dog, reappeared, found a way through the fence, and yelped and barked at his heels. Jordan was running blind now, it was dark and bushes were no more than bulky shadows. The weight of the woman on his arm was slowing him down, breaking his concentration. The dog again took his trouser leg and this time he kicked so hard he felt bones give way and the body of the Jack Russell flew like a baseball into the air, straight into the nearby river.

Bang! Bang! The double explosion swept pain in a million brilliant shards across his chest. He staggered and turned, shoving his captive sideways down the river bank, seeing his assailant under the suddenly bright, cloud-free moon—a man with a double barreled shotgun, a stranger. Jarvis stood erect for an eternal second, as though realizing his time had come. "Allahu Akbar." He cried as his body slumped earthward.

"I knew I'd get you, you cocky bastard." said the Irishman. "Comin' in here like it was a frigging party night, dragging your floos…"

The words were cut short in his mouth as something big, hard and angry bounced into him knocking him clean off his feet.

"What a hell of a night." Stewart White stood behind his neighbor, one foot planted firmly in his back and panted for breath. "Barbara… it *is* you, isn't it Barbara?" He asked the woman who came running up wearing a police raincoat.

"Me or a very good imitation, Boss."

"Got some cuffs?"

"Sure."

"Cuff him, for goodness sake. And caution him. I'd better check on Petty."

Sometime later, he said "I'd better call for a paddy wagon."

"Done, boss. Your dad did that as soon as we saw the bastard."

"My dad?" I knew I was going to have to have words with him later.

"Look, Boss. Can you unwind this thing from my neck?" Barbara undid the rain coat and Stewart realized she was wearing a plastic neck brace. "It's from Archie's department, reinforced."

"Sure." He worked on the chain garrote and got it free, then the brace itself. "You're not as tall as I thought you were."

"Got flatties on. Without heels, I'm pretty much your height. We're all more or less your height, those of us who've been camping out here in your dad's little bungalow. We thought it might confuse Jarvis."

"Ah, and that's why Dad's been sleeping in his old room."

"It was his idea, boss. His suggestion."

A shape moved through the orchard until it reached a spot where an old apple tree had fallen. Here the moonlight struck: a dog, a three legged dog, in obvious distress, seemingly heading home. With difficulty, the dog negotiated the small door entrance, drank a little water and curled up in its basket.

A half hour later, three cars and a police carrier arrived. The van held three uniformed police who took my neighbor away, they grumbled about paperwork and people's names. The three cars held sixteen people: Clive Bellamy and my team, apart from Barbara Patterson.

An impromptu party was just getting under way when a second police van nosed around looking for a parking spot and a dead murderer. I returned to the house chilled to the marrow, to see Connie and explain that I knew nothing about all this but I saw only a letter standing folded, center table.

Later, considerably later, long after I had picked up the letter Connie Cleghorn had left and long after I'd come to terms with the fact that she really had gone, a car called for me and chauffeured me in to a meeting in the boardroom with the Chief Constable. Joe Flowers was there along with Clive Bellamy and all of my team. Both Clive and Joe patted me on the back as I walked past and my guys fell silent as Joe ushered me toward the CC.

Not unexpectedly, the CC was in his bluff and hearty mood, jocularity oozed out of him. He offered me a port which I couldn't really refuse and he bent forward and said "Well done, Stewart," in a voice so quiet it was as though he felt guilty at saying it.

He turned to the meeting and said, "It's not often I get the opportunity to say well done to one of my teams but I felt in this instance it was justified. The villain you all played a part in bringing to justice was a particularly evil man who had carried out the most heinous crimes. The fact that his identity was a secret from everyone for so many years delayed his apprehension and that's why you're here to party this evening and…" He tried a joke which obtained the desired result, a few laughs, coughs and sniggers, "…blow the budget…"

He took me by the arm. "Tell me my boy, how did you figure out that the pillow-case murders and the chainsaw garrote ones were the same man? I mean it's not often a murderer changes his MO. Was that guesswork or what?"

Guesswork? I blew out a breath. "Well, sir, there were a number of things; firstly there were the blood samples, the same from two murder sites, the Morley victim and DC Stokes. If we assumed the samples had not been planted they must have been the killer's. Secondly, another of the samples turned out to be a pigeon although not exactly a pigeon. It was that of a dove, the kind of bird conjurers use on stage."

The interested expression was wearing a bit thin but I wasn't about to stop now.

"We'd proved Faulkner couldn't have killed DC Stokes as he was on a ship halfway across the Indian Ocean, and he was our conjurer, so it had to be a copy-cat conjurer, not just a killer who was carrying out the murders."

I grinned, letting him off the hook. "I could go on sir, but I risk boring you and I'd like to congratulate my team too."

He didn't take the chance I offered. "Yes of course you must, but how did you find out it was dove's blood?"

"Because I searched the trunk of his car he'd put through an auction. I found a whole load of conjuring gear among which was a bird cage, complete with blood traces and white feathers. One of the wires had broken in the cage door and that was where both man and bird had cut themselves. Now if that's all, sir?"

"Ah yes, of course, Stewart! That's how those drops got on the carpet. Well once again, good job. For the first time in weeks my phone won't be ringing with constant complaints about our not catching him."

"Not 'til the next time eh, sir?"

"What? Oh yes," the thought seemed to make him unhappy.

I joined the dedicated band of officers who were drinking heavily and loudly and picked up a glass and a can of beer. I thought of Dad who had accepted an offer to sleep over at Margaret's house while I was here and Connie whose letter lay heavy and expectantly in my pocket. But that was for later, this moment in time was for my team.

EPILOGUE

Dianna Summers, a staff nurse at Widdecombe Park Hospital, was checking the drip-feed equipment in the coma ward. She checked each bag of fluid, noted pulse rates, took blood pressure readings, all routine until she reached coma patient 243B12.

The patient had been lying here for almost a year with only ECG traces showing there was any mental activity. He opened his eyes, looked at her and started singing, hesitantly and with difficulty. *"You shake my nerves and you rattle my brain, too much love drives a man insane."*

More surprised than shocked, Dianna stepped back a little. "Hello," she said in as friendly a tone as she could manage. "I'm Nurse Summers." She picked up the limp hand and felt a tentative grip from the weak fingers.

The patient worked his mouth once or twice, trying to get the muscles to perform once more. "Hello, Nurse." He licked his lips. "I'm Robert Cleghorn. Have I had another accident?"

**Detective Inspector White
will return in:**

Damaged Souls

AUTHOR BIOGRAPHIES

DAVID COLES began writing fantasy and science fiction longer ago than he can now remember. His works have explored the local stars, killed off huge numbers of Roman legionaries, uncovered what happened to King Arthur and the Round Table—and hatched a few thriller plots. A founding member of the international Historical Novel Society, he has attended workshops run by Terry Pratchett and the late David Gemmel. David lives with his wife and a pet laptop in God's own county—Yorkshire in the UK—where he also designs and builds websites for friends and programs for fun.

JACK EVERETT is author and coauthor of a number of fantasy, science fiction, crime and thriller novels. Some are published, some are in progress and others are still in gestation. Jack also handcrafts stunning snooker cues and award-winning modern *objets d'art* from exotic and magnificently figured timbers. He collects books and playing cards though there is little space in a much overcrowded home. He dreams of having a bigger library, and hopes to one day have the extra room he dreams of.

WWW.ARCHIMEDESPRESSE.CO.UK

ABOUT
BARKING RAIN PRESS

Did you know that five media conglomerates publish eighty percent of the books in the United States? As the publishing industry continues to contract, opportunities for emerging and mid-career authors are drying up. Who will write the literature of the twenty-first century if just a handful of profit-focused corporations are left to decide who—and what—is worthy of publication?

Barking Rain Press is dedicated to the creation and promotion of thoughtful and imaginative contemporary literature, which we believe is essential to a vital and diverse culture. As a nonprofit organization, Barking Rain Press is an independent publisher that seeks to cultivate relationships with new and mid-career writers over time, to be thorough in the editorial process, and to make the publishing process an experience that will add to an author's development—and ultimately enhance our literary heritage.

In selecting new titles for publication, Barking Rain Press considers authors at all points in their careers. Our goal is to support the development of emerging and mid-career authors—not just single books—as we know from experience that a writer's audience is cultivated over the course of several books.

Support for these efforts comes primarily from the sale of our publications; we also hope to attract grant funding and private donations. Whether you are a reader or a writer, we invite you to take a stand for independent publishing and become more involved with Barking Rain Press. With your support, we can make sure that talented writers thrive, and that their books reach the hands of spirited, curious readers. Find out more at our website.

WWW.BARKINGRAINPRESS.ORG

Barking Rain Press

ALSO FROM BARKING RAIN PRESS

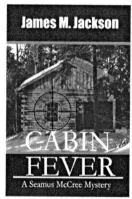

Lightning Source UK Ltd.
Milton Keynes UK
UKOW01f0112010416

271245UK00001B/176/P